Murders At Brent Institute

Also by Jerry Labriola

Famous Crimes Revisited

Murders at Hollings General

Forthcoming

The Maltese Murders

MURDERS AT BRENT INSTITUTE

BY
JERRY LABRIOLA, M.D.

STRONG BOOKS

To Gary, David and Sue

ACKNOWLEDGMENTS

The author extends heartfelt thanks to the following:

To his wife, Lois, and his son, David,
for their insights and encouragement.

To the entire staff at Strong Books,
especially Brian Jud, Nicki Hartonavich and Lucy Kanine
for their expertise and advice.

To the Connecticut Authors and Publishers Association,
many of whose members provided valuable suggestions.

And to the Goshen Writers Group for their understanding
of his many absences during the writing of this book.

CHARACTERS

—In order of appearance—

DR. DAVID BROOKS..... Physician. Amateur detective

KATHY DUPRE ..... Hollings detective. David's fiancée

BELLE..................... Secretary at the Hole

MANUEL MOLINA......... Director of Brent Institute

ADRIAN CLEMENTE ... Owner of Candies by Clemente

MUSCO DILLER......... Owner of Red Checker Cab.
World-class lock picker

JUAN CARLOS SALTANBAN....... President of Radonia

EVILINA RUEZ................. Saltanban's friend

HENDERSON HENDLEY................ Nationally
syndicated columnist

JACK OGLETON..... President of Howerton University

AGNES CROCKER............. Community activist

PROFESSOR J. KATER WELD ..... Associate Director of
Brent Institute

WILL BARLOW......... Radonia's Minister of Health

DR. SAMUEL CORLISS......... Director of the Center
for Behavioral Health

CHAPTER 1

✜ ✜ ✜

Thursday, February 7

D r. David Brooks flinched when his house lights went out. Neighborhood power outages had often accompanied violent storms, but it was a clear February night. For years, he had taken medical emergencies in stride; however, the unexpected hazards of amateur sleuthing were another matter. Something to do with experience. And he knew this had nothing to do with Medicine.

He drained the last of his coffee and fumbled his way in the dark toward the living room window, lifting its shade and lowering his six-foot-five frame to confirm that all the houses along the cul-de-sac were lighted. David fell to one knee—the good one—then eased the other down and, inching over to the telephone stand, put the receiver to his ear. He pushed it away and stared at dead silence.

He had to act fast, as fast as sweat dampened his collar

and breathing became defined and reasoning shifted into high gear. He could hear his heart pounding hard and fast. Forget a flashlight—or a candle—or the fuse box. Are they out back, whoever they are? But where's the blast, the bullet spray? David raised himself gingerly and flattened against the wall.

He ripped away the shade to borrow some outside light, then hit the floor and crawled into the den where he yanked a semiautomatic Beretta Minx .22 from the shoulder rig stuffed in his bottom desk drawer. Still on his back and relying on "feel", he attached a perforated suppressor to the gun barrel, then rolled onto his elbows before drawing a bead on the rear of the four-room ranch. David guessed at a correct line of flight and fired into the shadowy bedroom toward the far window—four rounds in rapid succession, the concussion pierced by shattering glass. He leaped to his feet and bolted out the front door, brushing against foundation junipers as he hugged the side of the house.

The roar of an engine sounded like that of a truck, not a car, but he couldn't be sure. Of no help, either, was the acrid stench of oil biting at his nostrils. The sound and smell came from the street behind the house and had dissipated by the time he had circled to the rear and reached the shabby spread of gravel he called a patio. Glass particles crunched underfoot; he picked one up and hurled it as far as he could.

Moonlight through the back trees cast a feathery pattern on the house, a backdrop to what David spotted at its corner, but he was less preoccupied with dangling power and telephone lines than with the intent of the intruder or intruders. What the hell were they up to?

He rubbed his chin at a thickened point near the cleft. It was his decision scar. The next few moves were clear: check the backyard as best he could, leaving for daylight a more thorough "snooping", a designation he preferred to "sleuthing." He would then use his cell phone to call Police Detective Kathy Dupre—his fiancée—to inform her of the cut wires and to ask about spending the night at her place. David bounded into the house for a flashlight.

The mid-winter night's air was still and fresh, and he had not bothered to add to the shirt and sleeveless sweater he'd worn all day, for even in ice storms, he would yield only to his trademark black scarf and gloves. Snow had not fallen on Hollings, Connecticut in more than a week, and the ground was spongy and bare as he scoured around in the open and among the oaks and underbrush, waving the flashlight like a watering hose. Everything appeared normal: no footprints, no broken twigs, nothing left behind. He leaned against a tree and, for a moment, believed he was about to be back in the thick of an investigation. But of what?

Inside, David thought it ironic to dial a digital cell phone by candlelight. From where he stood in his den, a sliver of illumination had reached each of the four rooms that made up 10 Oak Lane. He felt a peculiar mix of righteous anger and sadness, not because anything had been lost inside but because the source of brighter light that would perfuse over all his possessions had been taken from him. His home had been sullied and if he could have embraced it, he would have: the "shabby chic" pieces in front of the living room's fireplace; the kitchen wrapped by blue counter-tops and canary yellow appliances; the bedroom with its unmade bed; the den with computer, printer, fax machine, photo-copier, martial arts trophies, miniature deer figurines and books stacked on the desk—Bulfinch's *Mythology, Police Procedurals, Crime Scene Investigation, Cause of Death* and Dr. Henry Lee's *Manual of Forensic Science.*

There was a telephone on the wall in the kitchen and one beside the computer. He never installed an answering machine because he believed he'd be flooded with messages from the media; and anyone important to him had his cell phone number. Others would figure out, he reasoned, that he could be reached through the main switchboard at the hospital.

Even the outside surroundings were important to David. He felt comfortably anchored in his yellow wood-frame house, a block from Tower Park, a small children's playground with jungle gym, swing set, seesaw and other playthings encircled by yews, junipers and whatever colorful blossoms the Garden Club selected for the year. Each Spring he waited for their scent to drift his way. On weekends, he often wandered over to push kids on the swings or play ball, relieving mothers who tended to their other children at the rocking horse or the tiny whirligig. At its far end, the playground was guarded by a water tower taller than a house, the brilliance of its silvery paint subtly changing with the seasons. The tower was visible through his bedroom window and, in the winter, he could estimate the size of a snowfall from the height of white fluff piled on the railing of its upper perimeter.

"Kathy. It's me. You sitting down?"

"Not another homicide," she said in a husky voice.

"No, no. Are you sleeping or what?"

"David, it's after eleven—and I'm not sitting, I'm lying.

What's wrong, anyway? You okay?"

"I'm fine. Lying down, eh? Well, bunch up the pillow—I'll be right over." There had been many pillow talks to determine their best course of action in a crisis, talks they knew would end in reward before dozing off to sleep. And for David, the thought of such an aftermath eased the twin stings of having had his house violated and possibly being sucked into another investigation. There was no chance he would eschew a new case—after all, he *chose* criminal detection to complement medical detection. Why so soon, though? The string of murders ended but two weeks before. Five atrocities that almost closed down Hollings General Hospital.

"Dr. David Brooks, don't do that to me! What's going on, anyway? Is it good or bad?"

"It can keep. I changed my mind. I'd rather tell you in person."

"Look," Kathy said, clearing her throat, "the last time you asked whether I was sitting, you were calling about the hospital murders. Now c'mon, what's up?"

"Someone cut my power lines, then sped off, that's all." David didn't wait long for a response before adding, "Don't worry. I'm on my way over." He inserted the phone in its holster, clipping it onto his belt.

He slipped into the Beretta Minx shoulder rig and gathered up his attaché case to check its contents before descending the basement stairs. He had a name for the case: Friday. Nothing to do with Joe Friday or Girl Friday, just the day he bought it. It was an exact duplicate of the one that was battered when an Asian gang—the Yakuza—pushed his first Mercedes over the cliff at High Rock three weeks before. Rumor had it that no one ever saw him open up the leather case, and he liked that. He also liked the fact that with Friday in tote, people knew he was in the middle of an investigation, when he would parody to anyone within earshot, "Some wear two hats; I carry two bags." Then smartly, "Two guns, too." He never dared announce a snubby at his ankle . . . even when he anticipated the worst.

Like a conjurer working by flashlight, he pulled each item from the case, then returned it: an Undercover .38 Special wrapped in terry cloth, extra rounds of ammo, a pair of 7/30 Beecher Mirage binoculars, a Polaroid camera, additional film, a postage stamp-sized NT-1 Scoopman digital tape recorder, a flashlight, latex surgical gloves, various micro bugs and a digital thermometer. In the course of his readings, David had come upon numerous articles dealing with "concealment capability for tight situations." Thus, hidden behind a retractable panel beneath its lid were a compact SIG-Sauer P226 pistol, a Scout knife, whistle and a cylinder of Mace. Before the hospital murders, most of the items had been stored in a Campbell's soup carton in the trunk of his car, but things had turned different and he was more secure swinging his tools just beyond his fingertips. Bulkier items remained in the car: evidence vacuum, crowbar and other carpenter tools, and his pride and joy—a gift from Kathy—a Kevlar-lined raincoat that could stop a 9 mm. slug.

The single basement room was circumscribed by gun cabinets, their metallic odors unrestrained by glass doors. All widths. All heights. According to manufacturer: Charter Arms, Colt, Dan Wesson, Ruger, Smith and Wesson. According to calibers: .25, .32, .38, .45. Near the

Ruger collection, he opened Friday and replaced the .38 Special with a Super Blackhawk .44 Magnum. There was no reason for him to strap on the ankle rig for the Smith and Wesson snubby. Not yet.

* * *

At the start of the three-mile ride to Kathy's, David turned off Pavarotti from the tape deck of his black SL500 Mercedes convertible—top down—to focus on the cut wires incident, on its meaning and on what it might portend. Was it a scare tactic, or did the gunshots abort something more aggressive, more deadly? The five hospital murders were still fresh in his mind. Was there a connection to them or to the seemingly unearthed secrets of Istanbul, or Cartagena—or even of the daggers of the samurai? For two weeks, those crimes and secrets had dominated his thinking and filtered through dreams and now, alerted if not primed for additional action, he could feel his left foot press against the floor mat. It was as premature to question whether or not he was ready to take on another case as it was to expect another case to arise out of the circumstances of the past hour. But there were other matters now aflame in his mind. The issue of his medical practice, though confined to making house calls for other physicians, still growing larger since his key role in solving the recent crimes. The required experience to move from amateur to professional detective work. Competitiveness and the same love of combat— even as he approached 40—with its inherent dangers that propped him up in percussive karate all these years. And then there was one other thing: he was fucking mad. Not only because someone had damaged his property but also because someone dared to threaten him. He wanted, once again, to get even with what he considered the "criminal condition." In any event, he would sort it all out with his detective fiancée and, as he rounded the last turn, his foot relaxed.

Kathy's condominium complex—Hollings Hollow—was insulated from noise and neon by beige baffling on three sides. A row of hedge maples lined the fourth. Her corner unit comprised one of the smallest there: kitchen, living/dining room combination with fireplace, single bedroom with bath. It opened directly onto an interior roadway and, to the side and rear, a one-car garage, wooden deck and intervening section of yard occupied more space than the rooms inside. An American flag adorned the front of the garage, attached there by David shortly after the terrorist attacks of September 11. He and Kathy liked to barbecue year-round on the canopied deck which, confluent with part of the living quarters and garage, formed a secluded horseshoe. Rock ledge, half as high as the unit, ran along the driveway, defining her property line on the right.

David often referred to the kitchen as the family room for it was in a corner there, seated at a small white napkin table, that they spent much of their time—talking, planning and even watching TV. The "family room" was airy with pastel-colored appliances and matching overhead television set. Scant white curtains hung over double windows facing the driveway and on the bay window of the opposite wall.

David pulled into the driveway unable to recall ever arriving at that late hour—it was 11:30 on a Thursday. Halfway to the front door, a row of mushroom lamps suddenly lighted, and he hopped a step or two. The door burst open and Kathy appeared, tightening the sash of a white robe.

"Christ, lights snap off, lights snap on—I need a drink," David said, nearly missing a kiss as he swept by her.

"Are you all right?" Kathy asked, following close behind.

David continued into the kitchen. "Yeah, that's why I came by at midnight." He regretted the statement. Kathy, abreast of him at the sideboard and hutch, skewed her lips.

"I'm sorry, Kath—no need to take it out on you." He wrapped one arm around her waist and lifted her to his lips for a fuller, though not his usual, kiss, then eased her down. Without looking, he simultaneously removed a bottle of Dewar's Scotch from the hutch and his initialed coffee mug from a hook in an open cubby. He estimated two jiggers into the mug and gulped down half of it. Sighing, he added another jigger to the remaining supply.

"No ice?" Kathy asked, cocking her head.

"What? Oh, yeah . . . no, never mind, too late now." He drained the rest before Kathy could comment.

"David, I've never seen you like this. Would you shore up, please?"

David stared at her and, in a half-whisper, countered, "That's exactly what I'm doing. You want some?" He knew of her distaste of any whiskey blend.

"No, of course not."

"Your Chardonnay?"

"No, not that, either." She gave the response as if she couldn't wait to get rid of it, adding, "David, darling, let's go sit on the sofa." She took him by the arm into the living room where he gently disengaged himself and sank into a stuffed armchair, kicking off his shoes.

"Kath, I'm not tipsy, you know." He had trouble with the word.

"I never said you were, but even if you are, that's okay."
She stood before him and David imagined her reaching
only to his shoulders, were he to rise in his stocking feet.
He peered up at her, suppressing an urge to iron out the
pout of her lips with his own. Her raven hair was short
and wet, yet still kept a wave. A remaining breath of eye
shadow heightened the blue of her eyes and added a subtle highlight to skin like China silk. David had often nee-
dled her about cologne that didn't fit her profession and
about her being too petite and luminescent for a cop.
And too damn pretty.

They had dated on and off during college and then
veered apart. It was a decision of his choosing, colored by
a fierce determination to train hard for a medical career,
unencumbered by any serious personal relationships.
After working high school summers at his family's corner
store—Brooks Grocery—and graduating from Yale and
medical school, he had a two-year stint in the Navy during
which time Kathy had married and then was widowed.
Her husband, a fellow police academy graduate, had been
killed during a drug raid. And though he shared her grief,
in the decade since her husband's death, David came to
believe fate had gradually emboldened his love for her.
Over half that interval, he was transformed from the most
eligible bachelor at Hollings General to a one-woman man.

He gave her a concentrated, broad inspection before
asking, "Does that robe mean there's nothing under it?"

Kathy settled onto his lap and ran her finger through
his bushy mustache. "There's a time and place for everything," she said.

David left only her face exposed in an embrace and
said, "This is the time and place." It occurred to him that

he might have recoiled and mimicked Groucho Marx, but that would have trivialized the moment. Or he could have carried her into the bedroom with little or no resistance. Instead, heeding her admonition, he pulled away and signaled toward the kitchen.

At the table, David assumed a judicial expression. "You know what I say, Kath? What I say is . . . you're absolutely correct, it could have been worse." She had never made the statement. Kathy fashioned a slow smile and David followed suit, knowing the drink had worked.

She reached across the table, dwarfing her hands over his, and said, "Okay, give me the specifics because they can mean . . . ."

He stepped on her words, a habit he had worked hard at breaking. "You're interrogating me?"

Kathy looked wounded and replied, "Sorry, it's what I do for a living. How's this instead: What on earth went on at your place? I'm really worried because you happen to mean a lot to me." She listened as David, appeased, chronicled the events of the past couple hours— the blackout, the shots, the cut wires, a speeding vehicle, his inspection—editorializing on the possible significance of each detail.

"So you're more upset about what might have happened than about what really did happen," she said.

David raised his voice a notch. "You don't understand. They could have torched the place. All my stuff could have gone up in flames." He had long since removed his hands from the table and now waved them toward the ceiling.

"Including the gun collection?" she snapped.

Another notch. "Now cut that out! You know damn

well I don't collect guns. That dad gave them to me before he and mom moved to Arizona." He struggled to compose himself during her silence, then added evenly, "Besides, we have a deal . . . you know . . . move in with me, and after the wedding, we sell the house . . . including the guns."

"You keep getting it wrong. I'm not moving in until after it's official. Plus I'm not about to live on top of an arsenal for five months." She paused, unblinking. "Which reminds me: you may not collect guns but you sure do know your way around them. Anyway, maybe it's a good time to unload everything now, with the window and wire damage and all."

"When the guns were . . . how should I put it . . . forced upon me, I felt I should keep abreast of the field. So I began reading a lot. Big deal." He stiffened in the chair. "Sure helps in my new career. And as to unloading, we'd have to make the repairs anyway—whether we unloaded or not."

Kathy didn't budge. "David, you're a thirty-nine-year-old doctor still living in a pad."

He answered sheepishly, "But I like the place. It's all I need right now." He could feel the momentum shifting as he rose and walked to the refrigerator. "I suppose you're out of orange juice."

"Yes."

"You're always out of orange juice," he said, returning to the table.

"It's on my list," she countered, "so let's move on. Have you seen the hospital magazine? They sent me one."

"No, why?"

"Great spread on you and the murders."

"I read all the papers."

"You're on the cover and all through the thing." Kathy moved to a counter and, sorting through a pile of papers, found the latest quarterly edition of *The Hollings General Hot Line* and placed it before David. He paid more attention to the headlines than his photo:

THE HERCULE POIROT OF HOLLINGS?

"That's ridiculous," he said, unimpressed with the comparison to Agatha Christie's famed sleuth. "I'm just the opposite. Poirot was short, older, a dapper dresser—and he had an accent and a mustache that curled up."

"You miss the point. They're referring to detective skills. Read some of it."

Dr. David Brooks, Hollings General's own house call specialist, has become a regional and national household name. With assistance from the city's law enforcement and forensic authorities, including his fiancée, Police Detective Kathy Dupre, Dr. Brooks advanced his amateur detective status—and moved closer to full licensure as a private investigator—by solving the skein of murders ravaging the hospital in recent weeks. Operating out of The Hole, a makeshift office located in the hospital's basement, the tall physician who most in our medical family agree possesses the only handshake that hurts people, the one with "real" bow ties and an equally wide, blond bushy mustache, wasted little time in piecing together a complex puzzle involving drug cartels, international killers and mysterious samurai daggers.

David looked up and said, "But I know all this."

"Read on," Kathy said. "Get to the house call part."

David checked a sidebar profile: age, 39; unmarried; Navy veteran; private family practice, four years; hospital-based practice (Hollings General), four years; current practice limited to afternoon house call referrals by other physicians; criminal investigations, 6 years; black belt in karate; penchant for mythology, opera and trees. He skimmed through to the second page:

> Word has it that the hero doctor who began a sleuthing career by locating runaway teenagers and stray horses will soon be deluged with calls for his investigatory prowess in major criminal cases. Some say his house call load will similarly increase.

David read the last sentence again. "If this is what you mean, it's already started. I'm making calls that were requested the day before."

"So . . . are you getting some help?"

He put the magazine aside. "Funny you should bring it up. Bill Castleman from the ER asked about coming aboard. He's as fed up with managed care as I was."

"And?"

"And he's already informed the hospital. They might be short-staffed for a while but I think it'll work out."

"Soon?"

"Soon."

Kathy's face brightened.

Although David was pleased with the prospect of an associate and with the relief on Kathy's face, the magazine article rekindled the same disturbing emotions that had plagued him in the week following the apprehension of the murderer. Television, radio and print coverage; incessant phone calls from admirers; media interviews reluctantly granted. All the attention. Once a medical doctor, always a medical doctor. Will snooping take its toll? Can both be done?

After deciding that Kathy would handle the following morning's call to the electrical power and telephone companies, and David would contact a carpenter for the window repairs, they gravitated to her bedroom.

He felt perverse folding back a "country garden" comforter with its 3-dimensional floral appliqués blossoming across a soft field of white chintz. In bed, David said, "About the incident—what'll we do?"

"Wait," Kathy replied.

"Think we should call the police?"

"I *am* the police."

"I mean—to get it on the record."

"I *am* the record."

David, propped on one arm, said, "You're so into control."

Later, he reached down to retrieve a pillow that had fallen to the floor.

CHAPTER 2

✛ ✛ ✛

Friday, February 8

Hollings, once a vibrant manufacturing city tucked into a river valley, was on the rebound from the effects of a mass exodus south to warmer climates and better jobs. Many of its 100,000 people worked within four recently sprouted industrial parks that occupied high ground while above them, unpretentious homes stocked both hills, each a template for the other. The parks had changed the nature of Hollings' industry to high tech and service companies but had rescued its economic base. The city's color also changed—with regularity—a quilt in foliaged autumn, a shroud in the grimy sludge of winter. A few decayed but proud manufacturing plants remained behind, clasping hands along the valley, a stone's throw from the central district's shops, banks, churches and a splendid green with towering sycamores, granite war memorials and a gazebo.

Within the city was the venerable Hollings General

Hospital, one of two medical facilities there; the other—
Brent Institute of Biotechnology—was a complex of laboratories at the city's outer district. Brent, an arm of
neighboring Howerton University, was known as the
jewel of its Science Department, focusing on studies of
the human genome, stem cells, genetic engineering and
cloning. The Institute had prided itself in rising above
the debate between government sponsored scientific
research and that performed by private companies and, in
many areas, was further along than either.

Within Hollings General was the Hole, a tiny basement
space next to laundry rooms and the hospital pharmacy.
There were no windows: a clinking exhaust fan strained
to remove crosscurrents of medicinal and detergent
odors, and the door was usually kept open. The floor was
a cracked concrete slab, the ceiling a tangle of flaking
cream pipes. Its furnishings were two tubular steel
chairs, a pair of green metal desks not an arm's length
from each other and a matching file cabinet. It was
David's office.

The next morning, he arrived there at 9:20. He slid
Friday onto the cabinet, yanked a chair around and
straddled it.

"Belle," he said, "if I told you what happened last
night, you'd swear there's more to come." His secretary
was on loan from the Emergency Room—courtesy of the
administrator who spoke openly of the correlation
between David's work load and the time he saved other
physicians so they might see additional patients in their
offices. Translation? More hospital admissions.

"Good morning," Belle responded. "Problems?" She
and David were once an item throughout the hospital,

but their talk had never reached a serious pitch. Since Kathy surfaced, however, she had let straighten what was once curved and let curve what was once straight, although her hair still flamed, her smile was just as engaging and she continued to turn a head or two. More than a decade before, she had divorced an abusive husband and currently lived with her eleven-year-old daughter, Georgia.

"I'd guess someone's trying to scare me off a case."

"What case?"

"I don't know."

She gave him a puzzled look. "Then how are you supposed to know what case to get scared away from?"

"Beats me, but someone cut my power lines—unless they went to the wrong house." David was sure he'd recovered from the jolt and panic of the night before. He turned the chair around and sifted through some memos in a wire basket. "What's this afternoon like?"

"Your power lines?" Belle's voice had the ring of deep concern rather than inquiry.

He recited an abbreviated version of what had transpired, concluding with a wait-and-see expression.

"This afternoon?" he asked

"An avalanche. And everybody wants to be first." She handed him a list of names, street addresses and the chief complaint of each patient. "Incidentally," she said, "why not eliminate your morning investigations? Aren't you a bit beyond prowlers and stolen vehicles and all that other piddling stuff?" David saw through the transparency of Belle's return to business.

"Maybe so, but I still need to pile up credits in every category." He spoke with a tinge of resignation. Even though professional licensure was not far off, he wasn't looking forward to the prospect of losing certain advantages of his amateur status, like conducting searches without warrants or entrapping without legal worries. "Funny you should mention stolen vehicles," he said, "because those are the cases I've been putting off all week long. I'd better get going."

He picked up Friday and, at the doorway, turned and said, "Oh, and would you please call Tony Brown and have him send one of his carpenters over to replace the window. He can do it from the outside."

The phone rang as David left. While he jockeyed in the corridor between a laundry cart and the hospital's beeping robot, Belle caught up to him. "You'd better take this call. It's Dr. Molina from Brent, and he sounds kinda strange."

"What's he want, a house call for a rat?" David smiled as he recalled several times when he and Molina toasted imaginary people at out-of-town bars.

Dr. Manuel Molina, Brent Institute's diminutive and dapper director, appeared more cut out for hair designing than science. In his early thirties, he was born in Connecticut to parents who had emigrated from Radonia, South America. He was considered a wunderkind in anything scientific, earned a Ph.D. in molecular biology and was eventually lured back to Radonia where he taught in the local university's science department, only to be appointed the country's Minister of Science under President Juan Carlos Saltanban. Six years later, in 1999, Howerton University's president, Jack Ogleton, induced him to return to the states. Unmarried and an ardent skirt chaser and singles bar enthusiast, some wondered why his lifestyle hadn't precluded his assuming the reins at Brent. But Molina was a luminary in the international scientific community, a prolific contributor to its research literature and one of a handful regularly on the cusp of molecular discoveries. Most of his guest lectures covered genetic engineering, genome mapping and cloning possibilities. The Brent facilities had been established to coincide with his arrival and, early on, Hollings' citizenry speculated about the direction the Institute would take, about the details of its research and even about grant monies that flowed through its doors. But the initial intrigue subsided as increasing numbers maintained that since Brent was part of the university, its mission was on the up and up.

The tone of speech David heard over the phone was flat, spiritless. "You're sure it's okay to talk . . . nobody else is listening, right, David?"

"It's *that* important?"

"Yes, I'm afraid so."

"Well, you never know about hospital operators, Manny. Why not call me back on my cell phone." David gave the number and waited for the vibration at his hip.

"I followed your adventure through all those homicides" Molina began, "and I commend you on bringing the murderer to justice." He spoke as if he were reading from a script. "I have a special request. My life has been threatened and I wonder if we could meet to talk about it? I will pay you for your time." Again, a script?

Earlier, David had sensed the urgency of the call but had not expected it would grow deadly in its content; thus, for the first time since the hospital murders, his detective mode overcame him—with its quality of detachment, of formality, of official parlance. He cradled the phone on his shoulder, opened a notepad and made some entries.

"Forget money. Can you tell me why you were threatened?"

"It involves the research here—you know, stem cells, genomes and the like."

"And the threat stemmed from that?" David had not intended the pun nor did Molina pick up on it.

"A request was made of me over two years ago—26 months, to be exact. I agreed to cooperate, but now they say I'm reneging."

"Are you?" David had no idea about the nature of the territory he was in.

"We'll cover that if we can meet."

"And you say 'they'?"

"They or he." Molina paused. "David, please understand, I would really like to discuss more over the phone, but could you possibly come to my home later this afternoon at, say, 3:30? I'd come there but that might invite a . . . what is it you people call it . . . a tail?"

David paused in turn, cognizant of his house call demands and unsure of what he might be getting into, but he couldn't disengage the detective in him. He gave it a try, anyhow.

"I was never very good at preventive medicine, Manny. Why not contact the police?"

"They would create a big fuss over it, maybe botch it up. And, most of all, I was instructed not to—or else."

"I see," David said slowly, massaging his decision scar. "And so you want to give me the details and together we'll decide where to go from there?"

"Correct. I want you to have all the relevant data either to stop them . . . ." Molina's voice trailed off but David thought he heard "or in case they *do* get to me."

David finally understood there was no script, only the words of a pure scientist, much like the ones he remembered from medical school. "Okay, you're on," he said with the resolve of someone who had just had a stick knocked off his shoulder. He copied down directions to Molina's house, at the same time figuring on a likely connection between their conversation and his severed wires.

"By the way," he said, "do you know anything about a power failure?"

"Power failure?" Molina said without hesitation.

"Never mind." Although David had received the correct answer and timing, he returned to the same subject. "Did you tell anyone you'd be calling me?"

This time, Molina hesitated. "Not that I can remember."

David knew there were times when Dr. Manuel Molina might not remember much of anything, as in the late stages of most social events thrown by Connecticut's medical and scientific academia. He was often the last remaining pie-eyed raconteur.

"One last question, then. When was the threat made?"

"Two days ago."

"And you waited all this time to do something about it? Weren't you concerned?"

"Not till yesterday. I wasn't sure what to do—exactly." His voice turned severe. "Why are you going on with these questions?"

"Curious, that's all. See you at 3:30."

David hung up the phone and found Belle giving him her "Well?" expression.

"He's been threatened and wants to give me the details stat, so I'm going over to his house."

Belle shook her head. "How can you go at that hour when you have . . . ."

He stepped on her words. "I know, I know. But did you hear me? I stalled as long as I could."

"You won't be finished with your calls."

"I was stalling so I could figure out how to handle it. Phone Castleman. His ER shift ends at three. See if he wants to start with me today. I'll bet he jumps at the chance."

"Are you sure you want him?"

"Yeah, why? Is there something I don't know?"

"No, it's not that. But he may not want to give up Chief in the E.R."

"Chief or not—we've talked about it for months—and he complains about insurance forms and compliance forms and all the other garbage as much as I do. Trust me; give him a call."

David scribbled in his notepad, then strode toward the door with a slight bounce to his gait, awaiting the twinges of pain that were certain to reappear in his knee.

Belle had gotten up and was standing by her desk. As he passed, she grabbed his arm and said, "David, I have a funny feeling . . . ."

"Ignore it. I'll give him my best advice and that will be it. I'm certainly not going to be a bodyguard."

"You'll call and keep me up to date?"

"You can count on it." He detected a familiar nostalgic

look in her eyes, one that took him back to his pre-Kathy days, when he preferred her to scores of eligible women on the hospital staff: technicians, social workers, administrators, other nurses, other doctors.

* * *

It was 3 p.m. when David crossed off the final name in a foreshortened list of house call patients. In a phone call to Belle, he learned that Dr. William Castleman would make the later visits and work with the hospital in coordinating their joint house call practice.

"You were right, David. He went on and on about blankety-blank insurance forms and poor use of his time. I was surprised."

"That I was right?"

Belle giggled like in the old days. "No, that he'd complain so much."

David swung his car around and, top up, headed for home. He could feel the Beretta Minx .22 beneath his blue blazer and, though he realized he might be overdoing it, still wanted to increase his personal fire power. Once in the basement, he secured the Smith and Wesson snubby in his ankle rig and, grabbing his knee, hastened up the stairs and out toward Hollings' Marblehead district. Named after the city's most famous industrialist, there was no marble there except in the foyers and driveways at the fashionable end of its caste system of homes. To reach that end, Marblehead Proper, one drove up a gentle incline, through soporific rows of World War II capes and on through the middle zone, a grab bag of raised ranches, split levels, even a Georgian or two. The baby version of Levittown was named Mainline Road and the middle part, Veterans Heaven. Dr. Molina lived in the Proper section.

The sky was such a pure black that a paltry snowfall appeared out of place. It had started during David's trip to the Hole that morning and never gathered steam as would ordinarily happen in southern New England. Weather patterns have changed, he thought, launching into one of his internal monologues about nature and its surroundings: questions about global warming, ozone layers, tides, lunar influences, pressure variances. Were he on an idle jaunt through the countryside, he would have dwelled on the matter, introducing trees and vines into the mix. Or invoked certain scientific principals— Bernoulli's and Archimedes' were his favorites—or perhaps made up his own to fit the circumstance. Kathy was the only person who knew he even talked to trees. And, while he admitted it wasn't clear what kind of sensory apparatus they possess, he enjoyed rehashing, from time to time, what he believed: that trees thrive better when exposed to chamber music rather than to hard rock; that lie detectors indicate trees react adversely to moth infestation, fire or other threats against neighboring trees; that ultrasound stimulates growth; that an anesthetized tree is more likely to survive transplanting. She entitled such discourses the "Tree Sermons" and whenever David was inclined to add a new idea, she would be just as inclined to cover his mouth with a gentle hand, then a kiss— before he had a chance to finish.

But the trip to Molina's was no idle jaunt, and more immediate, powerful questions muscled past those of natural theory. Why 3:30 and not 5:30? Or after dinner? Why the urgency if the threat had been made two days ago?

Deep into Marblehead, at its outermost reach, was the house Molina had described. It was in an area David had never visited and, before long, he realized why it was considered the classiest in the city. Zoning regulations were clearly different among the three sections, as each of the Proper homes, mostly Victorian, was set on a lot that was the equivalent of two or three blocks on Mainline. Molina's was the last on the road, beyond a lengthy stretch of orchard grass grown tall around several empty barns, their red or gray sides faded and fractured.

The two-story house was a boxy Italianate with an adjoining one-car garage. A mansard roof, corner quoins and two balconies highlighted its red brick facade while two white columns guarded a central paneled entryway.

David turned into the driveway, pulled up to within inches of the garage and got out of the car. The air was filled with the loud chant of rap music. *Too loud. He's not that kind of swinger.* David tightened his expression. Even more when he found the front door two-fingers ajar. He tucked in his left arm and, though assured of the Beretta at his shoulder, turned and raced back to the car. Snapping his attaché case, Friday, open, he removed the terry cloth enwrapping the .44 Magnum and at first inserted the gun beneath his waistband but decided to hold it, after all, shielded in the hollow of his arm. He also decided to carry Friday with his free hand. David had a way of making even the most over-reactive moves appear necessary.

The light snow had not stuck to the ground, and there were no tire marks or footprints on the macadam driveway or square of front lawn. He trained his eyes over the property and along the street, then edged toward the right and lengthened his strides as he circled the house, leaning around corners. In the back, he passed by an open porch garden closed down for the season with wicker furniture pieces on their backs; dull tools, flower pots and watering pails in a heap; perforated bags of loam off to the side. He could smell old and fresh soil alike and briefly entertained a new theory that nature possesses greater pungency during winter months, that somehow in cold temperatures, odors trigger taste buds—two distinct senses in a symbiotic bond. David shook his head, "No, not now."

Returning to the front door, he rang the bell with the muzzle end of the .44. He could barely hear the ring through the music and eased the door open enough to squeeze through and into a shallow vestibule dominated by a staircase and an oversized chandelier. A stack of books rested on a nearby table and on the books was an unopened box of chocolates with a card taped to its corner, near a "Two Pounds" designation. The card's logo, matching the one engraved beneath cellophane, read, *Candies by Clemente* and a message, printed in red ink, was, "Happy Birthday, Manuel. From Juan Carlos."

David glanced ahead, beyond an archway to the living room, too absorbed in vigilance to process the specifics of stuffed chairs and sofas, pillows and quilts, worn tables, lace doilies, wooden boxes, candleholders, flower vases, books and magazines—hundreds of them—in bookcases, on shelves, piled high in corners. Just a melange because his mind was on the upstairs floor.

For a moment, he thought about not checking the first floor and, instead, proceeding to the second if only to stop the music whose repetitive rhythm had been poking him like a cattle prod. But he was on a higher alert and heeded the mandate that on such occasions, first secure the immediate perimeter. Thus, he put Friday aside and, both hands taut on the .44, finger on its trigger, stalked through the living room, dining room, utility room, garage and kitchen, whipping open closet doors on the way. In the kitchen, he struck his head on a cluster of milk glass lampshades, but felt no pain, engrossed in the significance of Molina's license plate: MOL544.

He'd forgotten to call out Molina's name during the search, and he overcorrected with a scream well above the music and directed to the second story. "It's me, Manny . . . David Brooks . . . are you home? Are you here, Manny?" No one answered.

There were moments when David savored his hunches. This was not one of them. He grabbed Friday, knifed around the banister post and took two steps at a time up the stairs, Magnum pressed across his chest, knee buckling but never breaking stride.

The upper landing ushered in a long claret-carpeted hallway whose walls were overfilled with paintings in frames twice their size and depicting landscapes, buildings and architectural designs. They reminded him of a museum. Dwarfed by the paintings was an occasional group portrait. David was in no mood to examine them up close. Gooseflesh pulled at his back.

He felt a give beneath his toes as he bounced slowly toward the first room on the left, the obvious source of the music. Coming to a crouch and leading with the barrel of the gun, he advanced his head sideways until one eye had cleared the doorjamb.

What he observed was what he had feared. A male body sat behind a desk, motionless, his bald head contorted back, salt and pepper goatee pointing toward the ceiling. He was fully clothed in a gray twill jacket, striped tie, brown slacks and buckled tan shoes. There was no mistaking he was Molina. David straightened, but before entering, surveyed the room—a cluttered study which appeared undisturbed, save for a few journals scattered on the floor to the right and probably once part of the pile skewed on the desk.

He walked over to Molina, felt for a carotid pulse and found none. A small circle of blood was clotted on the carpeting behind the body, in direct line with the junction of the body's head and the brim of the chair. Specks of red material dotted Molina's right hand. The lower part of his head had a purplish, liver color while the uppermost aspect was a waxy pale. David pressed his finger on the darker part, and it didn't blanch.

He opened Friday, put on the surgical gloves and turned off the radio that was on a rear counter. He then carefully lifted Molina's head. It was cool to touch. A slender ribbon of crimson lay caked across the shoulder. He could feel stiffness in the muscles of the neck and jaw but none in the muscles below. At the back of the head— its occiput—was a bullet entrance wound that was round with blackened and seared margins. There was no exit wound. He estimated the temperature of the room to be 70 degrees and, removing a thermometer from Friday, measured the body's temperature at 90 degrees. He looked around the room—its counter surfaces, chairs, cabinet tops, floor—and could see no gun or spent shell. In the process, he noted the journals near his shoes: *Human Biology, Journal of Human Genetics, Lancet, Science, Cell, Journal of Molecular Evolution*. He had all he needed for a few calculations and a preliminary crime scene reconstruction, one that included, to his consternation, the likely profile of the murderer. David swallowed hard. Bracing himself against a side wall while still staring at the body, he went through several mental sequences:

Body cool to touch with eight to nine degrees temperature lost.

Early rigor mortis in small muscles of neck and jaw.

Early fixed lividity with no blanching.

Therefore, dead four to six hours.

High velocity impact spatter on his hand.

Therefore, hand in close proximity to head when shot.

Edges of entrance wound black and seared.

No tattooing or soot smudge.

Therefore, hard contact by gun muzzle against skull.

A round, rather than a stellate entrance wound.

No exit wound.

Therefore, probably .22-caliber handgun used.

David knew that in a direct contact wound of, say, the breast bone, explosion gases expand between the bone and skin, thus blowing out the star around the hole. But the finding would be different in contact wounds of the head where a thin layer of scalp is stretched over bone. Also, if the bullet lacked the velocity to penetrate the skull bone a second time, instead ricocheting around within the skull cavity, a .22 was a good bet.

David's next move was to call Kathy but, before that, he

began to brood, beset by other forensic questions that would need sorting out later at his computer. For the moment, the larger question was whether or not he was ready for Murder One again—coming on the heels of the hospital killings, a mere two weeks before. He hated ambiguity though—a mindset he rendered as more disturbing than any of its components, much like the sting of anger generated by an accumulation of issues he cared little about in the long run. So, he took stock: this was the level of investigation he'd been training for; he had no control over the timing of criminal activity in Hollings; perpetrators don't wait for others to catch their breath. It was a continuum of his month-long baptism under fire, he concluded, and it was a matter of either staying in or getting out of the field. He looked at it another way: his single-handed solution to the recent murders had labeled him not only a celebrity but also a known quantity within the criminal justice system, and he had better muster up the necessary resolve—posthaste—if he expected to sustain such a label. David took a long slow breath, then lifted up and called Kathy on his cell phone.

"Kath, are you ready for this?"

"I should be sitting?" she asked innocently.

"You'd better be. You know Manuel Molina, Brent's top honcho? He's been murdered."

David heard breathing quicken at the other end and became conscious of his own.

"Where?" she asked.

"Here—at the end of Marblehead. I just found him." He gave a quick rundown of events leading to his discovery. "Would you know a mob hit if you saw one?" he asked.

Kathy's silence prompted him to remove the receiver from his ear and look at it. Finally, she answered with a firm question: "Why didn't you tell me you were going there?"

"To tell you the truth, I didn't expect to find him dead."

No silence this time. "Oh, come off it, David, you could have at least called. It's not like you had to rush out there."

He understood she was channeling the sudden emotion of the discovery into his having kept her in the dark about the impending visit to Molina's, and he could have said so. Instead, he settled for, "Why all the fuss?"

"It's not a matter of fuss. It's a matter of what if a mobster were still there?"

"So?," he said.

"Forget it. We'll be right over," Kathy blurted. David could picture her exasperation.

He figured she would dispatch the entire crime scene unit so, while he waited, he inspected the adjoining rooms, leading with his Magnum. Nearest was a bleak bedroom with a single working light—shades drawn, cobwebs at the corners—and little in it to explain its musty smell. A solitary bed—unmade—was surrounded by a mound of crumpled newspapers. David went straight for a pillow and was not surprised to find a pistol underneath. First tugging at his latex gloves, he picked up the gun and rotated it in his hands. It was a 9mm Super Star automatic, indigenous to Spain, and combined the Colt M19's outward appearance with the internal mechanism of the Browning Hi-Power. Now that's a thoroughbred, he thought, sensing that Kathy was right after all: since receiving his father's gun collection, he kept current, as the collection deserved. He replaced the pistol, then moved cautiously into a full bathroom, through a sterile sitting area, a second bedroom with no furnishings and, at the rear, into a room burdened with boxes, trunks, broken chairs, carpet rolls, disassembled beds and half-shredded books. Large-framed paintings and photographs, similar to those in the hallway, clustered all four walls. Without the music, the silence was stark and beckoning. He was unsure about what he'd find—the murder weapon, another body, a calling card, any small clue—but he encountered nothing suspicious. As for Kathy's concern, David doubted anyone would have remained behind, lurking for four hours or more, nor would that fit the M.O. of the killer or killers he reasoned had already left a calling card back at the murder site:

Loud music to muffle shot.

Hard contact of gun against back of head.

No punched out abrasion on scalp from recoil spring guide rod.

No spent shell.

Gun thus not an autoloading pistol, but a .22 caliber revolver.

Therefore, a mob hit.

During his examination of the body, he had glossed over the prospect of dealing with organized crime, but once he pieced together all the elements of a telltale pattern, he felt more convinced; and a stream of other questions surfaced. Was it really the Mafia, or did someone else want it to look that way? Was Molina into them for money? Was he a closet gambler? Did he cross them in some way? Did he know too much and, if so, about what? Or were they simply hired by someone else for God-knows-what reason?

David put aside other considerations for he had more work to do before the others arrived. He reinspected the first floor, then entered the garage, which he had eye-balled earlier from the doorway off the utility room. The oil smell reminded him of the fleeing vehicle of the night before, but even in the closed garage, it wasn't as acrid as then, an observation reinforcing his belief that the vehicle was a truck. He ran a latex-gloved finger along the length of the green Volvo S60 sports sedan. He looked at his finger; it was clean. The car's sunroof was in the open position. He placed his palm on a cold hood, then squatted at each tire to examine its treads.

David peered through the windows; only the front passenger seat caught his attention. It contained a two-pound box of chocolates like the one in the vestibule; this one, though, was without cellophane and its lid was askew. He angled into the car and flicked off the lid. He counted four pieces of candy missing.

He switched his .44 for the Polaroid in Friday and photographed the garage and its contents. Then hurrying inside, he included Molina's body, the murder site, and each of the other rooms in the house. He also snapped photos of the vestibule. Wanting some views of the exterior, he turned and opened the front door. The light snow had changed to a fine drizzle. David shielded the camera under his jacket and was about to negotiate the entrance stoop in a single leap. He jerked back. A fallen canary lay before him on the middle step, tiny raindrops bouncing off its underbelly. *He had not seen it there before.*

He squatted, confirmed that the bird was dead and quickly yanked out his nearest gun—the snubby from his ankle rig. He rose slowly, turned twice in a semi-circle, pointing the gun at trees, shrubs, along the road and into the mist beyond. Spotting nothing strange, he bolted once around the house's exterior, this time not pausing at corners.

After placing the bird under a nearby hedge, David stared off, pondering its meaning, having read about mafiosi's inserting a dead canary into a victim's mouth to inform rival groups who was responsible for the killing. But this was an outrageous variation of that ritual. Why announce their affiliation? Just honor the contract. And, since the bird was deposited while he was busy inside, how did they know the time of his arrival? Certainly, Molina didn't tell them. Or did he?

David covered his forehead with a hand as if to keep a vital thought from escaping. "Wait . . . a . . . minute . . . of course," he said aloud, drawing out the words. He hurried back into the house, straight toward the telephone in the study. He took the handset apart and found what he was looking for: a microchip transmitter, less than the size of a dime. Bugged!

A few minutes earlier, he had stifled any emotional, much less physical, response to so crude a symbol as a dead canary—disgust, fear, anger—but upon the additional discovery of microbugging by the underworld, he felt a blistering surge at his temples. Furthermore, the phone tap put a whole new spin on the past 18 hours because two and two told him that whoever murdered Molina also cut the wires at 10 Oak Lane; that they went to great lengths with the canary routine either as a self-congratulatory display or as intimidation aimed not at other law enforcement authorities but directly at him. His reaction? Jaw squared, he mustered the same fortitude that had carried him through the epidemic of hospital killings the month before. He snapped open his notepad. Yet, David was too absorbed to write, for he had been victimized in triplicate: mobsters vandalized his property, listened in on a confidential phone conversation and then mocked him by positioning a token of death under his nose. Sons-of-bitches! If he were about to become entangled with the mob, he vowed to be the spider.

He started to lower himself into one of two plush chairs in the study but stopped short of making contact, mindful that physical evidence might have been compromised. He checked his watch: ten of four. Forty minutes worth of inspection and deduction had been crammed into 20 minutes. He returned to the living room to pace and to await the screech of police cruisers, a predictable event that always amused him, for their arrival in such situations was never a matter of preventing death.

The screeches came, one after the other; David counted three. He opened the door and stationed himself midway on the front walk—in time to catch flashing lights cutting through the raw gray afternoon. The cruisers were lined up in the center of the road along with three other nondescript cars. Kathy, her supervisor, Detective Chief Nick Medicore, two deputies and a handful of uniformed police officers piled out. She walked to David's side; the others scattered as if they wanted to break the record for protocol execution.

"I put in a call to the medical examiner and Sparky. They should be here soon," Kathy announced in a manner belying her earlier displeasure. She squirmed into the blue London Fog which had been draped over a purse that hung from her shoulder. Bedecked in David's

favorite black suit, she sported a badge on her hip pocket as he had often requested. "Keeps the bird dogs at bay,"
he had advised her.

Compounding Kathy's transformation, she rose on her
toes to invite David's liberal kiss. "I expected to see
smoke coming out of your ears, you know," he said, wip-
ing his lips with a handkerchief.

"Sorry I chewed you out," she said. "I still think of you
as a neophyte, I suppose."

"I am," David said, wanting to wink.

She shook her head. "Five murders solved in two
weeks' time. Sure you are."

David, always uneasy with anything that resembled a
compliment, changed the subject by pointing to Nick and
several officers who were cordoning off the scene with yellow tape. "They've had lots of practice, lately," he said.

Nick came over and said, "Good to see you, Dr. Brooks."
Even after their shared investigations of the previous
month, Nick still used the surname. David briefed them on
what he had found. When he mentioned the canary,
Kathy's eyes took on a hunted look while Nick sucked on
his teeth. The Detective Chief, a recent transplant from the
west coast, wore his usual turtleneck—this one, blue—
under a checkered jacket. A badge was pinned atop the
swelling near his breast pocket. Fiftyish, bespectacled and
not much taller than Kathy, his snappy moves seemed at
odds with a compact frame. David believed they were
symptomatic of a lifetime of impatience, as were the
venous markings on a scarlet face. Nick folded his handkerchief to dab at the drizzle settling on his scalp, careful
not to disturb three or four strands of hair plastered from
side to side. He appeared to know their precise location.

"How are we doing this?" David asked with some enthusiasm. "You want me to handle it? Same arrangement as before? Same forensic support?"

"How else?" Nick replied, moving toward the house.

David—used to the Chief's brittle expressions—stared in his direction, then at Kathy and said, "What's eating him?" Since the solution of the murders at Hollings General, he wondered why on earth he had put Nick on his suspect list during the investigation. Until now. He took in a deep breath, then puffed up his cheeks before blowing it out.

Kathy grabbed his arm and said, "Look, David darling, this may not be the right time to say this, but not everyone's going to like you, or even defer to you—all the time."

David used a finger to swipe away the rain off his eyebrows. His voice took on a bitter texture. "No, it's not the time," he said, eyeing a small van as it pulled up behind the parade of cars. "And is it really a case of liking or not liking?"

"Maybe I put it wrong, but as I've told you many times before, he does like you."

"Pity his enemies." He didn't wait for an acknowledgment of the phrase he had just turned. "Do you know what bugs me the most about the guy, though? When city hall and the media and all of law enforcement this side of the Mississippi were after his ass, I saved it."

"David, don't you see? That whole scenario could have been a double edged sword because it . . . ."

He stepped on her words. "What's that supposed to mean?"

They both clammed up when Sparky and the medical examiner approached them.

"What have we got?" Sparky asked. The medical examiner nodded and went into the house.

Walter Sparks, the Hollings Police Department's criminalist, was a forty-some-odd throwback to a Western Union clerk in a 1940's B movie: slicked down black hair parted in the middle, wire framed glasses, suspenders. He sported a tan fur-collared jacket—open in the front—carried two black bags and was the only one at the scene wearing rubber overshoes.

David repeated the briefing before asking, "Will you be at the lab tomorrow?"

"Is DNA the rage?"

"It's Saturday, remember."

"Yeah, but murder's murder—and even if it weren't for you, I'd be there, at least till mid-afternoon."

"Thanks, I'll drop by."

David checked his watch for the second time in five minutes. He removed the cell phone from his hip and dialed the Hole.

"Belle, I found Molina murdered—so you were right with that funny feeling of yours."

"Oh my God, that's terrible!" After a deep sigh, she added, "What a waste of talent—and such a great guy. How?"

"A slug in the back of the head."

"Even I know what that means. You'll be in charge of the investigation?"

"I'm afraid so. I'll be in early Monday morning to go over my schedule."

"Here we go again. Be careful. This doesn't sound like just some crazy out there."

He believed her concern merited a brief summary of

what he discovered at the crime scene including the M.O., the canary and the box of Clemente chocolates. David's parting remark was, "Please don't get any more funny feelings."

After clipping the phone to his belt, he joined Kathy at the hedge which covered the dead canary. She was trying to turn it over with her foot. Temperatures dropping, he could taste the chill of rain which had not let up. She looked up at him and, in a voice edged in tension, said, "David, do you think it's the Mafia? Or made to look like it?"

"The Mafia."

"And you don't have some concern?"

"Of course not."

She regarded him as if he were challenging the law of gravity. "But a little fear might go a long way."

"What do you want me to do, develop a twitch?" he asked. Of all the two-bit indignities David ever suffered, he ranked the canary ploy at the head of the list and tried to disguise the scorching look he felt on his face. At the same time, he realized his question wasn't fair, for it was clear Kathy was mixing up her police detective role and her fiancée role. After pulling her into a bear hug, he arched back and said, "Don't worry, Kath. They may be hired-gun wackadoos but they don't have the intelligence for anything else." He wished he had faith in his last sentence.

"By the way," she said, "you'll be checking Molina's office at Brent?"

"What?"

"Molina's office. You'll check it?"

"Yes, of course," he replied, as if from another zone.

"Good. We'll probably send a crew there in the morning, but they'll leave things pat for you."

"That's fine."

"Do you see the treatment accorded heroes?," she said as she reached up to tweak his cheek, a move David never liked.

Jolted more by surprise than pain, it was enough to bring him back to earth. "I can do without the pinch right about now, Kathleen." He stepped away.

She stood her ground. "Oh, poor baby," she teased in her best new-mother imitation.

David managed a smirk. "Okay," he shot back, "let's cut the . . . ." He hesitated, then let the thought hang. "Look," he said, "you go do your thing in there. I'd join you but once with your boss in the same hour is enough. See you later?"

She moved away, her expression less than assured. "Yes, later—after dinner."

"Your place or mine?"

She returned and fixed him with a level stare. "David, you *know* I hate that expression."

"Pray tell me why. I forgot."

"Because it's what casual acquaintances say. It makes what we do sound trivial."

"Okay, do you want to do something trivial at your place or mine?"

"You're incorrigible," she groaned, pushing at his midsection. He doubled over in feigned distress.

At the door, she turned and said, "Make it my place."

✳   ✳   ✳

David didn't know whether he was like everyone else when it came to what he called "worry points." But when they bombarded him in bunches, he would store them in his mind until such time as he could sort them out. Now was that time. In the semi-darkness of the Mercedes, he listed the principal ones in his notepad: MURDER, MAFIA, NICK, CHOCOLATES, JUAN CARLOS. Next, he made a feeble attempt to sketch out the murder scene from memory, preferring inaccuracy over another encounter with Nick, inside. David recalled how the tone of his initial meetings with the Detective Chief differed from more recent ones, how easy and natural it was then, to explain the origin of his house call practice and the intrigue of police detective work, how he had soured on office-based and full-time hospital practice, both of which he had tried. It was a question of freedom. Freedom from staggering stacks of paperwork, from the annoyances of dealing with insurance companies and Health Maintence Organizations and from other elements in the Managed Care approach to medical care.

And, in turn, how easy and natural it was to receive Nick's explanation of why his police department would welcome the assistance of an amateur detective with limited experience. Having been given free rein in the hospital murders investigations, David had indicated he would check with Nick and Kathy on a regular basis. "That's important," Nick had said. "We're really accountable to city government." David remembered his every word. Nick went on to cite their cut-every-year budget, their meager staff, their need for help in the face of staggering responsibilities. He spoke of what was once an Electronic Unit, a Polygraph Section, a Forgery Squad— all now rolled into one under Sparky's command. Of the consolidation of precinct squads, a Narcotics Division and a Sex Crimes Task Force.

But from either side, it was no longer easy or natural. And David wasn't sure why.

CHAPTER 3

✝ ✝ ✝

David drove home with questions ferrying around in his head and anxious to sit at his computer to upload a schematic of the past day. He hated feeling unhinged. It was there that his thinking was the clearest, that his entries provided a kind of structure, a way of distilling chaos while cleansing his mind. But the motoring was slow on the black ice covering his usual route to Oak Lane and, never one to pile up empty time, he turned to the question of the chocolates. The card on the box was signed "Juan Carlos." Juan Carlos who? A relative? He knew that Molina was unmarried and probably had no children. Who would send *two* boxes? A friend? And what about the timing? David reasoned that if Molina had received them after the threat was made and had considered poisoning as a means for his demise, he had to have trusted the sender because four pieces of chocolate were eaten. On the other hand, if he received them before the threat, the matter of trust was irrelevant. But why would a murderer send chocolates in the first place? As a gesture to be perceived as kind, one that would divert attention, one not normally associated with a killer? In any event, the issue would be clarified when he visited Clemente's candy place in the morning.

Half-way home, the thought that Clemente's—a shop he had once visited as a youngster—might shed light on the chocolates question did little to quiet his mind. David tried to constrain his blinking, even as he wondered whether the events of the past 24 hours were influencing his thinking as much as his current readings about artificial intelligence and its burgeoning role in forensic science: crime mapping, crime scene logic, criminal profiling, getting into the mind of a killer. Or was he overdoing it by trying to store and process too much information in too little time, like being forced to drink from a fire hose. Even by leaping at conclusions too early.

Nonetheless, whether in medical or criminal detection, he had always preferred his own principle of logic, a simplification of its two basic components: deduce from a lot rather then induce from a little.

Approaching the last leg home and on the verge of cautioning himself about mental clutter, he felt his eyes widen. In the rear-view mirror, he spotted a set of lights similar to those that had often appeared throughout the skein of hospital murders—lights shaped like the eyes of a frog: Kermit eyes. They conjured up visions of the Yakuza underworld and their loyalty rituals such as self-mutilation and extreme tattooing; of the hospital atrocities, international killers and drug cartels. David felt anew the smart of the dart needle and the terror of barbed wire entombment in his Mercedes, hanging from a smelly tow truck in its climb up High Rock Road.

He whipped out the Minx and, after swerving onto Oak Lane, glanced over his shoulder and counted three heads in the darkened cabin of a black tow truck as it thundered off. Momentarily surprised by the truck's traction on the slippery road, he would later remember this as a rare time his spirits crashed over a hunch that proved correct.

The remote control gadget worked, and David heard the clank of bumper against trash barrel as he misgauged the direction into his garage. He thanked Belle silently for following through on getting the electricity restored.

He had expected to sit before the computer with only Molina's murder to review, but now he had also to contend with the posibility there had not been a complete closure of the circumstances surrounding the hospital killings. Was the truck following him the same one that sped from the house the night before? Were its occupants the same Asian goons with the dart gun? Although jarred by the possibility the Yakuza may have entered the picture again, he got out of the car, up-righted the trash barrel and marched into the house, all the while trying to ratchet up his resolve a peg or two.

On his way to the scotch in a kitchen cabinet, he noticed the repaired rear window and then tossed Friday onto a chair. Several industrial-size swigs failed to achieve an immediate effect, so he poured the rest of the drink into the sink. He would postpone his greater assault on sobriety until later—with Kathy—for there was computer work ahead.

Even as he inhaled the imagined pine in his paneled den—often a relaxing prelude to uploading—David was uneasy, weighed down with doubt. Within a month, his challenges had escalated from runaway teenagers and stray horses to murders on a grand scale. And with little more than a two-week respite, he now faced not only another murder mystery but also one possibly linked to a nasty faction of the underworld. Perhaps foreign. His problem was not fear of an adversary but uncertainty about whether or not his personal mettle could stand the test again. He was convinced there would have been less doubt had the hospital murders been strung out longer, allowing him time to adapt to a new level of danger. But they occurred so quickly, like tandem flashes on a continuous fuse. Thus, he hoped the process of consulting his notepad, organizing his thoughts and transferring them to the computer would bring the new challenge into sharper focus and help settle the issue: that he would have to sleuth as cases came to him, if he were to continue sleuthing at all. His recent celebrity notwithstanding, he could not yet afford to be selective. David felt the crease above his nose deepen as he began typing:

Friday, February 8
Manuel Molina Murder:
A) Summary
    Electrical & phone wires cut last night.
    This a.m., call from Manny at Hole. Stated his
    life was threatened. No particulars given. Urged
    me to go to his house where he would explain.
    Found him dead there at 3:30 p.m. Gunshot
    wound, back of head.
    Primary, organized crime scene.
    Dead at least 4 hours.

Contract killing?

Crime scene contents: chocolates from Clemente's, bug in phone, car's sunroof in open position (But snowing all day. Never went to Brent?)

Dead canary on front step—was not there when I arrived.

Complete photographic coverage.

Crime Unit summoned. Kathy, Nick et al arrived. Nick acted weird.

Sparky & M.E. arrived later.

B) Action Review

Done: Means of entry: door found cracked open.
Molina answered door or was ambushed and forced upstairs?
Angle weapon used.
Time of death.
Prints, etc. (Sparky).

To be done:
Check Molina's last 24 hours.
Identify suspects—attend wake, funeral, where else?
Check crime lab, Clemente's, Brent Institute.
Opportunity and Means settled. Motive?

Kermit eyes followed me home. Déjà vu all over again.

* * *

At 5:15, David's call to Kathy was brief: he would shower first and arrive there about six. Before hanging up, he asked when she had gotten home.

"Five minutes ago."

"I never expected you'd answer. You didn't stay there long."

"Long enough. That's your domain, you know."

"I'll be over in awhile." He replaced the receiver in slow motion, his mind focused on the go-ahead he'd just received.

* * *

A scotch or two would ordinarily blunt David's powers of observation but, well into their second drinks and seated next to Kathy on the sofa, his senses were on the qui vive as he stared at the living room drapes: full length, golden, woven check, raised accent dots, puddled at the floor, soft scalloped valances that tempered the bold lines of the furniture pieces around them.

"Great curtains," he said.

"You've seen them a million times," she said, arching back, "and, besides, that's not you. You notice what you want to notice, and it's certainly never drapes, for heaven's sake."

"Molina had no curtains—just shades."

Kathy nodded. "Why do you think?"

"Why do I think at all, or why do I think there were no curtains?" His sarcasm told him the drinks were kicking in. Squinting, he guessed Kathy looked the same as he'd begun feeling, then gulped down the rest of the drink with a flair of finality. Since he was about to start the we've-had-a-tough-day-and-we-deserve-it line of reasoning, he knew he'd had enough.

"No, silly. Why no curtains?" She stretched up, pulled down on his shoulder and blew gently in and about his ear.

He lifted her onto his lap and studied her face at close range. He pulled away and declared, "I love you, but no, let's eat first—next discuss the case—and then get on with what we just postponed." David knew if he let his guard down, he could easily slip into acting like a smitten teenager—having done it before—and there was plenty of time for such regression later. The puzzle at hand was too serious . . . dead serious.

Kathy stood and put her hands on her hips in mock indignation. "How can you be so scientific all the time?" She shot him a coquettish look before leaning over to kiss the tip of his nose. "And just for the record," she continued, "*you* made the decision to postpone, not *me*."

He watched her walk out of the room—she was wearing his favorite lavender skintight pants—and he wondered whether or not he had made the wrong decision. He also tried to remember if they had ever before gotten tight two days in a row. Perhaps during the week he'd given her the diamond, three years before. Or over the weekend when he decided to limit his practice to house calls for other physicians.

"We can eat inside or out," Kathy announced from the kitchen. "Maybe hamburgers?"

"Out—and hamburgers are fine." He was now leaning against the archway to the kitchen, arms folded, ankles crossed. "We've eaten there in worse weather than this."

Kathy was at the sink when he enfolded her tightly from behind, secured both her hands with one of his and, with the other, lifted her hair before pressing his open lips on the nape of her neck. She squirmed away and exclaimed, "David! Remember, you asked for it. Later."

On the deck, he lit the gas-fired grill and positioned two chairs and a small table merely inches from it. Even so, he tightened the scarf within his taupe flannel shirt and flexed his fingers several times after consulting a pie plate thermometer on the garage's cedar wood. It registered 29 degrees. He pulled a black stocking cap from his back pocket, put it on, took it off and returned it, deciding its warmth was not worth the tightness around his head.

Kathy—in a charcoal toggle coat—shuttled hamburger patties, rolls, potato chips, dishes and utensils between kitchen and table. She paused to watch David begin his usual overuse of a spatula—flipping the patties before they needed flipping, explaining once again the proper way to prevent burgers from scorching. She rolled her eyes and left for the kitchen, stating she forgot to make the salad.

There was little dialogue during the meal for David had insisted on forestalling any consideration of the crime until they became more lucid. Over coffee, he said, "Now let's get down to business." He never understood the sobering up process, particularly as it related to the interplay between alcohol and food metabolism. "You feel clearheaded now?" he asked.

"I guess. You?"

He pushed the coffee cup aside. "No problem," he said. "So I'll break the ice. You know Molina had no immediate family—at least that's my understanding."

"No, I didn't know very much about him, but I found out he was never married."

"How?"

"I called the Institute. They said he has one known survivor—a cousin."

"Who's that?"

"Adrian Clemente."

"Clemente the Candyman? A cousin?" David got up and paced, oblivious to a number of raindrops leaking from the canopy onto his shoulder. "That's where the chocolates came from."

"I saw that."

"Was he notified of the death?"

"I assume so. Nick was emphatic about telling him in person and driving to the store alone."

David stopped short. "Hmm . . . did you offer to go?"

"Yes, but he said he'd rather handle it."

The silence was but a fleeting impasse to a full discussion of the points he had earlier uploaded into his computer including forensic details, the bugged phone, a possible Mafia connection and time lines as applied to the chocolates and Molina's whereabouts. The one point David never mentioned, however, was the Kermit Truck that had trailed him to Oak Lane.

The issue they dwelled on—analyzing it from every possible perspective—was the significance of the cut wires and the canary left at the crime scene. Their eventual conclusion was that, in the first instance, David's shooting salvo through his back window possibly disrupted the perpetrator's deadly plans; and, in the second, since the canary was deposited while he was in Molina's house, it was not a scare tactic but a bold signal that David, himself, might be a future target. For if the bird's purpose had been to intimidate or to serve as a calling card for Molina's murder—Mafiosa style— it could have been left at the time of the crime, some four hours earlier. David had begun feeling relieved until he raised this possibility of his own demise.

Out of the blue, Kathy said, "Can I admit something, David?"

"Is it bad?"

"No, not bad, just dumb. I mean, sometimes I feel dumb."

David didn't dare touch it. "About what?"

"Genomes, stem cells, genetic what-ever-they-call-it—engineering. Sometimes I glance at the bulletins you get, or I might read about Brent in the papers and, more times than not, I don't have a clue. Have you kept up with what they're doing there?"

"I have. With what they do, and with what they can do. It's remarkable. Maybe scary when you come right down to it."

"Okay, doctor, you're the scientist; what's a genome?"

"It's the genetic code. The genome is the complete genetic code of one person and determines whether that person has brown eyes or blue eyes and anything else that's inherited. It's all in the person's DNA. Let's see. The way I remember how it works is to divide it up into parts. Chromosomes, genes and the DNA. That's about it. And cells with their nuclei. Everything takes place within the cell and especially in its nucleus. The body has roughly 100 trillion cells and each cell contains a nucleus. There are 23 pairs of chromosomes in each nucleus. A single chromosome is a long molecule of DNA. The chromosomes carry our genes, and there are 50,000 of them on each pair. The very same DNA is in every cell of our body and is different from every other person's except in the case of identical twins. Basically, the cell, under instructions from DNA, works like a miniature factory, pumping out proteins, enzymes and other material and, as I said, the same DNA is in every cell. The thing that boggles my mind is how a heart cell can have the same DNA as a brain cell and, even so, knows enough to pump blood rather than do arithmetic. And, Kath?"

"What?"

"You're not alone. It's complicated. I have it all written out on cards at home and periodically I go over it and over it, just to keep it straight. That's why I can rattle it off."

"What *don't* you have written on cards? But you make it sound so easy. You're that interested?"

"Yes, I am. Because it's in the forefront of medicine, and because it's absolutely fascinating. The same with stem cells and genetic engineering. You want another quick lesson?"

"Sure."

"Start with adult stem cells and embryonic stem cells. The adult type is taken from mature tissue like a healthy adult's bone marrow. They're harder to grow than embryonic stem cells and might or might not transform into other kinds of cells. The ones from embryos though, they can change into any of the body's tissue types."

"That's how many?"

"Tissue types? Two hundred."

"And the embryonic stem cell comes from . . ."

"Well, first of all, if we think 'naturally,' they're the ancestral cells of every cell in the body. If we think 'artificially,' they come from fertilized egg cells left over from in-vitro fertilization. So they're isolated and then cultured and can grow into any type of tissue. The idea here is for scientists to use the stem cells to replace damaged or diseased body parts, like brain cells in Alzheimer's and Parkinson's Disease . . . or liver cells . . . or cartilage to repair joints . . . or skin to treat burn victims. That's the good news: designer treatments. The bad news, depending on your point of view, is that there are many groups that oppose this whole process because what's called the blastocyst—that's the early stage embryo—has to be destroyed in the process of extracting the stem cell. Abortion opponents, for example, say that's the same as taking human life.

"The only part of genetic engineering I care about right now has to do with gene therapy—in other words, not fixing the symptoms of a disease but fixing the gene of a disease. They can now remove a 'bad' gene such as the one that causes colon cancer and replace it with one that suppresses colon cancer. Unbelievable."

"And, of course," Kathy said, "cloning always makes the papers. Dolly the sheep awhile ago, all the way to a human embryo—in Boston, I think. How does that work?"

"They took a woman's donated egg and sucked out the nucleus. Remember, that has the genetic core. Then they took what's called a cumulus cell and injected the whole thing into the egg. What happened was, it grew into a primitive six-cell human embryo."

"Could that embryo be implanted into a woman's womb and develop into a whole new cloned person?"

"It's hard to say. The research is at a very early stage."

Kathy massaged the back of her neck and said, "I feel more stupid than I did before." And, with a touch of resignation, added, "Maybe not stupid . . . no . . . more like helpless."

David crimped his mouth. "So with all that kind of controversial research going on at Brent, I'd lay ten to one that at least a dozen people had a motive to kill Manny."

"This could get nasty, David. I have bad vibes, and you know my vibes."

"I certainly know your vibes."

Kathy gave him a one-eyed stare and he leaned over and kissed her cheek.

She responded by shuddering. "You want a hard man

. . . uh . . . you know, a body guard?" she asked.

"No. Not last month, and I made it through in one piece. And not now, either." He didn't know whether to rub his decision scar or his sore knee. "That's not my style. I'll be okay."

"David, we're not talking about a poker game. We're talking about your life."

"I've had a good one."

"Now cut that out!" Kathy shrieked. She rose and walked to a supporting post for the canopy and pressed against it for a moment, her back toward David. She turned and said evenly, "Have you ever given any thought to a link between the hospital killings and Molina's?"

"No, not really. I doubt it, but I suppose anything's possible." If she only knew about the green-eyed truck.

Kathy seemed more satisfied with the reply to the murders connection than to her offer to supply him with protective support. She said, "I'm not forgetting a bodyguard—which is only common sense, my sweet—but let me ask you . . ."

David reacted to the patronizing edge of her remark. "Now, wait a minute," he said.

Kathy raised her hands in a defensive mode. "Never mind," she said, returning to her chair. "Stalemate, for now, but let me ask you: we'll attend the funeral, right?"

"We have to. And the wake, if there is one. I'll find out what's what from Clemente himself, tomorrow." He shuffled his chair closer to hers.

"About solving the hospital murder case," he said. The switching of subjects was seamless. "You mentioned back at Molina's that it was a double edged sword. What did you mean?"

Kathy appeared surprised that David remembered. "Just that Nick seemed happy over your success—and maybe a little bit jealous, too. It's only a hunch . . . but, please, not to worry."

"Okay, not to worry," David said feebly. "So what was he like after I left today?"

"Didn't say a word, other than he'd pay Clemente a visit."

"And the medical examiner?"

"Who, Reilly? He acted out of it, as usual. Too quick. Tight lipped."

"They're both tight lipped."

"Back to Nick again!" She rose and drifted toward him. "David, you're in charge. Just like before. Damn! Sometimes you can be a pain in the butt."

He reached around and pulled her closer. "And sometimes you're a tiger," he said.

"That's 'tigress,'" she snapped, her expression pinched.

"Oh, of course—a female. I'd certify that."

Staring at one another, each suppressed a smile and came together as if on cue.

They retired early.

CHAPTER 4

✛ ✛ ✛

Saturday, February 9

At 10:30 the next morning, David emerged from his car behind *Candies by Clemente*. The air had warmed overnight and, though dry, felt heavy against his skin. A biting sweet odor wafted over the parking lot, triggering memories of his visit there nearly 30 years before, and of the Clemente family's old homestead in a once fashionable section of Hollings, an imposing Tudor which the current generation had apparently inherited. David had often delivered groceries there when he worked Saturdays for his father's corner grocery store in the 70's. He remembered the front cement steps covered with vines and moss, the fragrance of lilacs, the barking dogs he could never see and the black letter "C" inlaid into all four sides of the giant, white chimney.

His nostalgia tempered what remained of a serious dose of annoyance with a local radio reporter an hour earlier. He kicked himself for having agreed to a phone interview in the first place—the reporter was a fellow black-belt.

And, in the second, for characterizing Molina's murder as a probable mob hit. But he had prided himself in referring to the killers as "goonheads." Before that, he'd decided to ignore a stream of answering machine messages left by both the regional and national press.

Candies by Clemente was an aberration, a mom and pop holdout among the giants of candy makers. Both candy store and factory, the small brick building still stood on the corner of Main and Church just as it had for five generations of the Clemente family. David had been inside only once when his father treated him on his tenth birthday. He could still recall the warm, mellow aroma of chocolate when they entered the store. And the two bags of candy he was permitted; plus the ten comic books his father bought him on the way home.

Friday in tow, David circled around front and noticed the same script lettering in Wedgwood-blue hanging above the storefront door: *Candies by Clemente*. A sign to the side of a *United We Stand* shield read:

Adrian Clemente, Permittee
Open Every Day

He walked in and moseyed about like several other customers. Surrounding an unattended checkout counter were room after room of candies, their containers labeled "Confectionary." The word "candy" was nowhere to be seen. It was a store with uneven floors of creaky pine planks and with metal ceilings, patterned and smoky, the traces of uncovered hot pans. Above archways were pithy sayings like, "A sweet tooth is better than a sourpuss." The sign above the next archway read, "But we have sourballs, too."

There were stands and stands of every variety of candy with different shapes, textures and taste, of chocolate and hard and chewy and whipped. Most chocolates were arranged in levels of bars and liquid-centered pieces. Others were combined with nuts or raisins or cookie crumbs. There were hard candies of fruit drops, butterscotch and brittles. One whole room was filled with chewy caramels, toffees and gums. Another had tables stacked with nougats, fudge and malted milk balls. Containers were as varied as their contents. Glass bowls and glass urns; wooden boxes, baskets and bins with tethered scoops; pewter saucers and tubs; chests and trunks. Some were covered, others were not.

At a confluence of rooms, David stood for a moment to take in the fragrance of the fruits and chocolates that triggered old memories. He was a ten-year-old again.

A woman, 50 plus, approached him. "May I assist you?" she asked in a husky voice.

"Yes, is Adrian in?" He noticed yellow stains on the fingers of her left hand.

"I believe so. Your name?"

"David Brooks."

The woman stiffened. "*Doctor* David Brooks?" She patted her hair on both sides.

"Yes."

"Oh, my! I saw your picture in the papers. All those murders. Are you here about the one over there in Marblehead? He was Adrian's cousin, you know."

"Yes, I know."

"Make yourself comfortable, Dr. Brooks. Feel free to look around—we're proud of our little operation. I've been here nearly half my life. I'm sure he'll see you." She disappeared into a poorly lit side hallway.

David spotted the morning's *Hollings Herald* next to a nineteenth century cash register on another checkout counter. A front page headline read:

Brent Institute's Top Scientist Murdered
Dr. David Brooks Called In

Sure he was . . . by the *victim*. Even before the police. He skimmed the article, learned nothing new and wandered through what was the rear wall, as he remembered it, but now, as an addition, opened into a spotless expanse of ovens and burners and mixers which worked the sugars, fruits and nuts or the cocoa, peppermint and vanilla. Refrigerators stretched to the ceiling. Stainless steel vats swung and tipped. Strings of copper skillets dangled above sinks. Along conveyor belts, he observed the blurred fingers of packagers who sat on their stools, similarly attired, their blouses, pants and caps immaculately white. The workers and their clothes blended into a starched look.

David heard footsteps and a voice in the shadows of the hallway. "Dr. Brooks! What an honor and a pleasure. I'm Adrian. Adrian Clemente."

A middle-aged, bony man rushed out, right hand extended. The other jingled change in his hip pocket. Of medium height, his handshake was firm and pumping. "It truly is a pleasure," he repeated, bowing. His head bobbed as he spoke and an etched smile pleated the dark skin around his eyes, cramping them half shut.

"So you're the Candyman. It's good to meet you, Adrian, and I'm awfully sorry about your cousin's death." David had expected a short, stubby man in an apron and tee-shirt, his hairy arms covered with flour, not one in dress shirt, paisley tie and cuff links.

"Thank you, Doctor. We were cousins but more like brothers." Clemente gestured toward the dark hallway. "Come, let's go up to my office."

He led the way toward a stairwell as David kept his fingers on the sidewall for direction. Halfway up, he moved laterally toward the end of the steps where it felt more secure under his feet. At the top, he stopped to flex and unflex his knee. Clemente had already thrown open the door ahead, as if he knew more illumination would help a visitor.

David entered a large room that was, in fact, two rooms in one, but without partition, railing or planter. Old cigar smoke assaulted his nostrils. Dented file cabinets lined the far wall, blocking the lower third of the only windows in the room. Strips of smudged linoleum, corners upturned, covered the floor to the left. Scattered narrow tables supported boxes split at the sides by wooden plates and molds. On one table, among stacks of newspapers, magazines and atlases, David spotted a pile of discarded airline tickets. A calendar, still showing January, was nailed crooked on the left wall.

"Come. Sit down, doctor," Clemente said from the direction of his desk to the right.

David was still running his eyes over the table tops as he headed toward Clemente, nearly knocking over a clothes tree angling up from the floor. It contained a beige leather jacket, brown beret and one black leather glove mounted loosely on a hook. Its mate lay on the floor.

The other half of the room looked like a set on a sound stage. It was carpeted to three walls. David had never seen a carpet end abruptly under a metal seam running across the middle of a room. The space was bedecked with red leather chairs and sofa, floor lamps and a cherry desk. The back wall was plastered with framed certificates and achievement awards for excellence in candy manufacturing. Some were in the foreign languages of South America and Western Europe. Computer hardware and a copier were tucked into a corner desk and hutch. David noted a closed door behind the desk.

Clemente motioned toward twin chairs in front of his desk. David sat in one. Clemente walked around and sat in the other. The level of his shoulders tipped slightly to the left, much the way David believed left-handers' did. A gold watch was on his right wrist.

"Please forgive the total office," Clemente said. "Right here's really it. That over there—strictly for storage."

"I can see that."

Clemente reached for a mahogany humidor at the corner of his desk and flipped it open. "Cigar?"

"No, thanks."

"Mind if I have one?"

"No, go ahead."

Clemente pared the end of a cigar with a device he had taken from his pocket. "You know, you shouldn't have said that," he said, throwing the cigar back into the humidor.

"What did I say?"

"'Go ahead.' You're a doctor. That's encouraging me— and I'm trying to quit." They both chuckled as David, his head tossed back, noticed a large black spot on the ceiling above the desk. He guessed there would be a smaller one above the computer. He looked and there was.

"Speaking of doctors, you do most of your work out of Hollings, I understand."

"Yes, I do."

"Nice hospital. I see Dr. Skopey there. Bad ticker." He draped his hand over his heart. "But" he continued, "what brings you here?"

David pulled out his notepad and said, "As you may know, I've been assigned to investigate your cousin's death. You might say I've been on the case from the very beginning since I discovered the body."

Clemente let his smile slip. "Yes, and thank goodness for that."

"May I ask you some questions?"

"Anything that will help get to the bottom of Manny's brutal killing."

"First off, then, who is Juan Carlos?"

"Ah, Juan Carlos. That would be Juan Carlos Saltanban." The smile returned. "He's the president of Radonia."

David readjusted himself in his chair. "The president? Radonia? You mean the country in South America?"

"That is correct," Clemente said proudly.

David briefly looked off into space. "If I'm not mistaken, he's been in power there for years."

"Correct, again. And, if I may be so bold, he's in power, yes, but he's instituted a true democracy in that tiny country."

"Sorry. Maybe I should have said 'in office.'"

"The point is, I've worked on some of his elections there. We go back many years—to when Manny introduced me to him. Manny was Juan Carlos' Minister of Science for a long time."

"Yes, I knew about his position, but didn't put two and two together about the president he worked under."

"In fact," Clemente said, "you can meet him tomorrow night. He's flying in for the wake. That is, if you're going."

"Oh, yes. In this business, we go to more wakes than politicians do. They go for votes. We go for leads." David crossed his legs, uncertain of whether he was more pleased about his analogy or with the prospect of speaking with Juan Carlos Saltanban.

"Well, I'm sure he won't be able to lead you to the murderer, but I understand what you're saying." What David didn't say was, since Juan Carlos' name was on the boxes of chocolates and since he was once Manny's employer, he had to be questioned sooner or later—and an encounter at the wake might save him a trip to Radonia.

"How'd he know about the death? Did you call him?"

"No, he called me. He saw the story on CNN."

David had been writing single words or phrases in his notepad, using Friday as a flat surface on his lap. Now, as he wrote an entire sentence, he sensed Clemente leaning toward him. David closed the pad and said, "Now then, are you in charge of the arrangements?"

"Yes, the wake tomorrow and the funeral on Monday. Actually, my wife, Dolores, is handling the details." Clemente excused himself, went to the phone and dialed a single digit. "Dolores," he said, "when you have a minute, could you come up and join Dr. Brooks and me? Thank you."

Clemente returned to his chair and continued. "Manny and I joked a lot about who would die first. He'd say I would because I sampled too much candy—and I'd say he would because he didn't eat enough. One day, he got serious and reminded me I was his only living heir and, if he happened to go first, would I take care of his burial? Right after that, he set up a little insurance policy—$20,000—to cover it all. I'm the beneficiary and . . . ."

"But wouldn't there be a . . . you know . . . a fancy state funeral in Radonia?"

"I doubt it, unless he died in office."

"On the same subject, do you care if I get a little more personal? And if you don't, please understand, I'm not insinuating anything—just asking routine questions."

"I'm only too happy to cooperate—but I know what the question is, and the answer is, no, I'm not aware of any inheritance for Dolores and me. Manny once said—in that same conversation, in fact—that upon his death, he wanted everything left to Brent Institute. He's been connected with it for a long time and thinks the place is terrific. I suppose his inheritance wish is in a will somewhere. I certainly hope so, for the good of research and therefore, the benefit of mankind."

"I get the picture," David said, slowly. One of his initial impressions of Clemente was still holding up: that the saccharin oozing from the Candyman's mouth could be bottled and used in his business. "And, of course, you knew Manny had some of your chocolates in his house?" David asked.

Clemente nodded.

"Who delivered them?"

"I did."

"When?"

"That would have been . . . Tuesday night, right after work."

"Directly to him? That is, was he home?"

"Yes. He asked me in for a drink but I refused. I wanted to get home." Clemente jiggled change again.

David reopened the notepad and, flipping back to a previous page, underlined a phrase and scribbled something in the margin. "Okay, then. Why two boxes?"

"Juan Carlos always did it that way. He said sending two boxes—two pounds each—was more impressive than sending a single five-pounder. I probably send out double boxes—I'm guessing now—maybe over 200 times a year for him."

"Really?" David said, looking up. "All in the States?"

"I'd say divided evenly between here and the rest of the world."

"All over the world?"

"Yes. Canada . . . . Europe . . . Latin America . . . Australia . . . Asia . . . all over."

"So what you're saying is that the president of Radonia is one of your biggest customers, and he has chocolates mailed to individuals in the U.S. and around the globe."

"*The* biggest. I wish we had a hundred like him. And it's not just to individuals."

"How do you mean?"

"He sends them to companies and businesses, too."

"What kind?"

"Oh, nothing I'd call large, like the major corporations. Places like hardware stores, book stores, supply houses."

"Any wholesale outlets?"

"Yes, wholesale outlets."

"Do you know any of the owners of these places?"

"No."

While David brought his notes up to date, Clemente removed the cigar from the humidor and put it in his mouth, unlit.

"Now back to the chocolates," David said. "Are they all the same—I mean in shape?"

"Yes, nothing fancy."

"And nothing custom made?"

"Right. The same as anyone else would buy."

"Speaking of which, does the president pay on time?"

"Better than that. He has a cash account here which he draws against."

"Oh, really? Does he maintain a regular amount in it?"

"Yes. When it gets to about a thousand, he sends us another four thousand."

David had been searching the air for some of the questions. He paused, looked directly at the Candyman and said, "I hope I'm not overstaying my welcome or flooding you with too many questions."

"No, no, please continue—however I can help."

"Okay. Messages. There's usually a card sent with the chocolates?"

"Yes."

"Are they pretty much the same?"

"Yes. Sometimes a birthday or anniversary greeting but usually just 'Best wishes'."

"Written in the language of the person or company he's sending the boxes to?"

"Yes, always. We type out the message and Juan Carlos' name."

"His full name?"

"Yes. Sorry. We type *Juan Carlos Saltanban, President of Radonia.*"

"Who does the translation here, say to French or Arabic?"

"No need to. He spells it out for us."

"How are the orders placed?"

"By phone."

"By him or an aide?"

"By him. And he always calls collect."

The door behind Clemente opened and the woman who had greeted David downstairs walked through. Of average height, she was about as stocky as he had expected her husband to be, and she had obviously tidied up her gray hair. A print shift looked recently ironed.

David stood and said, "I thought that might have been you downstairs, but I wasn't sure. Pleased to meet you." They shook hands.

"To be honest, Dr. Brooks, I was so excited to meet you, I didn't think to introduce myself." She pulled over a side chair and sat down.

David settled back, inserted his notepad into his pocket and addressed Clemente. "You have long hours I see by the sign on your door. Even Sundays."

"Yes, for sure" Clemente said. "Very long. On Sundays, only until one o'clock though. Many customers come in after church. It's probably our busiest time."

"And Sundays for you, too, Mrs. Clemente?"

"Please call me Dolores. And, yes, I haven't missed a Sunday in over 30 years."

David had received all the information he wanted but stayed on for a few minutes of chitchat before leaving, concentrating on the two Clemente children who were "finally out of the nest" and embarked on their own careers in New York City, and confirming that Adrian and Dolores did indeed live in the old homestead. He also secured the Clementes' home phone number and entered it in his notepad. Descending the stairs, he realized he had forgotten to ask them if they knew anything about Molina's death threat and, if so, had it been made by phone. He would inquire at the wake.

Back in his car, he spied two late model Volvos—one silver, one black—parked side-by-side against the rear of the building. Their marker numbers read: CANDY.1 and CANDY.2. He removed the cell phone from his belt and activated a number stored in its internal phone book.

"Musco? You game for a little house visit in the morning?"

Musco Diller, a cabby who worked Hollings' seamy North Square District, was an old friend and world-class safe cracker. David had used his services as a "freelance lock-picker" in such cases as 647 Vagrancy, 10-65 Missing Person and, most recently, 187 Murder. David himself could slip a credit card past a door latch with the best of them, but in many cases, that skill was too rudimentary.

Musco had once done time for a string of second story capers and now, having gone straight, was senior partner in the most popular cab company in the city, the Red Checker Cab Company. He had also lived on the streets, done in by muscatel wine, his favorite. Hence, the nickname. Musco was the only cabby David knew who handed out free passes to certain friends. He called them his "gold cards"—good for rides to any part of Hollings.

They agreed to meet in the auxiliary doctors' parking lot at nine in the morning.

*   *   *

David had intended to visit Sparky in the crime lab but opted to call him instead. Later. For now, he listened to his mind and body telling him he'd had plenty for 36 hours and, while driving home from the candy store, reinforced the message by extracting a three-by-five card from his wallet and reading what he had jotted down three weeks ago. It was during the intense hours of the murder spree at the hospital:

Do not force issues.

Know when to roll versus when to take stock.

Do not outpace circumstances. Let things settle out.

What else should he be doing, anyway? Checking out pet shops for canary buyers? Other than the trip to the Clemente house in the morning, an example of what Musco called, "a forced entry for enforcement's sake"—as if it legitimized the activity—the next major evidence-gathering event, Molina's wake, wasn't scheduled until the next evening. In addition, it was approaching Saturday night, the time of the week which, barring a catastrophic event and in spite of weeknights shared, Kathy and David had deemed reserved for them. She would be coming to Oak Lane.

Once at his computer, he entered:

Saturday, February 9

1—If Clemente and Molina were "like brothers" why doesn't Clemente appear distraught?

2—He said he consulted with Dr. Walter Skopey at the hospital. But Walter left the area over a year ago.

3—Who the hell is President Saltanban sending all those chocolates to?

* * *

For lunch, David scooped up a bowl of pork and beans, his excuse for catsup. But he was too pensive to appreciate taste. He used the wall phone in his kitchen to call Sparky at the lab.

"Hi, my friend. Are you all over it?"

"David, I want you to know I've checked for everything: fingerprints, footprints, shoeprints, tool marks, tire marks, fibers, soil, hairs . . . ."

"I'm sure you have, but . . . ."

"Animal material, glass, saliva stains, sweat stains . . . ."

"Sparky, wait. Anything positive?"

"What?"

"Did anything positive turn up?"

"Nothing."

"Anyone else's blood there?"

"No."

"And no fingerprints?"

"Just Molina's."

"Figured." David shifted his weight. "Dead four to six hours. You agree?"

"Yes, probably closer to four. And, in case you weren't aware of it, they already did the post. A single .22 slug lodged against the superior orbital plate in the skull. Lots of damage in there."

"That's no surprise. You *do* know that everything fits the M.O. of the mob?"

"Like a glove. Even the canary."

"Yeah, even the canary," David repeated, distantly.

"Do you think this is related to the crimes two weeks ago?"

"I don't know yet, Spark," David answered, the image of the Kermit truck flashing though his mind. "Anyway, many thanks. We'll be in touch. If anything turns up, buzz me. You have my cell phone number, right?"

"Right. Oh, earlier this morning, I went along to Molina's office at Brent. Saw nothing unusual, but I took some pictures if you need them. We left everything intact."

David couldn't help but appreciate that people were moving aside for him. He'd received plenty of deference before—in medical work—but this was something new, and he was ambivalent about the feeling.

"By the way, does Nick know about your findings—or lack thereof?"

"For sure. He called about an hour ago."

"He did? Why that . . . good, then I won't have to call him," David said, sorry he had inquired.

✳   ✳   ✳

David and Kathy dined at Olivio's, their favorite restaurant, at the junction of Hollings and Center City. He brought her current on the case including his encounter with the Clementes. Kathy, like David, was particularly suspicious of the Candyman's stated visit to the cardiologist.

The remainder of the evening was highlighted by a wager over who could stay awake longer. It was agreed upon that the stakes—to be paid later—comprised a win-win situation, no matter the loser. David lost.

CHAPTER 5

✛ ✛ ✛

Sunday, February 10

At 8:45 the following morning, Kathy was in the shower and David was about to leave to meet Musco. The phone rang. David said "Hello" three times, believing it unusual for a telemarketing system to be activated on a Sunday morning.

Finally, a male voice at the other end said, "This is Dr. David Brooks? . . . Am I correct?" David didn't like the two questions in a row and especially the pause in the middle. He decided to answer in kind.

"Yes, this is Dr. David Brooks . . . you are correct."

"I will be brief. You must realize you are getting mixed up in genetic engineering and stem cells . . . ." He blew into the phone as if expelling smoke. "Plus cloning." It was a strange sounding voice with a hollow timbre to it—like an echo—each word enunciated clearly. "And unless you bug off, perhaps all *your* genes will be available. Terrorists might try anything."

The click hurt David's ear and, after reacting by slamming the receiver into its cradle, his initial thought was that the caller was too uninformed to be a scientist. What good are dead genes? He would have preferred to sit and mull over the call, perhaps wait for Kathy to come out, but he was already late for his meeting with Musco. Thus, he gave it cursory attention at first. Besides, during the investigation of the hospital murders, he had become accustomed to a steady diet of threats made to throw him off track, and this he labeled as no different. Once on the road, however, he was struck by the caller's voice again, one he assessed as being exceptionally cultured for a criminal. He corrected himself: exceptionally cultured for an enforcer, not a solicitor. And all the way to the parking lot, he was intrigued more by what he had learned from the caller than by the warning itself. That, just as in the case of having been towed into the murky world of international killers a month ago, he was about to be dragged into the galloping field of genetics. And perhaps even into terrorism.

*   *   *

At 9:05, David smiled when he saw Musco leaning his head out the window of his cab, which was parked at the usual meeting spot near the back fence of the auxiliary doctors' parking lot. It was a little-used area large enough to accommodate no more than three or four vehicles, and it was separated from the main doctors' parking lot by a cement wall shrouded in vines. David suspected the private spaces had been created for the administrative hierarchy when their offices were on the first floor before renovations three decades ago.

"Dr. David, my boy, whatcha got this time? You said a house?"

David had pulled his convertible alongside. It was a September day in February and his top was down. "Hop in," he said.

Musco, easily in his sixties, was a short wiry African-American who always wore a black cap with a rainbow band and shiny visor. Several tickets sprouted from the band and even from the breast pocket of his scotch-plaid flannel jacket. He had a round face, small grizzled mustache and, at the center of his chin, a matching tuft of hair. David had heard that one of Musco's eyes was glass, but he could never tell which one.

"The reason I called . . . ." David began.

"Wait—hold on now," Musco said, hunching over in his seat. "Remember what I tell you every time. You don't never need a reason to call. And what else?"

"What else?" David maneuvered around and through the lot's exit gate.

"Yeah, remember—you never have to tell me why, just where and when. I don't want to know nothin'."

"Uh-huh," David replied. "You know Clemente's?"

"You mean the candy place over there on Church?"

David felt Musco's stare and nodded in the affirmative. "We have to check out their house."

Musco settled back. "You in on that new murder—the Brent guy?"

David turned his head to give a brief wry smile. "I thought you never want to know nothin'."

Musco chuckled. "Well, I *do* read the papers."

"The answer, Musc, is 'yes' and somehow . . . somehow . . . . let's say it this way: I have a strange feeling Adrian Clemente knows something about it. The murder victim was his cousin, you know. Name's Molina—

Manuel Molina. A world-famous scientist."

"A medical man."

"No, no. A molecular biologist and an authority on gene therapy and cloning."

"You mean like that sheep?"

David thought a moment. "Animals in general." He knew the lines around his mouth had deepened.

Musco pulled down on his cap. "Okay, got it. Let's get there."

* * *

The Clemente homestead was perched atop a severe incline at the confluence of three residential streets, its Tudor style setting it apart from the other homes in the neighborhood. Approached from below, one's eyes were drawn more to flights of cement steps that turned in a series of angular landings than to the house itself, even with its overdose of exposed beams.

David gunned his Mercedes up the incline and beyond the house to reach a level stretch of land whereupon he curved into a sliver of a driveway and to the right, coming to a stop behind a cluster of hemlocks. He heard its branches brushing over the car.

"No one's home?" Musco asked.

"They work Sundays. We should be okay."

David's expectation of howling dogs made the silence more palpable. They eased out of the car, closed their doors gingerly and, stealing past a two-bay garage, peeked through its door windows.

"Good," David whispered. "No Volvos."

They circled to the side of the house and at a covered stoop cluttered with stacks of newspapers bound with twine, he held open a storm door with his body. "You like to knock first, right?," he said.

"Right."

"Tell me again, though. What would you say if someone answered?"

"Anyone here call for a cab?"

"And who would I be?"

Musco scaled David's height. "My bodyguard?"

David let the door swing to near closure and put a finger to his lips. "But we don't have a taxicab here," he said with the finality of checkmate.

Musco, expressionless, said, "We're an advance team. Very busy company, you know, and we've had a lot of crank calls lately. I tell them that. Then when they say no one called from here, we just apologize and leave."

David was too keyed up over the task ahead to beg the question. He motioned Musco toward the door. He had watched the cabby use his homemade skewer tool only once and had appreciated his distress over someone looking over his shoulder.

"Okay, maestro, work your magic. I'll be right back," David said. He put his hands in his pockets, pretended to whistle a tune and ambled to the other side of the house. Moments later, he returned in time to see Musco wave a hand toward the opened door. "Another piece of cake," he said, triumphantly.

David shook his hand and asked, "What took you so long?"

Musco edged by him, saying, "I'll wait in the car. You go do your thing."

David was leery as he took his first step through the door into a mud room, concerned about tripping a security alarm. He closed the door behind him, pressed back against it and, tightening his grip on Friday, waited. There were no bells or sirens. He had a flashing thought that, upon his gaining full P.I. licensure, he would probably lose the luxury of forced—and illegal—entries. He also wondered whether either of the Clementes ever dashed home—for whatever reason. Their business was less than a mile away. Thus, he would skip a room-by-room search and settle for the one area toward which he leveled his eyes, through the kitchen and pantry, off to the far end of a spacious living room. It was in that rear location, he believed, he might best gather the most information in the shortest amount of time, amidst the computer equipment and bookcases he could make out from his vantage point, a room that was most likely Clemente's study or home office. He was focusing on any clue or two that might link the Candyman to the murder or clarify his relationship with the president of Radonia. Or both.

There was a hint of chocolate and old wood in the air. Not a disagreeable combination. The clicking of a clock in a room far ahead reinforced the urgency of his mission. Paying scant attention to the furniture pieces except a *Steinway and Sons* grand piano, he walked purposefully through the living room, past oak paneled walls, elongated windows separated by strips of quiet gray stone, and beneath a center chandelier that matched two others suspended from scrolled devices extending out from opposing walls. He peeked into two closets cut into the wall to his right and observed nothing of significance; he noted a third closet door in the opposite wall to his left.

The room at the far end—bracketed on two sides with tall built-in bookcases—was stuffed with three desks, computer and copying equipment, recording apparatus, several cameras on tripods and, in the near corner, a long-case clock in walnut, decorated with floral marquetry. Etched in a gold plate at its base was the date, 1702.

One desk seemed the busiest. David put on a pair of latex gloves which he had removed from Friday, and flipped through several piles of papers, mostly vendor invoices. He felt obligated to riffle random folders in its side drawers, then unfolded a newspaper whose mast-head read, *Radonia Hoy*, the equivalant of *USA Today*, he figured. It was dated 5 de febrero and had an address label affixed to its upper border.

But it was a red spindle that caught his eye. It pierced a three inch stack of *Candies by Clemente* invoices. David inspected those in the upper third. All were shipment copies for chocolates sent to Kabal and Mazur-e-Sharif, Afghanistan, and the buyer was not identified.

Another "worry point." Two, if you count the newspaper. However, he would deal with them later for his more immediate concern was to leave undetected. Retracing his steps out, he reached a point mid-way in the living room, then turned sharply to his right and tried the third closet door. It was locked. He continued on but looped back to try it one last time.

So a guy has a locked closet. But there wasn't time to fetch Musco to open it.

At the stoop, he paused at the stacks of papers and looked through enough to determine they were old editions of both the *Hollings Herald* and *Radonia Hoy*.

Back in the car, Musco straightened as he slid his cap off his face to his head and yawned. "Find what you wanted?" he asked.

"Enough. And it's getting fascinating. Maybe too fascinating." The Afghanistan shipment forms had set off the whole issue of global terrorism in David's mind, and he found it difficult to lay the subject aside. Clemente involved in terrorism? Who ordered the chocolates? Saltanban from Radonia? If only he were able to confront Clemente later at the wake, but how could he admit to unlawful entry?

There was little conversation on the drive to the parking lot. Musco returned his cap to his face, and David dwelled on his discoveries and whether or not to call Kathy about them. His preoccupation was breached only once when he swore they passed a silver Volvo heading in the opposite direction. As he veered into the lot, he had reached a decision: the time had come to cease and desist his constant running to Kathy with new developments. Separate their personal relationship from their crime detection relationship. Better to bounce ideas off himself at the computer and rely on the department for forensic support only.

He drove in next to the Red Checker cab. He reached into his shirt pocket for the hundred dollar bill he had stored there and peeled away two twenties from a wad he took from his pants pocket. Handing the bills to Musco, he said, "Thanks, old buddy, we'll be in touch. Probably sooner than later."

"Anytime," Musco said, "but why the extra twenty spots?"

"For your wait in the car."

"Aw, that was what, five minutes?" But long as you mentioned car, can I warn you about somethin'?"

"Of course. What?"

"It's only my opinion, mind you, but, like they say, 'Never get caught with your britches down.' In this case, 'Never leave your top down if you're on secret duty.'"

David felt his jaw sag. This latest installment of Musco advice had lost all the theatrics of before and began to sound like wisdom.

CHAPTER 6

✛ ✛ ✛

The consensus in Hollings was that Tilbud's, at 33 Park West, was the most elegant of the six funeral parlors that dotted the downtown district. Built at the turn of the century, it resembled a Gothic stone mansion from a distance, but up close, one could see more wood than stone. Above a green awning, which spanned the entire walkway from street to entrance, a keystone was etched with *Tilbud* in script. On either side, voussoirs were wedged between twin curves of dark hardwood, while a large American flag filled the concavity below, dangling waveless in the calm afternoon.

The parlor's interior, however, resembled the several others in which David had paid last respects: all plush, fragrant and muted.

He had called Kathy and arranged to meet her in the vestibule's side room at 3:30, a half hour after the wake was to begin. He was determined not to talk about his findings at Clemente's or about going there in the first place.

When he walked in, she rose and lifted up on her toes to kiss him. "There aren't many people here," she said.

"Not yet. All the academics will come later. It's Sunday, remember?"

Kathy put on a puzzled look.

"Their only connection with the real world is that they like pro football." He paused. "And, bow ties," he added, fondling his own.

"You're incorrigible," she said. "Let's go in. I already signed the book for both of us."

Inside, at the far end of a large receiving room, a short line of mourners stood before a closed casket surrounded by cascades of flowers. Reds, pinks, yellows, purples. Bell-shaped, funnelforms, tubulars, butterfly-forms. Here and there, a half-dozen husky men in dark wrinkle-free suits stood against the walls like sentinels, their expressions frozen somber. One pressed a walkie-talkie to his side. A like number of strapping women, hardly distinguishable from their male counterparts in dress and demeanor, were scattered about the periphery. David recognized the shortest two men as the Tilbud Brothers. To the right, quiet conversation droned from a receiving line where Adrian and Dolores Clemente hugged some of those who passed by and clasped hands with the others. A single row of people sat toward the rear. David knew none of them, but a few wore bow ties and he could make out the corners of plastic protectors in the shirt pockets of some. Off to their left, a half dozen rows of people sat stiffly, their mouths down-turned—a customary assembly David called the 'meditation section.'

He swung Friday forward, signaling Kathy to precede him, and after they knelt before the casket for an appropriate minute, they stood before the Clementes. David introduced her not as a police detective but as his fiancée, although he figured the longtime Hollings figure must have heard of her work with the department. During small talk, David glanced toward those who stayed behind in the meditation section and picked out Nick Medicore in the front row. Not surprised, David winked. Nick nodded. Kathy turned to move away with David close behind. She spotted Nick and walked over. Just then, Clemente grasped David's arm and gently pulled him back.

"I'd like you to meet someone," he whispered. Addressing his wife, he said, "Excuse us, dear, but I'll be right back." He motioned David to follow.

They were soon in a nearby alcove, one of three jutting out from the room. A sienna-faced man rose from his seat while two others, one at each side, rose simultaneously and stood more or less at attention, their eyes trained straight ahead. Broader and a shade taller than David, each was blond and untanned. An attractive woman in black, the youngest of the four, remained seated next to one of them, a gossamer veil trailing to her nose, hands folded demurely on her lap. She looked up and gave David an evanescent smile.

The man in the middle, hefty like a bouncer, stuck out his chest as if to highlight two silver medals that dangled from the jacket of his double-breasted dark suit. His hair, dense and curly, was solid black in contrast to a goatee sprinkled with gray. David guessed he was about 50.

"Dr. David Brooks, I'd like you to meet President Juan Carlos Saltanban. Juan Carlos, this is Dr. Brooks," Clemente said with a flourish. They shook hands, and if

Juan Carlos' hurt, he didn't let on. He was the first to speak.

"I have heard of you, and I am impressed. Impressed indeed."

David was startled by the English fluency. "It's a pleasure to meet you, sir. And you've heard of me? In South America?"

"Certainly. CNN is far-reaching. Before my position in Radonia, I was in telecommunications. I only wish it had been I who had the vision to create a CNN model with such international appeal. It is truly remarkable."

David had not yet heard a contraction of words. "But you've done fine for your country, and you should be proud," he said.

"Yes, I suppose so, and I am. But proud of my country, not myself."

"You two can get acquainted," Clemente said, "I'd better get back to my duties." He rejoined his wife near the casket.

On each little finger, Saltanban sported a solid gold signet ring, a "J" in script on the right and an "S" on the left. David noticed. "Why not simply 'JC' on one ring, Mr. President?," he said.

"No, no! Those letters side-by-side are reserved for someone much more important than I am."

David noted that Juan Carlos' face bore the marinated lines of hard experience and wanted to inquire how much in-fighting had to be waged before Radonia became a legitimate democracy. Instead, he looked past one of the other men and said, "And I presume this is Mrs. Saltanban? How do you do?"

"No, my wife is back home on official business. This is

my aide from Radonia, Evilina Ruez."

The woman, perhaps half the president's age, got up, curtsied, sat and said nothing. She was tall, trim and stunning.

Not sure of what to do, David settled for, "Thank you. It's nice to meet you."

After a brief awkward silence, he addressed the president. "I understand Manny worked for you at one time."

"Yes, he did. Our Minister of Science. And the best we ever had. Only there was nothing I could do to convince him to stay on. In Manuel Molina, the world has lost a great scientist. I was shocked when Adrian called me about it, and then I saw it on the television." Saltanban lowered his eyes and shook his head from side to side. "A tragedy," he said, softly.

Wait a minute! Clemente said Saltanban called *him*. For the moment, David balked at clarifying which one made the call. He would bring it up with Clemente sometime later. For now, he decided to cut to the chase while he had the chance. "As you probably know through Adrian, Mr. President, I'm investigating Manny's death— with the full support and cooperation of the local police, of course."

"Yes, and you should be. After your brilliant work last month, there is no doubt in my mind that you will bring the killer to justice. It was mentioned many times on the television, but Adrian also tells me that your fiancée is an important person on the police force. Katerina, I believe."

David answered, "A police detective, yes. But her name is Kathy. Kathy Dupre." He was fast becoming weary of Saltanban's clipped diction, of its formality and cadence. Deep down, he felt it was a customary ploy of the president—an attempt to disarm or, at the least, to establish a blockade between himself and others. And he didn't like being the target for either, head of a country or not.

"This is hardly the place, but I wonder whether I might ask you a question or two. Maybe out in the hallway would be better?" David said. Casting aside any thought of further amenities, he punctuated his new zeal by whipping out his notepad, running the tip of a pencil over his tongue and entering the day's date, February 10.

Saltanban responded, "I will do you one better. Is that how you say it in America? Since we are not flying back until tomorrow after the funeral, why not have dinner with me tonight as my guest? Wherever you choose. I will ask the Clementes to join us and please, you bring your lovely future Mrs. Brooks, and I will bring my associate, Evilina."

First an aide, now an associate.

"And, you can ask me all the questions you want there," the president said. "After a rum and Coca-Cola, my answers come easier, of course."

David jumped at the opportunity. "I'd like that," he said. "And I think you'd like Olivio's."

They established a meeting time of seven-thirty at the restaurant, exchanged goodbyes and, assured that Clemente knew the directions, Saltanban sat down. The two men followed suit. The president raised up to whisper something to the one on his right. The man cupped his hand to hear, and David noticed that one of his fingers was missing.

David turned and walked out along a line that had formed near the casket. Kathy had taken a place among the seated mourners—back from Nick—and motioned

David that she had saved an aisle one for him. He sat as silent as the others but within seconds, a short dapper man with a gray pencil mustache appeared opposite him and, bending at the waist, said softly, "Dr. Brooks, I'm sorry, but may I see you for a moment? In private, back there?" He pointed to a rear alcove. David got up instinctively, believing a medical emergency was at hand.

In the alcove, the man said, "I'm Henderson Hendley, and I won't keep you long. I just arrived to pay my respects, and I feel so lucky that our visits coincided." His baritone voice was well-modulated. Golden hair, perfectly demarcated at the forehead, registered as a poor imitation of his own. He straightened, then patted the side pockets of his pinstripe suit jacket.

David stepped back. "You mean the columnist?"

"Well, I do write one—and have for a longer time than I like to think about—maybe 40 years?" Straight teeth, his own, were crowded into a smile that seemed to take forever to disengage.

Hendley had started out in radio and television as a literary critic but later made his mark as one of the nation's most read political columnists, syndicated in a couple hundred newspapers. He had the clout, however, to venture into any newsworthy arena of his choosing.

David eased up on the handshake and said, "It's good to meet you. I admire your work."

"Thank you. I've been following your exploits, David. May I call you David?"

"Yes, of course."

"I've been meaning to contact you ever since the hospital murders here. You did a remarkable job."

"Thanks, but I had a lot of help."

Henderson smirked. "I also heard your comment on radio about the underworld and its possible connection with Dr. Molina's murder and with embryonic stem-cell research. It was picked up by national outlets, you know."

"Well, it's the truth, at least partly. I don't recall mentioning the tie-in with research."

"That's the way it came across. Besides, given the nature of Brent's work, I think people would make the assumption. In any event . . . "

"The police no doubt gave out particulars about the shooting, though, and the public can draw its own conclusions."

"No doubt. In any event, I liked the way you compared the Mafia to parasites that keep multiplying—so they never go away. But I believe you haven't been interviewed by the print media about that point of view—or about the murder, itself."

"I never say much to the media. Ruins my cover. Well . . . I mean . . . the more I can stay in the shadows, the better I can maneuver."

"That makes sense," Henderson said with authority. "A spook should act like a spook, right?"

David regarded him before answering. "Kind of, but that's a spy, and I'm no spy—just an amateur detective trying to help out."

"Certainly. Same church, different pew. But, let me get down to business, David. If you read my column . . . ."

"I do."

"Then you must have noticed, in the past I've tried to mix it up a bit. Since September 11, though, it's been solid terrorism, anthrax, a new kind of war, bin Laden, the caves of Tora Bora and on and on and on. Well, it's time to switch and along comes this murder—only it's not just another murder. Here we have as the victim, one of the leaders in stem cell and related research, and as his possible killer, the Mafia—at least, according to what you said on radio."

"I'm listening."

"So you really think organized crime is involved?"

"I do."

"Are you willing to discuss it in public?"

David hesitated. "Why not? Who knows? It might flush them out."

The columnist's laugh was tight.

They had been standing side-by-side, their backs to the alcove's entrance. David squared his stance and folded his arms. "Mr. Henderson . . . ."

" 'Hender,' please."

"Hender, then, I take it you plan on doing a column about the crime, and you want to interview me about it."

"Exactly. And maybe a quote about the Mafia would spice it up a bit."

"Why?"

"Because I want to assist in validating your claim, and later, I want to be the first to write, 'I told you so'."

"Wouldn't you fear for your life . . . well, maybe not that bad . . . wouldn't there be some danger in writing that kind of story?"

"A double answer. First of all, the underworld doesn't like to take on the media. When was the last time you heard of a reporter being exterminated? Same as in your profession— they don't often mess with the law. They'd rather intimidate than kill, the reason being, the heat would be greater. You know what they say: 'a cop-killer raises more fury among cops,' or something like that. And second, I'd write in such a way that the conclusions drawn would be yours, not mine. For your reasons, you agree to the interview—the flushing out thing. We don't state that in the column, of course. And for mine, I just want the story. Nowadays, new topics are about as hard to find as Jimmy Hoffa. Interested?"

Although David had already self-committed to a boy-cott of the national media, he had a hunch that working with Henderson might prove to be valuable. "Give me a minute," he said. He contemplated fast. His comment about flushing out the Mafia had been too impulsive but, on second thought, they don't like headlines. Their clan-destine operations suffer. Maybe giving them big time publicity might prevent further bloodshed. "I'm interest-ed," he said.

"Great. But, more specifically, are you suspicious that organized crime might be sensing something profitable in blocking stem-cell research?"

"Would that be the gist of your column?"

"Something along those lines. But I know how they operate. My feeling is that they're not against it per se. What they want is to force a bidding war between com-peting parties. That's their grab for power: playing one against the other, with the threat of deadly consequences for some depending on how they line up. Can you go along with that reasoning?"

"I hadn't thought about that, but I'd be willing to dis-cuss it with you at the interview. And, by the way, aren't *you* against that kind of research?" David knew the answer, but it was the most convenient thing to say while he tried to fathom what Hendley had been talking about.

"You must have read my column on the subject last year. Yes, I stand by what I wrote, the reasons I gave."

David didn't return to the question posed to him about the Mafia and stem-cells. Instead, he asked, "Will I be given a chance to review the copy before it goes to print?"

"If you'd like." Henderson handed David his business card. "I work primarily out of my office in Westport but I can come to your place or your office, if you wish."

David sized up the options before saying, "Let's make it your office. If you can come to a wake in Hollings, I can go to your office in Westport."

"You're sure?"

"It's not a problem."

"Agreed, then. How's tomorrow after lunch at, say, one o'clock?"

David looked at the card and said, "I'll be there."

"Excellent. In the meantime, you might be thinking about a juicy quote to get their attention."

"Do they read?"

"You'd be surprised. I hear from them all the time, and they can sound pretty nasty. If I believed it all, I would have quit writing a long time ago."

Hendley's face soured. "Incidentally," he said, "I couldn't help noticing you talking to my friend Saltanban over there."

"You know him?"

"Unfortunately, yes," he replied regretfully. "I'm surprised there isn't more of a stir here because of His Excellency's presence."

David had puzzled over the same thing before and chalked it up to the solemnity of the occasion or to lack of recognition of a tiny country's president. But why didn't all the security detail pique some curiosity? For the moment, he didn't want to pursue the meaning of Hendley's last remark but made a mental note to bring it up in Westport.

The columnist continued. "I did two pieces on him, one when he had just done some pioneer work in telecommunications a while back and then another when he came to power."

"He was elected though, wasn't he?"

"If you call it that."

"It was rigged?"

"Unfortunately, some of the smaller countries don't play by the same rules we do, but from a distance, it looks like they do."

What kind of answer was *that*? "So you're implying his election was fraudulent?"

"If one was, all of his were."

Another question for Westport.

David nodded, forced a smile and, as he left the alcove, observed Clemente waiting for the next mourner who was still at the casket. David cut in.

"Can we talk for a few minutes—later on before you leave?" he asked.

"Certainly, doctor," Clemente answered. He looked around before pointing to a side exit. "How about outside. I'm already thinking cigar."

"Thinking chocolate would be healthier," David replied.

Again in his seat next to Kathy, he sagged into his usual slouch, believing the day's tête-à-têtes had run out.

"What was that all about?" Kathy asked, partially covering her mouth.

"I'm scheduled for an interview with Henderson Hendley."

"Da—vid," she said, drawing out the name in a cautioning tone, "you know what those do to you—even if it's with a pro like Hendley."

"I know, but this one can help if I work it right. Before that, I met with the president of Radonia. You might say I've been alcove hopping." David scratched the back of his head. "Anyway, we're having dinner with him tonight. At Olivio's."

"Dinner? Tonight? Who?"

"You—me—the Clementes—President Saltanban. And his female aide. That's what they must call a concubine down in that country."

He looked for an immediate response from Kathy but received none. Instead, she spoke earnestly. "Think of what was accomplished in less than a half hour, David." She counted on her fingers. "Dinner with the former boss of the victim. An interview with a nationally syndicated celebrity—for what reason I can't imagine. And who knows, probably more if you stay here till the bitter end."

"You're not?" David asked.

"No, I've had enough." She took out a pair of gloves from her purse. "Personally, I think these affairs are barbaric, except maybe they help in closure for the family members." She turned her eyes toward the Clementes. "But that's hardly family."

Kathy got up to leave. "What time is dinner?" she asked.

"Seven-thirty."

"Call me when you get home." She didn't have to lean over to take his hand in hers. "Understand," she said,

"I'm not knocking the value of going to wakes and funerals for murder victims—really I'm not—it's just that I think one of us here for the last hour is enough."

David crimped his mouth in reflection. "And the funeral tomorrow?" he asked.

"They say it's at 10:30, but you've got plenty to do. Why don't I cover that alone. Just the church service though. I hate cemeteries. And don't forget, you better check in at the Hole. Don't let the practice slip entirely." She pushed up on an eyelash with her knuckle. "I think I'm sounding like a mother."

"No, not a mother."

Their eyes locked. "What then?," she said.

"A wife."

* * *

It was 4:30, a half-hour after Kathy had left. The line of mourners had thinned and David watched his foot tapping against Friday as he sat awaiting the wake's conclusion. In his experience, no one had ever stopped to talk to someone in the meditation section before visiting the casket and the relatives of the deceased. This was a first. Jack Ogleton, an old friend and the president of Howerton University from one town over, spoke as if he were in church.

"David. Good to see you again. Not, as they say, under these circumstance, but good to see you again, nonetheless."

Brent Institute was one of the divisions of Howerton and whenever David thought of Ogleton, he thought of the person most vehemently opposed to stem-cell research of any kind, whether using pre-existing embryos or starting from scratch. David often wondered why

Ogleton never tried to eliminate Brent from its umbrella, or why the powers behind Brent never tried to get Ogleton dismissed.

David stood and shook the president's hand with both of his. "Hey, Jack, it's *been* awhile," he said, his voice animated. At first, he didn't recognize the woman at Ogleton's side.

The president extricated his hand and looked at it.

"Sorry," David said, "sometimes I get carried away."

Jack Ogleton was a paunchy man, maybe in his late forties. People were not surprised that he wore wrinkled blue or gray tweeds and scuffed-up brown shoes. He had a fleshy face that devoured his eyes during a rare smile; a way of talking through the corner of his mouth like a ventriloquist; and a habit of clearing his throat while thinking of the next thing to say. There was something rough and pugnacious about him and his choice of words, unseemly for a college president, also set him apart. Recruited from within Howerton's Department of the Humanities a decade before, he was selected as a compromise over two candidates from less prestigious universities in the Midwest.

"So what are you up to, David? Keeping your ass out of trouble?" He answered his own questions. "Jesus Christ, what a clod I am. Of course: the killing. That's why you're here. That's why we're all here," he said, heaving his arms around and clearing his throat. David beat him to the next sentence.

"How's everything in the ivory tower?"

"Same old crap. Everybody drives me nuts. One week it's student activists, the next week the feds, the next week the alumni. But David," he said, moving closer and lowering his voice even more, "between you, me and the fuckin' lamppost, it all boils down to the green stuff. You know, that's what talks. They can go on about modern curricula or political correctness or beautification of the environment but, when it's all said and done, the bottom line is the bottom line." He covered his forehead with his hand. "Oy," he continued, "I should quit while I'm ahead. There's this friend of mine with a nice little cabin up in the Montana woods."

David slid to the side.

"And you have with you?" he asked.

"Oh, I beg you pardon. This is Agnes Crocker. Agnes, meet Dr. David Brooks. We met in the parking lot and walked in together," Ogleton said, apologetically.

"Ms. Crocker?" David said, "Of course I've heard of you but never had the pleasure of . . ."

"Meeting me? I can say the same about you, but thank you and congratulations on all your good work. Why do you say 'of course,' may I ask?," she said, extending four limp fingers.

David shook them saying, "Because hasn't everyone around these parts heard of you?"

"Not the right ones, I fear," she replied.

As Northeastern U.S. Director of *Life International,* Agnes Crocker was either admired or loathed depending on how one stood on the question of abortion. She had been a thorn in the side of the planners and developers of Brent Institute a decade before and continued to be the prime vocal opponent of all its initiatives ever since. A large top-heavy woman—way on the other side of menopause—her thick white hair was smartly moussed out around a dull face and back into a bun. She leaned on a cane though few believed she possessed a legitimate disability requiring one. The same few wouldn't challenge her routine of rarely leaving the chair at her desk at the local library. She was its Associate Director, a post she'd held since shortly after graduation from St. Joseph's College in Hartford.

David almost held back on making his next comment. "Frankly, I'm surprised you're here."

Crocker didn't seem offended. "Well, I can understand your thinking. Dr. Molina and I were at loggerheads most of the time, but I believe he was a brilliant scientist and shouldn't have died the way he did. His was a life, too. I pray you have the same success catching his killer as you did before."

Ogleton appeared impatient and said, "I'm going on ahead. Please don't stop chatting on my account." He extended his hand as he bolted away; David barely reached it. Ogleton stopped to say, "Give me a call, David. Let's talk. It's been too fu . . ." He looked at the woman, then finished the sentence. " . . . darn long." David nodded and turned his attention back to Crocker who was scowling at the college president.

Once he had left, she addressed David. "You and I have something in common."

"Oh? What? Certainly not the same motivation for being here."

"I guess you're right, but I'd have to chew over that one a bit. No, it's that I also drive a Mercedes."

David managed a grin. "You mean you know what I drive?"

"Of course. Driving with your top down in the cold of winter, doesn't everyone around these parts know you?"

She paused, but David gave no reaction except to shift his weight. "There, I said it to you, too," she added, and after a second fruitless pause, continued, "Only my car is red. Stands out, don't you know."

"I suppose you might say we're soul mates, then," he said but, finding such a bond distasteful, corrected himself. "Or better put, members of a club."

"Aha," she said, "what an opening. Won't you join my real club?"

"What club? At the library?" He knew what she was driving at.

"No. *Life International.*"

David felt outfoxed so he thought quickly. "Sorry, Ms. Crocker. I never was a joiner."

"But how do you feel about what they're doing over at Brent?"

"I'm all for research."

"Even when it kills human beings? Even when so-called scientists and educators are planning to ignore moral, philosophical and ethical considerations in creating new people in the laboratory? How can you be in favor of that?"

"I never said I was."

"Well that's the whole purpose of Brent, isn't it?"

"I think they do some things there that you *could* support."

"Support? Me? Never in a million years! Any good that comes out of that . . . that . . . place is far overshadowed by their wanton disregard for human dignity. If I were a spitting person, Dr. Brooks, I'd spit right now."

David wondered whether he might have preferred seeing her do that to suffering through a diatribe.

"No, don't do that, Ms. Crocker—you might miss the floor." He had no idea why he worded it that way and fully expected a mighty return salvo.

Instead, she chuckled and said, "Anyway, let me know if you change your mind. You'd be our most famous member from Hollings. Toodle-oo." She limped off toward the casket.

* * *

At five o'clock, David was the only one remaining in the meditation section. He was tallying up the benefits of attending the wake when he noticed Juan Carlos Saltanban leaving through a side exit at the far side, lost between his two overgrown sidekicks. Both had inserted their hands within their jackets at heart level. The one with the missing finger hesitated and turned back to look clear across the room at David. The four men stationed along the periphery funneled into a line behind them. Evilina followed but, at the door, turned, lifted her veil and made brief eye contact with David before walking out.

He had received similar contacts from various females in his day and, at first, was inclined to group this one with the rest. But, never one from Radonia. Never one who lifted a veil. The others had sexual import; this one did not, he was sure. As to "Mr. Missing Finger" he didn't know what to make of his behavior. He stared at the closed door, half-expecting one or both to return.

At that moment, he felt a hand on his shoulder. Clemente, overcoat in hand, said, "I have a few things to settle with the brothers but let's go out and talk first." David planned on glancing out the door anyway, to corroborate his reading that Saltanban had an entourage of seven—and no doubt others patrolling the environs.

Outside, it had grown dark, and a chilling wind had kicked up, jerking David's trouser legs to the side. He quickly donned the scarf and gloves which he had removed from Friday. Clemente got into his coat and steadied a cigar in his mouth but had difficulty lighting a match in the gusts. They watched—and David counted—as the president and an entourage of twelve filed into two black vans. All but Evilina who had drifted off into the shadows. As if on command, one black Lincoln town car shot in front of the vans, two others behind, and all five vehicles headed for the parking lot exit as a tight motorcade. In the dim light, dark tinted windows unified the vehicles, a single column snaking along, emergency lights flashing, yellow and green flags snapping in the breeze. As it veered onto Park West, a white compact sedan materialized and, like a caboose, brought up the rear. Evilina was behind the wheel. David squinted. He couldn't be certain, but her car appeared to bear a Massachusetts license plate.

David turned to Clemente. "The trappings of heads of state," he said. "Does Radonia have an embassy in Washington?"

"Yes, it does. Juan Carlos has invited me to dinner there."

They descended four or five steps down to a macadam driveway but, shivering, nodded in agreement to retreat up near the door, beneath the overhang of the small portico.

"This won't take long, Adrian, and I certainly appreciate your taking the time when you have other things on your mind."

"As long as a cigar lasts?"

"Not even. Maybe a couple minutes. You got that thing lit?"

Clemente drew on the cigar in short bursts and stopped to look at it. "Voilà. Go right ahead, doctor."

"First off," David said, "I have to clarify something. Did you notify President Saltanban about Molina's death, or did he call you?"

Clemente removed the cigar from his mouth, inspected its tip and answered, "He called me."

David, maintaining a flat expression, took out his notepad and made an entry.

"Next, were you aware that before the murder, a threat was made on Manny's life?"

"No. How do you know that?"

"He called to tell me about it, and that's why I went out to see him and why I was the first to discover the body." All the while David spoke, his mind was on the day before—at the candy store—when he informed the Candyman of his being first at the crime scene. Why didn't Clemente ask how that came about? Had Molina phoned Clemente first in order to mention the threat and his decision to summon assistance?

"So you say you didn't know about the threat?" David asked.

"That's correct." Clemente's voice showed no sign of wobbling.

"Okay," David said, flipping to the next page.

"Wait," Clemente said, "did he say who made the threat?"

"I tried to pry it from him on the phone, but he wanted to discuss it in person and, as we know, it was too late.

I kick myself for not being firmer on the phone."

"Well, you had no idea the end would come on that precise day."

"Did he travel in bad circles?"

"If you mean with criminals or prostitutes, the answer is no. At least not to my knowledge."

"Jealous husbands? We all know he had an eye for the women."

"I think Manny was smarter than that."

"Was he a gambler?"

"For money?"

"Yes."

"No way. He was too cheap. We kidded about it. He made me look like . . .what do they call them . . . high rollers? He made me look like a high roller."

David had assessed Clemente's every word. "Only one more question, Adrian: do you speak Spanish?"

"For sure. My heritage is Spanish. Then there was all that time I spent in Radonia helping in Juan Carlos' political campaigns. I still have Radonia's biggest newspaper delivered to my door."

David was relieved, for he'd been mulling over whether or not to introduce the newspaper topic, fearful that no matter how indirectly he presented it, it might raise the suspicion of a forced entry to the Candyman's house.

He slammed his notepad shut, thanked Clemente, repeated his condolences and left.

CHAPTER 7

✛ ✛ ✛

Olivio's was a turn-of-the-century restaurant with elegant atmosphere, elegant meals and elegant prices. Set in the industrial valley near the junction with Center City, it was secreted within a sagging stockade fence smothered by ivy, euonymus and other assorted vines. The structure was ash faced and stucco framed, reminiscent of those in ancient Florentine villas, and it was not without design that the restaurant's menu derived from the tastes of Tuscany, even as its name reflected one of the dominant crops of that region.

David had picked up Kathy and, as he wormed his Mercedes through a congested side parking area toward a little-known spot behind a utility shed, he detected Saltanban's motorcade double-parked along a row of cars. He would have guessed the president was already in the building while some bodyguards maintained a watch from within the cars of the motorcade, much as had probably transpired at the funeral parlor.

Within, all was light and airy. Outer walls of casement windows, each set straddled by stained-glass lancet sections, lent a bright ambience which complemented the building's exterior. Rows of polished stone columns separated groupings of old wooden tables and chairs. Some of the corner tables had initials and dates crudely carved into them.

David put his scarf and gloves into Friday, helped Kathy remove her overcoat—the blue number he gave her for Christmas—and escorted her into the basil aroma of Italian cuisine. Not waiting for the maitre d', they headed straight for the back of the main dining room, past the table of the two blond bodyguards who looked up from menus and teased out smiles. David obliged with a wink. On the way, he touched the shoulders of some patrons he knew, addressing them by name, and received congratulatory remarks and best wishes from many more. Mellow Sinatra competed with the hum of diners in designer clothes and the chitchat of fawning waiters and waitresses in white gloves. Definitely upscale but, as David's favorite spot even when alone, he wouldn't have it any other way.

In the corner ahead, Adrian and Dolores Clemente, Juan Carlos Saltanban and his woman friend stood around two tables which had been put together for six. All smiled broadly at David and Kathy as they approached. The president stepped forward and gave David a firmer handshake than before as if to brace himself for the crunching return.

Saltanban wore the same double breasted suit but had added another medal. "Ah," he said, "this must be your fiancée. He reached for Kathy's hand and raised it to his lips, but before kissing it, shifted his eyes toward David and said, "What have you done, doctor, to be so lucky?"

Kathy answered for him. "I'm the lucky one. Lucky and most honored to meet you, Mr. President."

"But the honor is mine . . . Kathy, is it?"

The Clementes looked respectfully at Saltanban while David strained to keep his eyes from rolling. Evilina's face was vacant. She had changed from somber black attire to a red slit dress and, to David, she was more appealing than he had imagined through her veil.

"But you are. . . how shall I put it . . . too petite? Too fragile? . . . to be doing police work," Saltanban said, staring at Kathy..

"I like the 'petite' better," she said.

"I like the 'fragile' better," David added devilishly, not certain of what he meant.

"Looks are deceiving," Clemente said. "Her reputation is that of an excellent detective— and an excellent police officer before that."

The president switched his stare to the Candyman. "On your recommendation then, I must ask our police authorities back home to recruit women like her."

Chagrined, Kathy slid her chair closer to the table while the others displayed various degrees of amusement, Evilina the least.

After a round of drinks was ordered, Saltanban said, "Now if you do not mind, I would like to get a piece of business out of the way. Not my business but Dr. Brooks'." The president's fingers assumed a church steeple pose and, tapping them together, he continued, "That he and I postpone the little interview he requested earlier at the wake— until after dinner. Do you normally eat dessert, doctor?"

"No, not normally." David anticipated a punch line.

"Nor do I. While the others do . . ." Saltanban waved a hand across the table . . . "you and I can move into the empty room over there and close the door behind us. I already arranged it with the maitre d´. Then you can ask me all the questions you want, just as I promised."

David nodded. "No holds barred?" he asked.

"No what? What is the meaning?"

"I'm sorry, Mr. President. Will you take all questions?"

"Yes, yes. With the reporters in Radonia, I must be careful, but with a doctor like you, please ask anything you would like."

Soon after tossing off a scotch, David addressed the president. "So before you went into politics, you were in telecommunications. How did you get started?"

"It is a long story." Saltanban settled into his chair as if he planned to spend the night. "As a boy, I was always taking radios apart. Later, I became an aficionado of the history of communications. Even in high school, I knew that would be my field someday, and in the meantime, I read all I could about the history." There was a palpable charm not only about what he said but also how he said it, and the table responded with riveted attention. Even David relented to his brittle way of expression.

The president continued. "I do not mean to bore you . . ."

"Are you kidding?" Kathy said. "Please go on. It'll be ages before we get a menu here, anyway."

"At the beginning, the first form of long distance communication was what?" He allowed no time for a response. "Smoke signals." He drained a rum and Coke and, smacking his lips, went on: "Then some people called the Sumerians developed the first known system of writing; the Romans started the first newspaper; and the English introduced the first pencil. Next, the French developed photographs and three of your Americans—Morse, Bell and Edison—invented the telegraph, the telephone and the phonograph. The radio came in there somewhere and I think a Canadian was involved.

"As I have said, Samuel Morse invented the telegraph. It was in the early 19th century. Of course it was he who later developed the Morse Code. The telegraph was a very important instrument during your Civil War for both the press and the armies of both sides. And it helped at your stock exchange and at your railroads.

"What can I mention about the telephone? Bell discovered it in the late 19th century. And you know, a funny thing. One never thinks of it, but at the beginning, there were no switchboards. They came during the next year. Then dial phones, service between countries, and the technology I am most interested in: commercial satellites. Think of these as relay stations that . . . but I have said enough about these devices. I am afraid I ramble once I begin. Some other time, perhaps, I might discuss the radio and the phonograph."

Saltanban signaled the waitress for another round of drinks. Only David complied; the others, shaking their heads, covered their first wines with their palms.

"So you see, it is all related—all these forms—and all the countries, somehow many of them wanted to—how do you say—wanted to get into the act."

David had little doubt the president had given the spiel many times before. The table remained focused.

"Anyway, my friends, we are now up to the things I used to do and hope to resume when I step down. That is, if I can convince my son to take over as president of my country. I believe the people will elect him." He stared wistfully into his glass before continuing. "That is the desire of my early twilight: the presidency of Radonia for my son, Luis, and advanced telecommunications for me." He made no effort to disguise a fine hand tremor.

David put aside his drink, took out his notepad and said, "I'm learning something here."

"You mean about my son and my plans?"

"That too, but I mean about telecommunications." He jotted down some notes.

Saltanban looked pleased. "Then forgive me, but I shall become more technical. "Bell Laboratories discovered the transistor; Xerox, the copier; and Corning Glass, the first optical fiber that could be used for long range communication. Fiber-optics uses a laser to send signals through glass or plastic. The transistor, which replaced the vacuum tube, is a tiny device that controls the flow of electric current in T.V. sets, radios, computers and . . . but there I go again. I am sorry."

Now David was convinced the remarks had been delivered many times before and probably to audiences just as indulgent. Saltanban waited for him to look up from his notepad.

"I spoke about satellites already. Telstar is a satellite that was launched in early 1960. It relayed telephone calls, television shows and other communications between your country and Europe. My company dealt with fiber-optics and satellites primarily, but I have recently become interested in cybernetics. In point of fact, three months ago, I completed a book on the subject, and I am now anxiously awaiting word from the

publisher. I want to advance knowledge about how information is transmitted by the control mechanism of
machines and the nervous system of living things."

David pricked up his ears. "Like animals?"

"Yes, animals . . . humans. Yes, anything living. But I
believe I have rambled on too long." The president
gulped down the remainder of his drink. "You asked me
the time and I made you a watch!"

"Nonsense," David said, coming around even more.
"That was most informative." He wanted to write down
the "watch" comment. "One last question, though. What
about computers? Where do you think they're taking us?"

Saltanban exhaled like blowing out a match. "I am
concerned. The Internet with its encrypted messages can
be such a tool of secrecy that crime of every kind will
become electronic and will take place in an instant once
the decision is made. Drug operations, fraud, embezzle-
ment, prostitution, blackmail, government conspiracies,
military coups, murder. Much is possible now, but it can
get worse. In the matter of terrorism, for example. And,
even in business or education or government work, face-
to-face meetings may no longer happen, and I think
much will be lost there. It is really a sword with a double
edge. E-mail. The Internet—an Information Super-high-
way, but one that is filled with—what are they called—
potholes? It is the secrecy that is my worry. Split second.
Cheap. Yes, cyberspace is good but can become evil. And
too little has been done to prepare for the evil. I am afraid
this hemisphere and perhaps the whole world has an ana-
log intelligence dealing with a digital threat. That is how
I see it."

There was a hushed pause before Clemente began to

applaud softly. Dolores and Kathy joined in. Evilina, her eyes fastened on David, finally broke her silence.

"I've heard it all before," she said, "but some things, you know—they get better all the time." She spoke without an accent.

David found the comment more titillating than elevating. He reached over to shake Saltanban's hand and said, "I hope you get your wish. And by the way, how old is your son?"

"Luis? Sixteen. He will be out on his own soon."

"How old do you have to be for the presidency?"

"In Radonia? Twenty-one, but we are trying to reduce it to 18."

After that, dinner and conversation of little consequence lasted about an hour, less for David who waited for Saltanban to finish his third rum and Coke.

The two retired to a small poorly-lit room which was antiseptic in appearance but smelled of stale cigarette smoke. It contained a single square table and two straight-backed chairs; they sat opposite each other. Saltanban folded his hands tightly and placed them on the table to control the accentuation of his tremor. David removed his notepad from Friday.

"Proceed, doctor, please," Saltanban said. He twisted his mouth and snorted—a trademark of some chronic imbibers David knew.

He had been eager to begin his interview of Molina's former boss but didn't have a list of questions formulated in his mind. Often, in both taking a history in medicine and in criminal interrogations, he would learn more by body language and by what wasn't said than by the responses themselves.

He wasted no time but started cautiously.

"How long did you know Manny?"

"About ten years."

"Can you think of anyone who might have killed him or wanted him killed? Someone from either your country or here?"

"No, no one. He was well-liked in Radonia—no political enemies, no jealous colleagues in the scientific community that I know of. I assume the same was the case in the United States."

"Are you going to the funeral tomorrow?"

"Yes, I expect to, unless I receive a call from my country that needs my immediate . . . you know . . . my immediate attention. Sometimes that will happen . . . you know . . . not often, but sometimes. I can handle most situations by phone, however, so I am certain I will attend most of the funeral. Even if I am needed in an emergency, our flight home will be soon after. From the airport in Hartford."

"Bradley International."

"Yes, that is it."

"Do you come to the States often?"

"Once, maybe two times a year—on official business," Saltanban answered, a smile pasted on his face. "I would often include a visit with Manny at his office. A famous place, that Brent. I have given them financial help since Manny took the job. They are doing wonderful things but now, unfortunately, they must carry on without him."

"Did he visit Radonia very often, do you know?"

"Oh, yes, more times than I came here. He has . . . had . . . many old friends there."

David stopped writing. "Will any come to his funeral?"

"No, and I do not know why." The pupils of the president's eyes seemed large. "Some should," he added. "He remained close to a few. They would tell me about it."

"Now, on the question of chocolates. I know you sent Manny some for his birthday. Do you send many people chocolates?" David didn't know any other way to word the question without tipping his hand: Clemente's information that Saltanban sent chocolates regularly throughout the country.

Saltanban's smile disappeared. He dropped his hands on his lap and said, "May I ask you a question, doctor?"

"Yes, of course."

"Why are you asking me questions like these?"

David rubbed his decision scar. "Partly because you were a chapter in Molina's past but mostly curious, that's all. I believe you said I could ask you anything. I must have misunderstood."

"Forgive me, then. I thought you meant there would be questions about my friend, Manny, and his job in my country, not about chocolates I might send to my other friends."

There was a knock on the door and Kathy stuck her head through. Her face was ashen and hard. "Sorry for interrupting, David, but could I see you for a moment?"

In the hall, Kathy led him to a corner. "There's been another murder," she said.

David felt his forehead wrinkle and, looking around, said softly, "Where? Who?"

"Nick just contacted me. He got a call from the funeral parlor. They found a dead woman in a red Mercedes—in the parking lot."

"A red Mercedes? Agnes Crocker?"

"Yes."

"Shoot!" David said, shoving the notepad into his pocket.

Back in the room, he found Saltanban hunched over, pacing the floor. "Sorry, Mr. President, I have to leave. There's been another killing."

Saltanban came to full height and went over to David. "I am sorry to hear that. Your work never ends, does it?"

David checked his watch. It was 9:10. He rushed through his next statements while prolonging a hand-shake. "It was a pleasure meeting you. I'll probably not attend the funeral tomorrow. Have a safe trip home. May I call you if I have further questions?"

"By all means. Please call even if you have no ques-tions. Or consider coming down to visit sometime." With a looping of the hand, Saltanban produced a business card and handed it to David. "My private number is list-ed there. Do not hesitate to use it."

David pocketed the card after noticing, at its upper half, a color photo which appeared to be a capitol build-ing. Halfway out the door, he turned and said, "By the way, any chance you might have come across an Agnes Crocker?"

Saltanban snapped his fingers twice. "Crocker," he said, "do you mean the Life lady? She walks with a cane? Is that the one?"

David shot him a sidelong glance. "You knew her?" He reentered the room.

"Knew her?"

"Yes, she's the victim."

The president put a hand to his cheek. "That is terri-ble!" He walked in a circle, stroking his lips. "But why?," he said. "She was part of a noble cause—not one I believe in—but nevertheless noble. There is a chapter of her organization in our country."

David was in no mood to be discreet. "So is it that you heard of her or that you've met her?" he asked firmly.

Saltanban stopped. "I met her right here in Hollings—at a party for Manny when he was installed as Director at Brent. But I had heard of her before that. I must admit I never understood why she was at the party because she was opposed to everything the Brent Institute stood for." His voice turned pontifical. "What do they say: it is best to know your enemies up close? Maybe that was the reason."

* * *

David and Kathy pulled in behind an ambulance that was parked near the main entrance to Tilbud's Funeral Parlor. She stepped onto the sidewalk and he, grimacing, stabilized his knee as he lurched around the front of the car. A police officer, coat collar pulled up against the hissing stiff wind, beckoned to them.

"They're waiting for you," he said and lifted a line of yellow tape for them to walk under.

What had been a dimly lit parking lot, as David had remembered it from a few hours before, now resembled a highway construction site illuminated at midnight. He could feel the warmth of floodlights on his head. The staccato of shortwave radiospeak blared from the center of four police cruisers, their convergence an arrowhead pointed at a red Mercedes. It was the kind of scene David was familiar with: flashing lights, faint smell of burnt rubber, uniformed police, plainclothes officers, oversized van of the Hollings Major Crime Scene Unit.

At the open driver side door of the Mercedes, Sparky

was taking flash stills in rapid succession. The criminal-ist gave them a solemn two-finger salute.

"You check it out first," Kathy said, nodding toward the car as she made her way toward the van. She stopped short, returned to David and whispered, "Remember, darling, same as before—you're the lead. We're as short-handed now as we were last month—look at Sparky tak-ing his own pictures. And don't worry about Nick, for heaven's sake. He may be chief but he needs all the help he can get even if it means . . . well, you know what I mean." She walked over to the van.

David approached the Mercedes but before looking in, said to Sparky, "I can call you tomorrow?"

"Certainly. Doesn't seem to be much. Midmorning would be fine. I left the weapon undisturbed in there for you to see. Then I'll take it with me to the lab." He moved away.

Once again, David withdrew a pair of latex gloves from Friday and snapped them on.

Detective Chief Nick Medicore appeared from nowhere and said, "Help yourself, Dr. Brooks—this gets more interesting everyday. But also increases our goddamn work load."

"I'll do what I can," David said. "Did anyone hear gun-shot?"

"There wasn't any," Nick scowled, taking off toward the van.

David thought it was another patented snide remark until he peered into the car. He had expected to find Agnes Crocker slumped against the steering wheel, the rear of her head matted in blood and—since Sparky had mentioned the weapon—a handgun on the seat or floor.

Instead, she sat erect on the driver's side, her head extended backward at a severe angle. Neither blood nor a gun was visible from David's vantage point. Lips thinned, he removed a flashlight from Friday, then leaned in.

Crocker's eyes were open and opaque. Her dark blue face was set in a look of horror. Embedded in a straight line across the front of her neck was a length of wire, each end fastened to a brass handle.

David drew back sharply as his mind went into a rapid search-and-retrieve mode. A garrote hit by the American Mafia was rare. Not so in the case of foreign mobsters, especially those from Spain. He would check his reference materials later at home. In the meantime, he feared that once again he was being sucked into a conspiracy of international proportions.

He reached in and put his hand against the side of Crocker's face; it was cool. The muscles in her neck and jaw felt stiff. He pressed a finger against her cheek; it blanched pale. These findings were compatible with the time he calculated she had left the parlor and entered her car: four-and-a-half hours before.

David directed the flashlight across the front interior. A cane lay on the floor of the passenger side and a small purse on the seat. He opened the back door and lifted the corner of a neatly folded blanket on the seat. The edge of a cellophane-wrapped box came into view and, after throwing back the blanket, he stopped in mid-breath and looked over both his shoulders. It was a box of chocolates. A card taped to it read: *Candies by Clemente.* He stood by the car, stroking his lips, trying to decelerate the throb of the moment.

*   *   *

Back home, David was preoccupied with his upcoming computer entries, shrugging off concerns about the peculiar silence he had shared with Kathy when he drove her to her condo from the crime scene. He rationalized she was allowing him the freedom to think alone, to be the "lead" as she expressed it. Or to drive without distraction through a steady drizzle.

He referred to the entire den at 10 Oak Lane as his computer corner. Hardware, writing materials, major reference books, a radio and a telephone rested on an oversized oak desk. A well-stocked portable bar was positioned on the wall to the left, within easy reach during computer tasks; he preferred the scotch supply in the kitchen cabinet, reserving occasional refills from the bar. Above wainscoting, two other walls bore shelves overflowing with papers, books and folders.

It was 10:45 p.m. when he walked in and sat at his desk, drink in hand and the entries sketched out in his mind. He approached the computer as if he were about to write the preamble to a monumental opus but, once in his chair, he recalled the garrote hit and his decision to read up on foreign organized crime families. He pushed on his feet and rode the chair to a nearby reference book, *Criminal Elements, Here and Abroad*, and flipped to a dog-eared page with a heading, **Murder for Hire**:

The Mafia or "La Cosa Nostra" had its roots in Palermo, Sicily in the thirteenth century. Later, the Italian states were dominated by the Bourbons who had spawned another secret organization, this time in Seville, Spain. It was called "The Camorra" and was composed of out-and-out criminals. Its favorite weapon for contract killings was

the garrote. The organization still exists today, but its pri-
mary arm—"The Camorra N'Drangatta"—reigns in
Naples. Before long, the Camorra and the Mafia merged
but maintained headquarters in Naples and Sicily. Most
experts believe their alliance is an uneasy one as they
compete in criminal activities among themselves and
other organized crime factions such as the Chinese Triads,
the Japanese Yakuza and the Russian Organizatsiya.

David clenched and unclenched his jaw as he slowly
reread a sentence: *Its favorite weapon for contract killings*
was the garrote.

The information confirmed what he understood all
along, so he plunged into his entries:

Sunday, February 10

Manuel Molina Murder, continued:

(A) Ongoing summary

Sparky call: .22 slug within skull. M.O. of
American mob.

Phone call threat. Mentioned genetic engineering,
terrorists. "Bug off."

Searched Clemente homestead with Musco.

Radonia newspapers.

Invoices for chocolate shipments to
Afghanistan.

Locked closet.

Wake at Tilbud's.

Pres. Saltanban. Bodyguards (Big suckers).

Girlfriend, Evilina (Mysterious knockout).

Henderson Hendley (interview tomorrow in
Westport).

Jack Ogleton

Agnes Crocker. Her last wake.

Saltanban and Clemente give different versions of who called whom.

Dinner at Olivio's:

Saltanban knows stuff re telecommunications.

His wish: son to become president of Radonia and he retires to telecommunications field.

Evasive on chocolate issue.

Open invitation to Radonia (May go, depending on developments. Alert Musco).

Agnes Crocker Murder:

In Tilbud's parking lot. Primary, organized scene.

Garroted after attending wake. (? Camorra).

T.O.D. about 5 p.m.

Body found about 9 p.m.

Box of chocolates in car (Candies by Clemente).

(B) Action Review:

Done, continued:

Wake (skip funeral—Kathy to attend).

Clemente search.

Crime lab.

To be Done:

Molina's last 24 hrs. (Start at Brent tomorrow).

Crocker's last 24 hrs.

Check Clemente's locked closet (?)

Call Clemente re chocolates in car.

Check with Sparky.

Evilina (?)

(C) Unresolved:

Crimes related (?) Chocolates at both.

Motive (?)

American mob, Spanish mob or both (?)

Where is Kermit and the Asian mob?

(D) Key considerations:

Kathy and Nick again giving free rein, an entreaty.

Events stacking up as international in scope.

Terrorism included (?)

Musco essential as sidekick.

The entry took less time than he thought. It was 11 p.m., and in a fifteen-minute time span, transferring his thoughts to print had worked its magic once more. For before he began typing, twinges of self-doubt surfaced, like the searing pains of opposing muscles gone taut.

He'd had a taste of international killers before, but not the terrorist variety. And was that the case at all, or was the Mafiosa—and possibly others—capitalizing on a new fear? Were the Yakuza still on his tail? If so, why? The threatening phone call with its remark about terrorism. The garrote with its shiny handles. The nation's prevailing mood since the Trade Center calamity: anger, but also apprehension. He felt waist-high in territory not covered by the mantras on his three-by-five card. And, Kathy's and Nick's reaction were important to him. Was he up to their summons and its strain? Was he in over his head? Should he be bothered in the first place? He wanted to wait until the entry was completed, when he knew he'd have a better chance at finding some answers.

So now, as he thought about his phone call to Musco, he experienced tension draining away, and if there had been someone there to hear him—like Kathy—he would have shouted for her benefit, "Come ahead, you bastards, I'm ready for you!" He viewed his new resolve as nothing short of an epiphany.

*   *   *

"Are you sleeping?" David asked.

"Not now." Musco's voice was weak and scratchy.

"Sorry."

"Don't worry about it. What's up? You in trouble?"

"Depends on what you mean by trouble. Look, Musc, I'll get right to the point. There's been another murder and I've got my work cut out for me. You say you don't want to know nothing, but what if I want you to? Two eyes and ears are better than one. What I mean is, can I borrow you from Red Checker on and off for a couple days . . . uh . . . maybe more, depending? I'll double what you pull in as a hack."

Musco's reply was swift. "We've been through this before and . . ."

David stepped on his words. "So it's 'no'? Guess I don't blame you."

"You're wrong, old buddy, but that's too many clams."

"You mean it's 'yes'?" David asked, perking up.

"Yeah. But let me get this straight. You want I should be your deputy? Temporary like?"

It was exactly what David had in mind. "That's a great title. I'll buy you a badge. A badge for Deputy Musco Diller." Musco gave a genuine laugh which allayed David's momentary fear that he had parodied the cabby's role.

"Then why not the usual place tomorrow morning at eight," David said. "I'll buy breakfast." He felt a surge of confidence, reinforced by the support of a trusted, cagey sidekick.

"You got it."

"Good. Two more questions. You're sure it's okay with the company?"

"Okay? I'm boss around there, remember? And don't forget, this gives all our other dudes in the field more passengers."

"Understood. Second question. You own a gun?"

This time, Musco hesitated. "Do I have to tell you? Wait—that's dumb with a friend like you. Yeah. I keep it at home."

"What caliber?"

"Forty-five."

"That'll do. Can you bring it with you?"

"Sounds serious. But, like I said, you got it."

"Terrific. And one last thing."

"You want I should come over now?"

"No, no, of course not. What I want is to let you know we'll talk high finance later." David hung up without waiting for a response.

CHAPTER 8

✣ ✣ ✣

Monday, February 11

The following morning, David's descent on the slick road toward the hospital was an adventure. But not unexpected. He had put another blanket on his bed during the night and figured that the drizzle would turn to a freezing rain, that he would end up slaloming down the road or hugging its shoulder. He shifted into low gear and did a little of both, all the while questioning why the main approach to a hospital hadn't been sanded yet.

Hollings General, a labyrinth of new and hundred-year-old buildings—grays and tans and glass surrounded by red brick—lay set into the eastern hillside. Halfway down the hill, David was automatically drawn to the clock tower, a reflex he was certain all visitors shared at that point. Seven-fifty-eight. In his nine year association with the hospital, this was the first time his mind's eye connected the descriptive word "tower" with the commanding structure ahead of him, its copper cupola rising half again higher than the buildings it towered over.

In the auxiliary parking lot, he heard the rasp of sand as he skidded his Mercedes into the usual slot, cracked open the window, looked up at a menacing sky and put on his scarf and gloves for the long walk to the doctors'entrance. He would have donned the stocking cap reserved for deep chills but never liked wet wool pressing against his head.

Musco maneuvered his cab alongside, got out and took quick midget steps to the trunk, fumbling around until, in one motion, he extracted an umbrella and snapped it open. It was gray and grungy, had several collapsed struts and leaked at the center.

"Good timing," he said.

David climbed out, put his hands on his hips and began laughing.

"What's the matter," Musco said, "you never seen a guy in fancy duds before?" He unbuttoned a brown checkered jacket—a tad long at both sleeves and hips. His shirt was off-white and open at the collar, and a brown sweater was tucked into his waistband. He wore tan creased trousers and no cap, exposing a bald, finely contoured head which David hadn't ever remembered seeing. "And don't tell me they don't match," Musco added firmly.

"No, it's not that. You look great. It's the umbrella. I'm sorry but I can't help but think of Columbo's car—or, better still— his raincoat. It's antediluvian."

Musco cocked his head as if he hadn't heard right. "Show-off," he said, then pulled back one side of the jacket. A pistol was lodged under his belt. He grinned proudly. "So?" he asked.

"Good," David said, "I'll bring you a holster."

"Nah, they're too much trouble. I can pull this baby outa my pants just as fast. C'mon, get under. But don't get near the middle. And you'd better take this yourself or I might poke your eye out."

Even while stooping under an umbrella with one arm around a fledgling deputy and trying to dodge icy raindrops slithering down his neck, David felt a swagger to his gait. He ignored Musco's soft comment, "Maybe I should buy me a blue blazer like you got."

David led the way into the hospital and toward the cafeteria, slowing down now and then to allow Musco to keep pace. Near the pharmacy, the cabby's nose quivered. "Smells like a hospital," he said.

"Well?"

"I wouldn't be caught dead in this here place."

"You wouldn't know, so don't worry about it." Musco shot him a touché glance.

They had a light breakfast in the corner of the doctor's dining room where several medical colleagues came over to offer encouragement and best wishes—even advice in the case of a surgeon or two. David introduced his table mate as his deputy and could tell that the cabby was trying to look important. Between visits, Musco agreed that during their investigation of the crimes, he would be at David's side as much as possible.

"Like a bodyguard," Musco had said. It was more of a statement than a question.

David looked over and beyond Musco's head and replied, "Sort of, but really like a lookout." He was sure the distinction hadn't offended his deputy. "I just want people to get used to seeing you with me—for a few days anyway."

In the Hole, Belle was about to hang up the phone, but before the receiver hit the cradle, she blurted, "Now you have two murders on your hands."

After tossing Friday and his scarf and gloves onto a chair, David stood before her desk, his hands pressed on its surface. Musco stood behind him.

"Have you seen this morning's *Herald*?" she asked.

"No."

"Your friend, Nick Medicore, is quoted as saying that because chocolates were found at both sites, chances are whoever killed Dr. Molina also killed what's-her-name. The activist."

"Agnes Crocker," David said, then rubbed his decision scar thoughtfully before adding, "He said that publicly?"

"It's all over the front page. Even his picture."

"Christ, as a law enforcement professional, he should know better. What a tooter." It was a euphemism David chose for "big-mouth." In another mood, he might have strung out his condemnation of the Detective Chief. Instead he moved aside.

"Belle," he said, "this here is . . . I mean . . . this is Musco Diller. He'll be helping me out over the next few days."

"So *you're* Musco Diller. I've heard a lot of good things about you and about your company. I use your cabs whenever I need one," Belle said, extending her hand.

Musco stepped forward and shook it, then withdrew a "gold card" from a pocket and handed it to her, saying, "Pleased to meet you. You're the one who keeps my old buddy here on the right road."

Belle inspected the solid white card and said, "I've heard about these passes for free rides, too. Thank you."

David had gone over to sit at his desk and was flipping through some lab reports. He stopped to address Musco. "Aren't those freebies taking away the fares your cabbies would get? Or do you reimburse them?"

"In a pig's . . . ." Musco looked at Belle. "In a pig's eye," he said. "They know that's the way it is at Red Checker—or else they don't get hired."

"So there," David said as they shared a laugh, Musco's the lustiest.

David stretched as he got up, then crossed to Belle's desk, checking his watch. Eight-thirty-five. "Okay, my Belle, we're running late. About the house calls—you know, it seems like ages since I thought about medicine. I feel like I'm completely abandoning my profession."

"Don't be silly," Belle said.

Musco sauntered away to an opposite corner, his hands clasped behind him.

"Think about it," she continued. "On Friday, you missed an hour at most and Dr. Castleman covered. And today, the most unusual things—well, really only one about the practice."

"Like?"

"Well, you know how busy we get on Monday after-noons—all the docs over the weekend promising their patients you'll handle the house calls?"

"Tell me about it—like till eight or nine."

"They've eased up again—only two offices have called."

"What do you mean 'again'?"

"The same thing happened the last time you were investigating. It's as if they all know you're preoccupied."

David scratched the back of his head. "Now I'm really

worried. Do you think it'll pick up again when it's all over—whenever *that is*?"

He glanced over at Musco who was glancing back.

"It did last time. They all need you, remember? This is just their little way of saying, 'we're helping you to hurry back.'"

For a second, David thought she should have been a psychiatrist.

"Now it's my turn," Belle said. "Two questions. First, you're not attending Molina's funeral?"

"No, Kathy will cover it."

"Okay. You plan on visiting Brent, right?"

"Right. This morning. We're leaving after I talk to Clemente about the subject of chocolates. Why?"

"Because some guy phoned here just before you arrived. He said I'd better tell you to stay away from Brent."

David rolled his neck a few times. How the hell did anyone know? But it's obvious, isn't it, that the place has to be checked out sooner or later. Yeah, that's it.

"Did he imply when I'd go?"

"Imply? No, he seemed to know."

"When did he say?"

"This morning." Belle uttered the words with a hint of resignation. She fingered the locket around her neck.

Musco had been inching closer to the conversation. "Excuse me for butting in," he said, "but the way I figure it, someone's trying to scare you . . . uh . . . us off. That's all."

David squeezed the cabby's shoulders into his grip and gently shook him. "You may be right, my friend," he said. He then waved at the air as if signaling contempt for the circumstances. He hadn't even bothered to ask Belle to describe the caller's voice.

David's call to Clemente revealed little about Agnes Crocker's box of chocolates except that he had no idea who might have ordered them. He would check the records but suggested that someone simply gave them to her or that she might have bought them herself. And, yes, he knew what she looked like and no, he didn't remember seeing her in the store lately.

After putting down the receiver, David got up and wished the office had a window to gaze through. Instead, he leaned against the wall and pondered for a moment. Is Clemente lying? Did Saltanban send Agnes chocolates just like he did Molina? If not, who did? The Camorra? If so, why?

The two men looked at each other. Musco opened the door for David to exit first. But he strode back to Belle who appeared contemplative, staring into space.

"That caller," David said, pausing. "The voice. What did it sound like?"

"Deep. Smooth. And it had—like—an echo to it."

"Hmm," David said. "Echo-man." He pulled out his notepad, scribbled down a single word, twirled the eraser end of his pencil in his mouth and added another word.

"Do me a favor, Belle," he said crisply. "Call ahead at Brent that we're on our way over. They'll alert the gate."

"You got it, but be careful, will you?"

David ignored the admonition, his face a mask of intensity. "And another thing," he said, "See if you can find out if Agnes Crocker had a birthday recently."

"Sure, but why?"

"Oh . . . curious, that's all. Plus say 'Hi' to your Georgia. Is she noticing boys yet?"

"Please. More than I'd like."

* * *

If Hollings General Hospital were considered molded into an eastern hillside, Brent Institute of Biotechnology had been dropped into a decaying western flat surrounded by fast-food restaurants, chain stores and several tenement houses. One would have thought the only thing holding up the houses was the paint. And the paint was peeling.

Not yet four years old, Brent was a three-story, sprawling complex of glass sheets and steel spines, its aluminum-rod brise-soleil mounted at roof level protecting the northern elevation and extending out to form a sun-dappled entrance court in summer. Alongside, the highest flagpole in Hollings flew its largest American flag.

It was a scientific research arm of Howerton University in neighboring Center City and employed 400 administrators, scientists, nurses, laboratory technicians, computer experts and other assorted technocrats. Its nursing component assisted in experiments among human volunteers.

Security was tight, with trappings more like a munitions facility than a research center, from an armed guard at its front and back gates to its strikingly high chain-link enclosure. Cameras were conspicuous along the sides at both first and third floor levels. Long-distance parabolic sensors and sweepers kept watch from their central locations at each side wall. The hardware for a night surveillance system was perched at each upper corner, while a network of antennas and transmitters sprouted from the rooftop. All external and selected interior doors required encrypted "smart" cards for admission.

David termed it an electronically armed camp and often wondered why radar equipment and a sharpshooter in a lookout tower weren't part of the landscape. On more than one occasion, the same questions popped up: Who are they trying to impress? What's so top-secret? Aren't universities in a constant pinch? Where did the money come from?

By 9:00, the rain had stopped and the cold morning air was sharp against David's cheek as he lowered the window of his Mercedes at the main gate.

"You're expected, doc," a burly guard said. He leaned out from his booth and, after handing David a parking pass and an entrance card, gestured as if loosening stiff fingers. "Circle around ahead, park over there and, remember, when you get to the front row of doors, only the one on the far right will take the card. Insert it this way."

David laid the pass on the dashboard and slipped the card into his shirt pocket. When he did, his hand brushed against the cold butt of the Beretta Minx under his jacket.

"Thanks, Alex. You want me to sign?"

"Not you, doc."

It was all a ritual that took place during every one of David's visits.

"Hope you get to the bottom of what's going on around this town," the guard said. He stretched closer to the car. "Who's your buddy, there?"

"Oh, sorry. This is Deputy Diller." Musco nodded his head and, as they drove away, pushed back against the seat and beamed.

Brent's internal architecture and ambience were as outrageous as its external, the visual counterpart of radio stat-
ic. Curved ceilings, curved window panels, curved furniture pieces. Automatic this, retractable that. Direct lighting
here, indirect there. In more expansive areas, curved struc-
tural sections gave way to those supported with Glulam
beams, corrugated metal and painted drywall to create a
clashing palette of materials and colors: soft reds and yellows, strident blues and greens. David had long ago concluded that its interior design had something to do with
light and power conservation or air currents and nothing
to do with eye appeal. He often referred to the physical
plant as an avant-garde celebration rather than a basic science building in which promising new discoveries were
being hatched, and spoke openly of funds wasted on
building, security and furnishings instead of directed
toward additional research. And whenever he did, he
reflected on where the funds came from and whether or
not there were strings attached to their use.

After being let into a central corridor splitting an
ocean of spotless laboratory rooms, Musco kept pace
with David initially, but then fell back as he paused at
each open doorway to gawk at technicians in scrub
suits, caps, gowns, shoe coverings, goggles and strange
plastic masks that looked like pig snouts. Some worked
silently and swiftly at benches below suspended fume
hoods—benches of Bunsen burners, beakers, wire
loops, petri dishes, scales, centrifuges, microscopes,
incubators, chemical jars, rubber hosing, glass tubing
and oxygen tanks. Others deftly manipulated extension
rods through glass partitions, transferring the dexterity
of their hands to metal claws inside.

David navigated the circuitous but only route back to the administrative wing, beneath a parade of overhead cameras, through pungent chemical odors that smarted his eyes, toward the office of a long-time acquaintance, Brent's Associate Director, Professor J. Kater Weld. He passed, in turn, an immense laboratory outfitted with scores of DNA sequencing machines, devices resembling the photo-processing units at retail photo centers; a section labeled "Imaging Network"; a larger one labeled "Peptide Synthesis Facility"; a conglomerate of rooms assigned to Radiology, Ultrasound, Nuclear Medicine, Spiral CT Scanning and Open MRI.; and a closed cast-iron door with a sign above that read, "Sample Evidence Control." He had toured the complex on more than one occasion with Dr. Molina and was informed the room was utilized to coordinate labeling procedures to assure that a legal chain of controls for evidence was maintained and to avert mix-ups that could thwart proper DNA identification. David's interpretation? It prevented screw-ups.

Near Weld's door, he strummed his fingers on his thigh, waiting for Musco. The door burst open and Jack Ogleton emerged, his face red against his white shirt, anger sweat at his hairline. He was breathing fast and recoiled upon seeing David.

Confident that Ogleton wasn't about to collapse, David said, "Well, I'll be darned. What's a university president more interested in the humanities doing in a science emporium?" He felt smug over his descriptive choice.

"Shit, man, that guy's impossible to reason with!" Ogleton said with effort. "And insubordinate, too." He leaned back hard against the door jamb, emitted a single heaving breath and seemed to gather some composure.

"Sorry you have to see me like this, David. Just bad timing." He straightened up. "So what brings you here? The investigation, I suppose. Terrible about Agnes, wasn't it? Right after we saw her, too. Here one hour, gone the next. It's a goddamn shame. She meant well."

"Yes, that's why I'm here," David said calmly, and sensed that Ogleton wanted to leave in a hurry. He was right.

"Well, my friend," Ogleton said, clearing his throat, "I've got to run off somewhere to chill out." He raced by David, saying, "Good luck in catching the bastard." His voice trailed off as he rounded a corner, but David thought he heard, "Or bastards."

Within seconds, Musco arrived and said, "That fella looks like a cabby whose hack's been stolen."

"Maybe something *has* been stolen," David said, dismissively. He rapped on the door and smiled into the camera above his shoulder. Hearing a click, he and Musco went in.

David was struck by a gargantuan human genome chart pinned to the far wall. Weld, at a window, turned and showed no agitation over what might have transpired with Ogleton. He walked over to shake David's hand.

"They told me you'd be coming," Weld said. "Let's sit over there." He pointed to a cramped sitting area tucked off the office proper and equipped on three sides with built-in benches of cherry wood. They sat, Musco straining to plant his heels on the floor, David adjusting the angle of his legs. With knees at near shoulder level, he imagined he was seated in a children's playroom. He would have preferred the office's pastel chairs, modular yet contoured and adult.

The Lilliputian professor was not much taller than Musco. His build was slight, complexion ruddy and abundant gray hair fluffed out at the temples. His old but eager face was too small for the rest of him, its features severely scrunched as if cast in response to a foul odor. David supposed that if Weld scrunched further, no one would notice a difference.

Eyeglasses dangled from a cord looped around his neck, and he appeared lost in a long white coat with pockets brimming with reports, memo cards and lab chits. He, too, wore only "real" bow ties and, at one time, had joked with David about forming a club.

Trained as a biochemist, he had earned a doctorate at Howerton and stayed on as a teacher at the main university but transferred to full-time research and eventually to Brent upon its inception.

David and Musco sat against one wall, Weld against the opposite one, a folder on his lap. "So you must be training for your detective's license, too?" he inquired of Musco.

David answered for him: "In a manner of speaking." Musco looked like a cross between a celebrity and a smoked out imposter.

David immediately switched the subject to Ogleton. "I bumped into Jack as he was leaving. He had fire in his eyes, you know."

"He's always got fire in his eyes, lately," Weld said, shrugging. "And now, he's making the rounds here."

It was Weld's turn to switch the subject. He pulled out a sheet of paper from the folder and clutched it like an IBM stock certificate. "I assume you're here to discuss Manny's death but first, could you listen to half this page?"

David leveraged his leg to cross it over the other, then decided it wasn't worth it. "Sure," he said.

"I'm writing an article for *New Approaches in Medicine.* Imagine. They asked an ordinary biochemist his thoughts on the subject."

"Don't sell yourself short, Kater. You've done more clinical work lately than some physicians."

Weld got up and paced in a narrow path before them as he read:

My judgment is that far too much attention continues to be paid to those clinical entities that scientists have researched for years. Studies have been repeated over and over, ones on the east coast of this country duplicating ones on the west coast—or those from our country almost carbon copies of those from Great Britain or Germany or France or Italy. I have in mind illnesses like heart disease, stroke, cancer, arthritis. To a lesser extent, Alzheimer's and Parkinson's. It is my firm conviction that a moratorium should be called on all grant monies dedicated for research on a specified list of diseases to be determined by an impartial group of specialists. The monies saved, however, should not then be redirected to the study of other diseases or other causes but rather should be used to compensate a pool of dedicated, skilled individuals to pore over all the medical literature accumulated in all the great libraries of the world. Collate the material, get some computer help and make some sense out of it all. This is not to say there should never be a return to analysis of those specific topics, but let us pause, catch our breath, step back and interpret what the scientific body politic has amassed. Perhaps by arranging fragments of knowledge in the correct order—as we did with the human genome—there may be more complete answers. Who knows until we look?

The professor put the paper back in the folder with a flair and said in a dramatically hushed voice, "There you have it. The premise of my article. I've thought this for years, David. How did it sound?"

"It definitely makes good sense," David answered, teasing out each word. But inwardly he queried where Weld's approach left stem-cell research, genetic engineering and the potential of one day curing most serious illnesses. It was an approach that contradicted the mission of Brent Institute, as he understood it. Unless Weld's thinking excluded such basic research in the moratorium.

Through the corner of his eye, David could see Musco squirming about. And probably Weld saw it, too.

"I'm sorry," Weld said. "Thanks for taking the time to listen, but let's get on with why you're here. Besides, I have a funeral to go to at . . . ." He glanced at the boxy appointment calendar on his desk. ". . . at 10:30. You no doubt have some questions for me about Manny Molina."

David answered by tilting his notepad on his lap and scrawling Weld's name in bold letters so that the professor could read it backwards.

"To begin with, Kater, what's your take on the way Manny was perceived, not in the scientific community, but around here—at Brent?"

"You mean interpersonal relationships with his staff and the employees?"

"Yes, that's it."

Weld leaned forward and said, "This place is a hotbed of cold feet. Manny was the only one with guts—and everybody knew it and respected him for it." He let his hands fall flat on the desk and stared for an instant at David and then at Musco.

"But everyone else here is still alive," Musco murmured, sheepishly.

David turned and gave him the once-over. Wisdom again?

Weld ran his finger back and forth over his lower lip.

David squared back to the professor. "Can I come back to a statement you made earlier? That Jack Ogleton came here this morning to make the rounds. What did you mean by that?"

"Simple. He's plotting even before Manny's buried."

"Plotting for what?"

"His successor. I won't have any part of the way he goes about things."

David rubbed his decision scar. "You don't have to answer this, but is that what he came to talk to you about—and why he left in a tizzy?"

"Yes. He asked how I felt about curbing some of the things we do here."

"Like stem-cell research?"

"Yes. He knows damn well what my position is—that we should continue forward. That my suggested moratorium does not include ongoing study of embryonic stem-cell study. Only he's afraid I might slip in as Director, even though he's the lofty President." Weld flung his hands upward.

"So he's against that kind of research, and you took it as arm-twisting to his point of view?"

"Not exactly. He's against *most* of the things that Brent does, incidentally. But I took it as sort of a threat. That if I expected to be considered as Manny's replacement, I'd better change my priorities. Well, I don't work that way, and I told him so. But more than that, David: the poor guy's not even in the ground yet. What timing. How insensitive can you be? I told him that, too, so he goes bonkers—well, screw him." The professor's words were coming faster. "He's always gotten his way by bullying. Well, not me." He rubbed under his nose with a knuckle. "No sir, not me."

David interrupted his note taking. "You mean you're not interested in the position? Seems logical—you're second in command as it is."

"I could be interested but not in plotting for it. That's the only way I can describe it. The successor should be named in due course, and only through a search committee. Fair and square. With all the regulations and equal opportunity stuff—you'd think the deck couldn't be stacked. But," Weld said scornfully, "I've seen the way Ogleton operates."

David placed his pencil on the notepad, closing it.

"Help me sort this out, Kater. If he's opposed to the work going on here, why the hell does he support keeping it open?"

No hesitation. "Because, between you two and me, he's probably funneling some grant money through this place and using it on other things at the main university. You know: creative accounting. I'd bet my life on it."

"Hmmm," David said. "Tell me. Did he and Manny ever argue?"

"Are you kidding?" Weld's voice tightened, his smile

distorted. "Every time he came here—which was too often for my money—they had *screaming* arguments. They threatened each other. From Manny's office next door," he explained, pointing to the nearest wall, "I could hear them going at it."

David flipped back to a previous page and jotted in a margin. Then he asked, "Did Manny take early lunches? Did he go out? Did he eat here?" He raised his hand in a stop position. "Wait, I mean the day of his murder—Friday—what did he do?"

"He called in sick." Weld cocked his head. "Come to think of it, that's the first time he did that since we started."

"I see. What time was that? Did he speak to you directly?"

"He did. It was about this time in the morning. I remember distinctly because we were supposed to have a meeting."

"Just the two of you?"

"Yes."

"About what? Do you mind saying?"

"No, not at all. We had received an inquiry from a family in Washington that had suffered through more than its share of colon cancer, and they wanted to know how far along we were in genetic engineering. Specifically, in trying to remove that cancer-causing gene from its living members, if any of them had it."

David recalled his explanation to Kathy and considered the irony of such a disease coinciding with the example he'd presented to her.

"So you were going to discuss that case—and the possibility of helping out?" he asked.

"Helping out, but also advancing our knowledge and even, selfishly, our position in the field."

"Did you have any idea how Manny felt about it?"

The professor gave a slow meditative reply. "David, I really can't say for sure. About that or about many of what I thought were solid beliefs of his."

"How's that?"

"He seemed to be wavering about practically everything in recent weeks."

"Was he acting scared?"

"Not scared. I'd say . . . confused. He e-mailed me just before his death and said he felt locked into something but didn't specify. Said he'd explain when he saw me." Weld lowered his eyes. "Of course, that never came."

David saw him check the clock on the wall. "Just two more things, quick-like," David said. "Did you go to the wake last night?"

"Yes, I did."

David didn't remember seeing him there. Maybe he came and went during the conference with Saltanban.

"And you're attending the funeral?"

"Yes, even if I'm late—but I think I'll have time." Weld jumped up as if stimulated by the end of the interview. David stood and, observing Musco who was still sitting, tried to contain a laugh. The cabby was scribbling in his own notepad.

*　*　*

Before they left the professor, they had received his permission to examine Manny Molina's office, one door over, and were informed some uniformed and plain clothes police officers had been through it two days before.

Molina's square office was not much larger than the

Hole but with more furniture and more daylight. Its walls were overtaken by casement windows beneath which tables abutted in tandem, their back surfaces weighted down with books and scientific journals neatly propped between sets of bookends. The remaining table space was occupied—not so neatly—with heaps of manuscripts, documents, Manila folders and loose papers. Straight-backed chairs, a dozen or more, were snug under the tables, and they, too, were saddled with various books, magazines and journals. In a corner to the right, a computer, printer, copier and fax machine were housed within a hutch of blond-colored wood.

To the left, in the only corner where tables didn't join, a yard-high stack of newspapers rested on the floor. Despite the schizophrenic arrangement of materials in the room, the stack was the only component that appeared out of place, and David was drawn to it. He checked the top few. Their mastheads read the same as those he'd seen at Clemente's house: *Radonia Hoy*.

Musco sat on the stack and withdrew his notepad.

David spotted an appointment book at the hutch, went over and leafed through it. The only appointment that caught his eye was one scheduled with Jack Ogleton at 2 p.m. on February 7—the day before the murder. He booted up the computer and hoped that Molina's e-mail messages, though password protected, didn't call for verification—that, rather, Molina had instructed the computer to bypass the step for easier access. He had. In scrolling through incoming and outgoing messages for the past two weeks, David reconstructed an exchange between Molina and Juan Carlos Saltanban. It was dated 2/7/2002 8:06:16 AM Eastern Standard Time:

Seguimos comunicandomos por e-mail?

Si.

Cambiemos a clave? Si?

Los cidigos se rompen, major no. Ademas, debes saber que a mi gobierno nole agrada mi idea, pero yo voy a prevalecer. Y quien les dijo, que yo todavia no se.

David's knowledge of Spanish was tenuous but he was confident the gist of the dialogue was:

Should we keep communicating by e-mail?

Yes.

Shouldn't we switch to code?

Codes are meant to be broken so why bother? You should also know that my government does not like my idea, but that I will prevail. Who told them, I do not yet know.

Another incoming message was from Agnes Crocker. It had arrived five days earlier:

Why were you so—well—nasty last night? My plea deserves better.

There was no response from Molina.

David walked to the center of the room and, hands in his pockets, slowly spun around, trying to absorb everything in his line of sight. He watched Musco for a second or two.

"You about ready to leave?" David asked.

The cabby, his face set in concentration, was brushing his pencil back and forth over his pad. "There," he said, "Ain't no Picasso—that's him, right?—but it'll do."

David walked over and peered down at Musco's pad. He had sketched out the entire office and its contents.

"You like it?" Musco asked.

"Good job. It may come in handy."

"How'd you make out?"

David decided to detail the events of the past 48 hours including a vague assessment of Saltanban. Musco took notes.

"There's something fishy about that guy," David said. "Maybe with the whole Radonian operation."

Musco hopped off the stack and said, "Should we fly down and find out?"

David massaged his decision scar before answering. "Not quite yet, my friend."

CHAPTER 9

✜ ✜ ✜

Outside in the Mercedes, David called Sparky at the crime lab.

"Too early?"

"No, but the physical evidence doesn't yield much, David. No prints other than Crocker's. I vacuumed the whole car. Zip. The cane, the purse? Zip. Nothing unusual in it. The chocolates though, that was strange."

"I've got a theory on that."

"We need one," Sparky said, giving credit for it but not asking what it was. Rather, he moved on. "There's only one thing left to say and . . . "

David stepped on his words. "And what?"

"And I hope this doesn't sound off the wall, but I have a theory, too. In darned near 20 years in the field, I've never come across anything like this weapon. Quite a few killers use that M.O. in the States but they use rope, twine, maybe nylon stockings—you know—the usual ligatures. Never one with shiny brass handles. That was professionally made for a specific purpose."

"Meaning?"

"Meaning 'imported'. Or maybe I should say 'import-ed?' because I'm really not sure."

It was sure enough for David and supported his hunch about a Camorra involvement. "That's a real possibility, Spark. The playing field could be getting larger."

*　*　*

In downtown Westport over the noon hour, people scur-ried into luncheonettes, strolled into fine restaurants, traded places at fashionable shop windows. The affluent city was part of Fairfield County, Connecticut's "Gold Coast" home to multi-million dollar mansions and many Fortune-500 companies.

David and Musco made the hour-long drive southwest on the Merritt during weather more characteristic of the Shenandoah Valley than New England, out of central Connecticut's chill, into a calm, consoling afternoon.

David *needed* some consoling but not as much as in the early days of the grisly hospital spree. He had hardened for that investigation, relaxed all too briefly, then found himself bracing once again for an ordeal with interna-tional implications. More at hand, Ogleton's outburst, Professor Weld's revelations, the Saltanban and Crocker e-mails, Sparky's theory—all would have conspired to jangle the earlier version of David Brooks. Consolation? The weather change sufficed.

David found a parking spot within a block of the address on Henderson Hendley's business card. They were 20 minutes early and could have stopped for a sand-wich but decided against it. Musco, capless, had stripped off his jacket. David rolled up his sleeves, and while they walked toward the three-story building ahead, he felt the vibration of the cell phone at his hip.

"Where are you?" Kathy asked.

"Just outside Hendley's office."

"Where?"

"Westport."

David waited for Kathy's turn to speak but she didn't take it.

"Did you make it to the funeral?" he asked.

"Yes, I did," she answered flatly.

"Anything unusual there?"

"No."

"Did you stay for the whole thing?"

"Yes."

"Did you go to the cemetery?"

"Yes."

"You remember Ogleton and Weld from all those stupid socials we stopped going to?"

"Yes, how could I not? One's a cussing embarrassment in my humble opinion, and the other would back me into a corner and go on and on about the wrong kind of research done around the world. Except at Brent, of course."

"They're the ones. Did you see them at the funeral?"

"No, but the place was mobbed and I didn't pay attention. The only guy I looked hard for was our friend from Radonia, and he was nowhere to be found."

"Saltanban? You said you stayed till the end?"

"That's what I said, and I arrived early, too."

David readjusted his weight against the side of the building.

"You recall seeing Ogleton at the wake last night?" he asked.

"Yes."

"Did you notice Weld there?"

"No, but I left early, remember?"

For the most part, David believed he was on the receiving end of an automated phone system, and he hadn't even initiated the call. She agreed to spend the night at his place, however, and if something were bothering her, it would have to wait till then. He signaled Musco not to enter the building yet and then leaned against it near the entrance. He had more to cover with Kathy whether something else was on her mind or not.

"Wait," he said, "don't hang up yet. Can you please check on a couple of key things?"

"Yes, like what?" Her voice took on a lilting quality. Maybe she wanted more of a role after all, more than just attending a wake and funeral. The reason for her curt responses?

"First, would you call the Radonian Embassy and see if they have the time their president arrived here, and when he's leaving or left? They're more likely to give out that information to you than to an amateur detective. And, second—the same thing—they might tell you and not me: see if you can check with whatever airline and find out from their manifest whether anybody from Radonia arrived yesterday, and if they're leaving today. Also the airports and times."

"Okay, I'll get right on it. You want me to call you?"

So that was the reason for the curtness.

"No, it'll keep till tonight."

* * *

The directory in the lobby indicated that the columnist's office was on the third floor. They took the elevator.

Stepping out, they were greeted by a raven-haired receptionist in a red suit that matched the carpeting. David identified Musco and himself and gave her more than a glance. It was the lines of the suit he liked, not the color coordination. Her station of desk and computer console was directly opposite the elevator door and against a wall that ran about 30 feet to the right and 30 feet to the left of her. From the names on the wall, it appeared she was the receptionist for four separate offices that opened off the corridor.

Gold-framed reproductions of *The Seven Wonders of the Ancient World* paraded along wall spaces between entrance doors and above posh furniture pieces. The lighting was soft, background refrain soothing.

"Mr. Hendley's suite is the last to your right," she said. "Please go right in. He's expecting you."

David opened the door slowly and they walked in. Hendley sat facing the far wall, his fingers flitting to and fro over the keyboard of a word processor. Brassy music blasted from a grungy radio squeezed sideways among reference materials crammed onto a rack.

The room was puny, no larger than a prison cell, and nearly as bare. Astonished at the stark contrast to the elegance of the reception area, David thought it was like walking from a smartly appointed salon through a door marked, "For Employees Only" and finding yourself in a storage closet. He wondered why the receptionist called it a suite.

"Mr. Hendley? Hell—o," David shouted.

Hendley turned down the radio volume, swung around and rose nimbly. He was in white shirt-sleeves, unbuttoned collar and a drab brown tie.

"David. Good to see you. And you brought company."

After introductions and assurances that Musco was an incorruptible confidant, Hendley invited them to sit, pointing to the two other chairs in the room—wooden, unstable and recently painted.

"As you can observe," he said, "my quarters here are rather Spartan. I'm not associated with a newspaper or other media outlet. Always been a freelancer. I like it that way. More freedom to do my thing—and when I want to."

"Well, you've been at it a long time," David said.

"Yes, the business has been good to me. I love the writing, and I'm fascinated with most of the people I write about." Hendley lifted a notepad with one hand, tapped it on the palm of his other and said, "But let's get down to business, shall we?" He left no room for a response. "There's been another murder, of course, since we spoke last and . . . ."

"I want to ask you about that," David saidwhile opening his own notepad with a flourish as if to serve notice that what was to follow would be a two-way interview. Particularly in view of the comments Hendley had made about Saltanban the night before. David noticed Musco glancing alternately at him, then his hands, and the columnist, then his hands. David fancied his deputy was questioning whether this was going to be a battle between notepads.

"Did you know Agnes Crocker ?"

"Very well. I served on her Board for a spell. A fine woman."

"You had the same views on the kind of research going on at Brent, right?"

"Right, but for reasons other than hers. There's a fine

line of difference there. Maybe we could go into it someday. All I can say is that if she was killed because of her
views, it's a real shame because many, many people think
like that."

"Then do you have any idea why someone would kill
her?"

"No."

"Or who that someone could be?"

"No."

"Foreign elements?"

"Could be."

"Was she ever married?"

"I doubt it."

"Any relatives?"

"I think none around here. She came originally from
Idaho, so there may be some there."

"She moved here when? Do you know?"

"I'd say 20 years ago. Maybe 25."

David was surprised at the amount of slack Hendley
was granting him thus far and decided to take advantage
of it since the time would come when media-type questions would arrive in blocks.

"Could we go back to a comment or two you made
about Juan Carlos Saltanban last night?"

"I knew you'd raise that. I thought about it later. It was
perhaps too harsh. Better we move on?"

David gave him a bemused grin. Clever: drop the seed
and drop the subject. But he had no intention of letting up.

"But before we do," David said, "between two
Americans, what do you think about the guy?"

Hendley put the side of a fist to his lips. "Well, I'd
say—strictly from the point of view of a newspaper

person—that he knows something about the murders."

David, feigning indifference, took longer than usual for a notepad entry.

"Do you think the two murders are related?" he asked.

"Definitely. I'd say definitely."

"How so? They were at opposite poles on stem-cell research, genetic engineering, cloning and all that."

"Regardless. There had to be a common thread—that's my hunch. But getting back to Saltanban. I think he's in trouble down there in Radonia."

"Politically?"

"That and militarily."

"A coup in a democracy? Then it wouldn't be a democracy."

"Exactly. Maybe it isn't to begin with."

"That reminds me. At the wake, you said you thought Saltanban's elections might have been rigged."

"And I stand by that."

"Bought?"

"Possibly."

Hendley scribbled down his first sentence. He leaned forward and spoke almost in a whisper, as if to share a secret. "This is all speculation on my part, David. I mean the business of knowing about the crimes—and, understand, I'm not insinuating he was involved. Or about problems with the future of his leadership, although my sources tell me there are some peculiar doings there. You know, sometimes it's hard to get a real feel for these things from a distance."

David got the message and said, "If there's even the remotest chance he can give some insights about the murders—which is really all I'm interested in, not the politics of third world countries—then maybe he should be confronted about it. In person. I was too easy on him when he was here."

"That might be a good thing," Hendley said. "Should you elect to go see him, I'd suggest you include a talk with Molina's successor. He's still Radonia's Minister of Science. Man's name is Barlow—Will Barlow. He's an American transplant who married a Radonian lady. Prior to that, he spent time in Washington—Centers for Disease Control. I've interviewed him. Pretty level-headed guy."

To that point, David was still astonished at receiving much more than he was giving.

Hendley leaned back. "More to the purpose of your visit here, however. Remember, I wanted this interview in order to write a timely column, and you wanted it—or at least agreed to it—in order to flush out the Mafia somehow. Because, as you put it, they hate media coverage. That sums it up, right?"

"Right. Not only the Mafia, *any* criminal organization. It's clear that whatever their origin, they're involved in both killings, don't you think?"

"It sure seems that way. The American Mafia is everywhere. Even in Radonia. And the Spanish version is trying to horn in."

"There?"

"Everywhere."

Hendley's face became stern. "You realize," he said, "that organized criminal gangs have permeated virtually every continent on the face of the globe. You name it: all three Americas, Europe, Asia, Africa . . . you know, all of them . . . the American Mafia, the Sicilian Mafia, the Southern La

Cosa Nostra, the Corsican League, the Chinese Triads, the Russian Mafia, the Japanese Yakuza, the internationalist terrorist cartel. The Chinese gangs are particularly strong and getting stronger. They control most of the world's heroin supply and their yearly take is more than the total of the United States currency now in circulation. Can you believe it? And their manpower is just as staggering. In Hong Kong, there are about 300,000 Triad members— that's the name of just one of their groups, one of 50 in that area alone. Think about the others scattered around the globe. In contrast, it's estimated there are only 2,000 members of the American Mafia operating today.

"And it's common knowledge that all the gangs' usual activities are things like gambling, prostitution, extortion, drugs, murder. But more and more they've gotten their tentacles—some say their testicles—into big-time corruption of public officials at the highest levels."

His pace gathered steam. "Once upon a time, that was the exception. Nowadays, I wouldn't necessarily say it's the rule, but it's certainly more prevalent. Or, maybe it's simply a matter of better detection. In any event, having top officials in their pocket makes their other activities even more lucrative."

The columnist took a breather. David puzzled over the dissertation. And Musco was writing furiously.

David's conclusion was that it was a rehearsed speech. "You seem to know a lot about them," he said.

"I've made a living writing about people of every stripe. But never about a famous M.D. sleuth." He chuckled.

David grinned brightly, masking a deep concern about all he had been told or, more specifically, about what he might not have been told.

"But I'm afraid I tend to digress," Hendley continued. "Could you give me your opinion, David? It's really the same question I put to you last night and I might have misunderstood your answer. Are criminal organizations sensing something profitable growing out of stem-cell research, genetic engineering and the like?"

David shrugged. "My answer is that I can't be sure . . . yet."

"The 'yet', I take it, means you'll be investigating that possibility?"

"Unless clear evidence falls into my lap."

All three took time out to write in their notepads, Hendley the fastest this time.

David thought this was the best opportunity to approach the topic from a different angle, one left over from their conversation the day before.

"Another thing you mentioned at the wake, and it's related to the question you just asked me," he began. "Was the Mafia's grab for power—your words as I recall—connected with stem-cell research? I came away thinking they were both for it and against it. Not the power, the research. Could you run that by me again?"

"Take Agnes, poor soul. And you're the Mafia. You promise her you'll help block the research, but for a price. So that promise makes her happy, she goes to her well-endowed organization and gets practically a blank check to hand over to you. Naturally, it would be laundered in some way. But behind the scenes, the research goes on, so if, eventually, they get to the stage where they can cure diseases genetically—extract a bad gene here, insert a good one there—you know more about this than I do—then they can flourish in all kinds of black market schemes. It's a matter of control, David. If you control the industry, you make money. In this case, you make it early—from gullible people like Agnes—and you make it later, when the techniques begin to work."

David was impressed—and Musco looked it—with the ease of Hendley's explanation, more impressed than his simple nods conveyed.

Hendley went on, "So I pose our question again: Could there be a relationship between that background and the Molina and Crocker murders?"

"Let's put it this way," David responded, "It's a good bet the Mafia—and their counterparts from wherever—are infiltrating the field of science, and especially cutting-edge science. And that some people are either getting in their way or trying to dismantle projects before they get off the ground. The gangs aren't about to cave in."

"Crocker, I can see. She was the grande dame of opposition in that area. But Molina? He was a trailblazer and everyone around knew he was committed to his work."

From the way Hendley was framing his inquiries, it was clear to David that the columnist—being a columnist—had pre-conceived answers but wanted to draw him out. However, David didn't mind.

"True," he said, "if we limit ourselves to the mob's motive, then that's the piece of the puzzle that doesn't fit, and the margins are all filled in. But let's remember, others might have hired them. Hell, someone else might have called the shot in one case and, in the other, mobsters might have rubbed one out for their own personal reasons."

"Okay for me to include that in my column?"

"Absolutely. Nothing I've said to you here—or back at the wake—is off the record. Which brings me to the juicy quote you wanted: 'The scum-bags of organized crime wouldn't recognize an honest living for themselves if they fell over it. Their behavior is animal, and they prey on society because their instinct tells them to.'"

David had planned every word of the quote, hoping to stimulate more discussion on the streets, to incense the mob. Who knows? They might even make contact.

Hendley's grin appeared devilish as he wrote. He ran a firm quick line across the page as if he were about to announce, "There! Roll the presses!"

They got up simultaneously and, after an exchange of pleasantries, David asked when the column would appear.

"I'll write it today, you'll get a fax of it Wednesday and, if you approve, it'll be in the New England editions next Tuesday. It's always been Tuesdays around here. Of course, syndication means any time around the rest of the country, but I think most of the papers will handle it by the middle of next week."

* * *

It seemed to David that, in recent days, he'd done most of his serious thinking in the Mercedes. Once strapped in, Musco was the first to speak.

"Smooth character," he said. "You get what you wanted?"

David nodded yes, clasped his hands behind his head and kept a smile in check, believing if he appeared smug, he might feel it.

"Think about it, Musc. Hendley pulled Saltanban into the equation; he made sense in explaining the mob's motives; he wrote down my quote as if it were gospel; and, most important . . . most important . . . he advised us to fly down to Radonia."

But receiving all the information hadn't settled much, in a sense: David's mind remained a tangle of questions.

Musco slipped his thumbs under his belt. "I'd say it was a home run," he said. "Like, you played it cool and let him run off at the mouth. But he knows a lot, that guy."

David fastened his seat belt, turned on the ignition and, latching onto a single question, said, "I guess we're closer to deciding on Radonia." He turned sharply toward Musco. "If it's a go, are you game?"

"Hey, I'm your deputy, right?" the cabby answered.

They agreed to forgo lunch and to meet at nine in the morning for a visit to the Hollings Public Library where they would question Agnes Crocker's former staff associates.

*   *   *

It was well after four when David called Belle at the Hole.

"You're psychic," she said. "I was about to buzz your cell phone."

"For what?"

There was a long pause before Belle's answer. "You're tired," she said.

David was seated before his computer, doodling on a pad—a dead giveaway that he was indeed tired. He was aware that Kathy knew the sign when she saw it. And so did Belle. But they also knew the sound.

"You were about to call to tell me *that*? And what makes you so sure?"

"The 'for what?'. The just-short-of-short-tempered. That's a weary David Brooks."

"You always read into things. So what's going on? Is Castleman working out?"

"Very well. I think you'll be pleased when you get

back. The two of you will be a great fit. But that's not why I wanted to reach you."

"Then shoot."

"First, you asked me to check on Agnes Crocker's birthday. It was the day before her murder."

David was not surprised and began shading in a triangular figure.

"But the real reason I couldn't wait till tomorrow: a man just got off the phone with me, and it was the same voice I heard this morning—the one that warned you to stay away from Brent. I'd swear to it."

David dropped his pencil and shifted the receiver from one ear to the other. "Echo-man?" he asked.

"Yes, him all right."

"What did he want?"

"He wanted to speak with you. He said it was important. I said you wouldn't be available until later on. Then I gave him your home number. Was that all right?"

"Why not? It's in the phone book, isn't it?"

There was a pause, longer than before. "Get some rest," Belle said.

After offering a half-hearted apology and asking how her daughter, Georgia, was doing, David phoned Kathy at police headquarters and invited her to dinner and a sleepover. He mentioned his classic grilled cheese sandwiches and potato salad, and she responded with a delight he interpreted as feigned.

Whatever fatigue David experienced had nearly dissipated after half a glass of scotch before showering and the other half while toweling off and dressing. He didn't agree with Belle that it was fatigue in the first place— more like turmoil. And he never understood why, but a turtleneck from a growing collection always seemed to relax him the most, despite noticing Nick Medicore in his own collection. Recalling that Kathy had bought him several in the past year, he managed a difficult smile and selected the dark red one.

Shortly after six, he heard a key in the door. Kathy walked in, carrying an overnighter and a garment bag. David took the bag and flung it over his shoulder while, at the same time, he used his free arm to yank her off her feet and into a brief but tight embrace, then released her and kissed her forehead lightly. Her fragrance was one he'd never experienced before.

Kathy, breathless, said, "If I hadn't learned how to make myself into a rag doll when you do that, I would have been long gone by now."

"You should complain?" he shot back. "How about when you tweak my cheek?"

She removed a black raglan coat, hung it in the closet, then spun around and assumed a model's pose. Everything about her looked different to David. Her hair was pulled back in a gold bumblebee tie, and earrings of tiny yellow finches hugged her lobes. She wore a wrap-around black blouse, stretched tightly and fastened in the back. He thought the contour of her breasts was lower than usual. Her skirt was white, tight and slight, barely reaching her knees as she straightened and extended her hand. David took it and drew it slowly toward his mouth.

"Am I supposed to kiss here or where?" he asked. "If you're trying to do a job on me . . . ."

"Complaining?"

"No, but I'm sorry, Kath. The usual impulses are deep frozen right now."

"I can wait."

He kissed her hand with the same light touch he'd given her forehead.

At the kitchen cabinet, David poured another scotch for himself and a Chardonnay for her. She took a giant swallow, gripped his wrist and led him into the living room where she aimed him toward the sofa and shoved gently. He complied and she eased down, facing him, one leg tucked under.

"Now, let's get back to the tweaking business," she said. "What's that all about?"

"Simple," he said, half expecting a return to the subject. "Are you planning on pinching my cheek tonight?" He pantomimed the act in the air.

"What do you mean?"

"My cheek. You plan on pinching it tonight?"

Kathy pulled back and fired her classic one-eyed stare. "You're serious, aren't you?," she said.

"Shouldn't I be? You know I don't like it."

She squared her gaze, hesitated and spoke submissively. "Okay, you win. You don't like it, so I won't do it."

David had begun to hear his breaths leave through his nostrils, a sound signifying a slow burn, and it always bothered him more than the initiating cause. Relieved, he said, "Good. Once and for all, it's agreed?"

Kathy nodded. She reached out, enveloped one of his hands in both of hers and pressed it against the side of her face.

"Look, darling," she said, "I know it's been a tense few days. But you've had them before. What's wrong?"

"Goblins."

"Goblins?"

"Yeah, like Saltanban—and Clemente—and Ogleton—and now, Hendley—and maybe more. Even faceless goblins, like whether or not to fly to Radonia."

"You're going to Radonia?"

"I don't know yet. The president invited me, and Hendley urged me to go. He said there might be some things going on down there that I should know about."

"Even so. Don't drop everything for a trip like that."

"I'm not dropping anything. But Molina worked there six years, for Christ . . . ." David pulled the complete phrase, polished off his drink and surveyed the glass.

"Well it seems to me that it could be a wild goose chase. Do you suspect him?" Kathy asked.

"Of course I do—just like any of the others. But it's not only that. There's the Mafia connection, too. Look, we just had two hits in a row in this city, probably by two different gangs. Then we get strong advice to check out the damned place down there from an internationally respected journalist who's got connections all over the globe. What am I supposed to do, ignore it all? As far as I'm concerned, most of criminal detection is a *series* of wild goose chases, anyway. So I come home empty handed. That still tells me something, doesn't it?"

Kathy kept wrinkling her nose as if she were trying to sniff the essence of everything he was saying to her.

David, who had been gesturing with his hands while he spoke, suddenly collapsed them in his lap while releasing his chin to his chest. He raised his eyes and, in the deepest voice, said, "Sometimes, Kathleen, you can be . . . ."

She broke in: "You're tired."

"I've heard that already."

"What?"

"Never mind. I should have stuck strictly to medicine."

She transferred to a nearby easy chair. "Well," she said, "tired or not, whether you're ready or not, you've got to hear what I found out about one Juan Carlos Saltanban."

"Now what?," he said, his voice tinged with exasperation.

"I had to pull all the official strings but apparently Mr. President didn't arrive in the States yesterday as he said, but the day before. Saturday. And his flight home wasn't scheduled until about two hours ago, so he had plenty of time for the funeral—if he'd wanted to go."

David slid forward on the sofa. He ran his fingers along his mustache and down to his decision scar. "Strange," he said. For the first time since Kathy arrived, his face felt alive.

"And there's more," Kathy continued. "Didn't you say his flight was in and out of Hartford—at Bradley?"

"Don't tell me . . . ."

"You got it. He didn't land at Bradley, or take off from there, either."

"Then where?"

"Boston. At Logan."

"So the bastard lied."

"Sure looks like it. I don't know why he had to, though."

"That's the second time, if I can believe Clemente."

"But wait. I'm not through." Her sips of wine took longer. "That Evilina broad? She wasn't on either flight. His group included four other guys, description unknown."

"So where in hell did she come from?"

Kathy shrugged.

David remembered that Evilina drove away from the wake in a separate car, and that it appeared to have a Massachusetts license plate. "Why not?," he said, slapping his forehead. He informed Kathy about the car and asked if she could check with that state's Motor Vehicles Department on whether or not an Evilina Ruez lived there.

By now, the second drink had begun to kick in, and he began weakening on his recent vow not to consult with Kathy about every investigative detail. Separate the personal life from crime detection, he had instructed himself. Yeah, sure. But why? What's to be gained by withholding information? Running to her on the spot was one thing; sharing with her at the appropriate time was another. This was an appropriate time.

David leaned back and chose his words carefully. "I didn't get a chance to tell you, but yesterday Musco and I paid a visit to Clemente's house."

"If you went with Musco, that meant they weren't home."

"Correct."

Kathy's unperturbed reaction wasn't what he'd expected. He went on to describe what he'd found, including the invoices for chocolate shipments to Afghanistan, the Radonian newspapers and the locked door.

"What's behind that door really bothers me," he said, shaking his head from side to side.

"Why couldn't Musco unlock it?" she asked.

"He was waiting outside, and I was worried about time."

"I'd bet on a return visit."

"You'd win. And it probably should be soon."

They seemed to sense what each was thinking as they rose, downed what was left in their glasses and walked into the kitchen together. David decided to include sliced tomato and ham strips in the grilled cheese sandwiches while Kathy combed the refrigerator and found a bowl of leftover potato salad. She mixed in some olives, eschewed asking David about his preference as she filled both their glasses with Chardonnay, and declared the meal fit for a king and queen.

While they ate, David brought her current on his findings at Brent and the encounter with Hendley—particularly about the columnist's knowledge of the underworld, his estimate of unrest in Saltanban's Radonia and the Barlow fellow who replaced Molina.

They were clearing the dishes when the phone rang. It was only five of David's paces to his desk in the den and he took the call there.

A woman in monotone who identified herself as a telephone operator asked, "Is this Dr. David Brooks?"

"Yes, it is."

"I have a person-to-person call from Chicago, Illinois. Go ahead, please."

"Hello, Dr. Brooks. My name is Anthony Stonzo. I have a small business in Chicago and was wondering whether we might discuss some things that I'm sure will interest you." His voice sounded hollow.

"Now?"

"No, in person."

"What kind of business and what things?"

"You might say I deal in services. I understand some nasty things have happened to you recently. And some unfortunate things in your community. Perhaps I might be of some assistance."

David decided not to draw out the caller further, for it was precisely what he was waiting for. And the column hadn't even been written yet! He waved his hand for Kathy to lift the receiver of the wall phone in the kitchen.

"All right, Mr. Stanza, where?"

"That's Stonzo."

"Oh, I beg your pardon."

"That's okay. On Thursday, I'm flying into New York City to receive an award for my work with underprivileged children. I can catch an early flight and we can have a discussion over lunch. How would that be? Would you mind traveling to the city?"

"Let's see." David pretended to consult an appointment book. "Why not? Yes, I can shift my schedule around for that."

"Good. That's a very wise decision. And if I might get personal, do you think you might have the time to fly to Radonia before we meet? My friend, Juan Carlos, tells me you two have already met. I can assure you, doctor, that you wouldn't be sorry if you made a trip there. It doesn't have to be long. You'll see what I mean when we talk in New York after the trip."

David wasn't totally surprised at hearing the country mentioned by a person who was either Mafiosa or a damned good facsimile. But its timing—its out-of-the-blue emergence in a phone call from Chicago, the nonchalant manner in which Stonzo brought it up—rattled him like a thunderclap. He figured him for a capo bastone, the second in command, certainly not a don.

"It's definitely in my plans, and I'll try to get it in by

Thursday," he said, mustering a degree of firmness.

"That would be smart. Now, I'll put my secretary on the phone to give you details." Stonzo's voice became louder and less hollow. "Frankie, would you speak to Dr. Brooks, please?"

"Hello, this here Dr. Brooks?"

David diagnosed frayed vocal cords. "You got it," he said brusquely. It dawned on him that while he welcomed the call, he was still livid over organized crime's likely role in the affronts to his personal property and his ego—the cut wires at Oak Lane, the phone tap and the canary left at Molina's. Not to mention the two homicides.

"How's twelve-thirty at Sorrento's Restaurant? I don't have no address but it's in the middle there, right there in the Big Apple."

"I'll find it."

"Good boy. Oh, I almost forgot. One other . . . whatcha call . . . deal. Mr. Stonzo likes to have his meetins, uh, structured."

"Structured?" David was shocked Frankie knew the word.

"Yeah. Each side can have as many outside men as they want. They stay outside, in the next room maybe, so they can do the, you know, advisin', if they have to. But at the table, you can have only one inside man wicha. Okay?"

"Thus far, everything is copacetic." Take *that*, Frankie.

"What?"

"Yes."

"Whadaya mean yes?"

"I mean I understand the business of outside and inside advisors."

"Good. That there's important."

"Will you be there?"

"Don't know yet. There's this here other job I might have to do. Mr. Stonzo's figurin' it out. We don't like to do too much during Lent, bein' that it's holy, so maybe he wants me to do it after Easter. Also, he says Thursday is Valentine's Day and we don't like to do too much then neither. He says it makes people remember that there big Chicago job—you know, the massacre— and it would put the heat on . . . wait, we had nothin' to do with that, you know—not in the twenties—but all the cops and them wiped out. Too bad. So I might make it in New York."

"Fine, I'd like to meet you."

"Likewise, I'm shur."

They wished each other Happy Easter in case they didn't meet.

"And to your family too, Frankie. Do you have a big family?"

"Inside? Nah, just my mother and brother. Outside? Yeah, big. *Real* big."

After they hung up, David leaped from his chair. "Golden, so far, Kath," he said and shoved a fist through the air. "Are you convinced now that I should go?"

"To New York?" Kathy's face had lost color.

"Well, yes, New York."

"You have to, I guess."

"And Radonia?"

"Yes," she answered, reluctantly. "Who's your inside man for New York?"

"Who else? Musco."

"Can you take Nick and maybe some of the guys on the force as your outside men?"

He reached down to put his arm around her and shook her tenderly. "I can handle it. I have a plan. I was waiting for the time and it's about to arrive. It goes with the flushing out thing."

"You have a *plan*? You're taking them on?"

"No, not taking them on. Out-foxing them. I'll explain later." He sat again.

David had never seen Kathy pace before. From the den to the kitchen and back to the den. In little steps. Head bowed.

She stopped before him, clasped her hands around his head and said, "You can't fly with hardware, you know." He nodded.

"Take Musco with you."

"Of course. And questioning the library about Crocker will have to wait."

He checked his watch. Ten after seven. He rummaged through a small varnished box on his desk and withdrew the card containing Saltanban's private number. Utilizing both house and cell phones, they made calls to Bradley International Airport, Musco and Radonia. Within 15 minutes, David and his "deputy" were booked out of Bradley at 7:05 in the morning—Tuesday—with a scheduled departure back to Connecticut for Thursday at 2:45 p.m. Musco stated his bag was already packed. Saltanban insisted on having his personal driver pick them up at the airport and providing private transportation during his stay, but David vetoed the idea in favor of more independence. Assuming his plane landed on time, after a brief stopover in Miami, he assured the president he would honor his invitation to visit him between four and four-thirty. Saltanban explained that his office was known as the El Cielo House or simply El Cielo.

The process seemed to transform Kathy from anguished fiancée to steely detective.

Though revved up, he suggested they retire early.

She responded coyly, "Do you know what would be nice right about now?"

"What?"

"Let's take a shower."

"But I just took one."

"So you'll be the cleanest guy in town," she said, alighting softly on his lap. Her miniature kisses around his ear lasted but a minute.

In the bedroom, David, the first to undress, tiptoed into the shower stall. Kathy joined him, covered his mouth with her lips and, as steam rolled around and warmed their bodies, pulled away and said, "Is this taking your mind off the goblins?"

CHAPTER 10

✛ ✛ ✛

Tuesday, February 12

The plane departed from Hartford ten minutes late. David and Musco sat side-by-side toward the rear. Neither removed his beige trench coat. About 20 aisles ahead, a man brushed back his blond hair. His was the only head visible above the backrests, and when he brushed a second time, David could swear that one of his fingers was missing, yet, throughout the eight-hour flight, he hesitated to stroll up front and check for fear he would be right.

Musco twirled his cap; David was certain the cabby would eventually place it over his eyes while he dozed.

"I don't like it that I can't pack my forty-five and that you don't have your usual bulge—know what I mean?" Musco whispered.

"Those are the rules."

"Maybe when we get there, we can buy what we need." He tapped David's side with his elbow.

"Let's just hope we don't need anything."

Earlier, before leaving Oak Lane, David and Kathy had discussed what she would carry out in the following 48 hours: contact Bruno's Martial Arts Studio about having someone else teach David's beginners class Tuesday night; dig up what she could about Agnes Crocker and her position at Hollings Library; check on whether or not Evilina lived in Massachusatts; and call Belle to inquire if the house calls were going smoothly.

In a series of phone calls, Kathy had determined that the best lodging in Radonia was the Hotel Husa. And David had photocopied a page from his encyclopedia collection which, in a single column, defined the newly democratized country of Radonia.

He had elected to bring Friday along, minus its guns and gadgets. From it, he dug out the article on Radonia and skimmed over several snippets:

> ... the Spain of the South with all the Andalusian ambiance and touches of Seville including a scaled-down version of its giant cathedral, a bullring and a replica of La Maestranza with its Plaza de Toros.
> ... a relatively new democracy, but still a country of haves and extreme have-nots.
> ... It's first and only elected president, Juan CarlosSaltanban . . . in power for 12 years . . . recruited from a highly successful telecommunications business . . . a rags-to-riches story for, during his entire early life, his was an obscure family among the have-nots.

David had mixed emotions, aware of an inherent danger in his mission yet responsive to the spate of signals that he *must* investigate Radonia firsthand. Stonzo's polite but certain advice was the clincher, although he couldn't believe he'd been swayed by a probable organized crime figure he had never even met.

He looked at Musco who had, indeed, fallen asleep. David decided on one last rationalization before he, too, might succumb. In the overall investigation of the crimes, was this trip taking a disproportionate slice of his time, or was it justified because of what he saw as the "underworld factor?" The two crimes, after all, had all the earmarks of gangland slayings. Not to mention that Saltanban, an obvious suspect, needed more questioning: the chocolates, the link to Molina and to the Institute; the air flight misinformation; the claim that Evilina was his aide from Radonia—or did she live in Massachusetts?

At 2:40 p.m., they landed in the country's capitol, Copa, a name derived from the Spanish, meaning the crown of a hat. It referred to the city's configuration, a reversed valley with farmland in its center elevation and commercial and governmental properties around its lower brim.

In the modern airport terminal, David phoned the hotel and had no difficulty booking two rooms. The receptionist spoke fluent English as did a man at the terminal's information kiosk who offered general directions and arranged for a car rental. Lobby signs were printed in both Spanish and English. By three o'clock, they stepped out onto a concrete island between two lanes of honking fast-moving cars, all jockeying for position. Awaiting their car, they put down small suitcases and, in David's case, a garment bag and Friday. Musco pulled down on his cap and David shielded his eyes from the brilliant sun, remarking how much the air felt and smelled like a

New England Spring. They removed their coats and, in a switch that surprised them both, David sported a brown print golf shirt that matched his tan slacks, while Musco wore a blue blazer and a short-sleeve white shirt with a four-in-hand necktie and Windsor knot.

The car arrived—a black compact—and David drove toward center city, along the quays of a lesser Guadalquiver, on streets that twisted and convoluted only to emerge into plazas of orange trees and fountains. Pale green foliage cascaded over stucco walls and white blossoms punctuated the still air with the fragrance of jasmine. A grassy knoll featured a billboard which read: "Welcome to Radonia, the Sevilla of the South." Musco commented that apparently most visitors were from the States.

They cruised around a block-size bullring, its wooden façade dotted with graffiti, its pit quiet and resting now, poised to echo the brass fanfares and chants of a delirious crowd at another time. Three blocks behind, the multi-spired Copa Cathedral rose up, not as high as the gothic original in Seville, nonetheless proudly, its bulk anchored by the tower of an old mosque in one corner. It was but a replica of what the Moors had built in the southern cities of Spain during the eighth century.

Along a constricted street beyond the bullring, David slowed down. "There it is," he said, "just as they described." He pointed to a three-story building with balconies stretched between turreted walls of granite. The only hint foreign to old Spain was a sign at the top— HUSA— attached to a superstructure and encircled by garish neon.

The interior was a display of elegant décor reminiscent of Spanish alcazars. Balconies, fountains, sculptures and staircases rimmed the main lobby while its many arches were supported by marble and onyx pillars. Fine reproductions commanded every wall: El Greco, Goya, Dali, Gris, Picasso.

For a moment, David and Musco gawked. Then David marched over to an ornate counter and verified that their rooms were set for later. The receptionist informed them that El Cielo was two blocks west of the cathedral, within walking distance. She landmarked its location as the only nearby building with a tunnel.

They checked their bags and headed for Saltanban's. The way was studded with flowers, overspread with the scent of bougainvilleas. They moved through scores of both tan and white-skinned pedestrians who were milling around, and David was startled as much as Musco by the sudden lift of hundreds of white pigeons from one of the plazas.

"That's it, up ahead." David pointed his chin toward an isolated two-story structure, its whitewashed walls glistening through poplars and acacias. In seconds, they arrived at the entrance to the tunnel mentioned by Husa's receptionist. A single sentry stood at attention armed with a rifle David recognized as a Russian AK 47. David instinctively tucked in his left shoulder. His Minx .22 was not there. The sentry, burly and somber, asked who they were and what their business was. David gave the answers. After giving them the once-over and making two calls on a walkie-talkie, the sentry waved them in.

The warren-like building before them was a reconstruction of an old corrales, common in Seville centuries before when communal living flourished. As one used to the majesty of capitol and government buildings in the

States, David wondered where Copa's were hiding. No statues, no memorials, no edifices commemorating national pride? There were no nearby structures that might pass as administrative offices.

He led the way through the damp tunnel as if he had done so before. Near its end, they recoiled when they looked into an alcove carved into rock ledge. A platoon of guards in faded blue uniforms, their Uzis prominently displayed, sat on a deck of three-tiered bleachers. They seemed disinterested as if they had been forewarned.

Further in, David and Musco emerged onto hard-packed Alcala earth lined with wooden railings. A second-story veranda coursed around a rectangular courtyard below, its walls comprised of bays of cross-hatched windows.

"Now what?" Musco asked.

"Let's try here." David walked purposefully to an open stairwell. He could feel Musco on his heels.

On the landing at the top of the stairs, they came upon a door with a sign that read, "El Cielo: Oficina." They passed through and entered an anteroom where two more sentries flanked another door, AK 47's at their sides. No words or smiles were exchanged and one sentry opened the door for them. A sultry raven-haired receptionist sat at the far right corner of a large waiting room, deeper than wide, its right wall a casement window of immense proportions, facing the veranda straight away and the courtyard below. A radio blared soupy Spanish music.

She was tall, full–figured and, with a simple change in the curve of her lips, alternately sent sensual or severe messages.

"Good afternoon, gentlemen. You're here for the president, I understand," she said, her words enunciated evenly and in perfect English. After introducing herself as Gloria, Saltanban's special assistant, she lifted a receiver off its cradle.

"Yes, I'm David Brooks and this is my associate, Musco Diller." David extended his hand and Musco bowed.

She ignored both motions and said, "Yes, of course. He's expecting you. One moment, please."

They stepped back from her desk while she brought the phone to her ear, pressed on a key and swiveled around in her chair. David couldn't hear the soft conversation but saw her lips moving in a broad mirror panel behind her.

He leaned over and whispered to Musco, "See that? It's a one-way mirror." It occurred to David that the angle allowed the president to look through the mirror, beyond the solid glass wall of the reception area and directly into the courtyard below.

"One-way? How do you know?" Musco asked, barely moving his lips.

"You can spot them after awhile. There's one back at the Department. Helps in interrogations."

Gloria turned, rose and said, "One more moment, please. Won't you please be seated?" She slipped through the nearest of three doors to her right.

Neither man sat. Musco straightened his tie in the mirror. "Why?," he said.

"Why what?"

"The mirror."

David turned his back to it and answered, "Probably so he can keep his eye on the courtyard and this waiting room at the same time."

As David spoke, he glanced out the window and did a double take. He spotted four men racing through the middle of the courtyard, fists clenched, arms swinging one step ahead of their legs. One of them looked up toward Saltanban's office.

"Je—sus Christ!" David said, straining to keep his voice down. "That's Hendley!" He wheeled around.

"You stay here, Musc," he said, emphatically. "Offer my apologies. Say I forgot something at the hotel. Anything. If I miss them, I'll be right back." He walked casually out the door and past the two sentries. Once on the landing, he bolted down the stairs and by the time he reached the right edge of the courtyard, Musco was leaning over the veranda's railing.

"And if you don't miss them?" he shouted through cupped hands.

David slowed to return a brusque answer. "Who knows? Just stay there. Give my apologies but stay there."

The men were nowhere in sight as he raced in the direction he'd seen them run, trying to ignore the pain in his knee. He heard Musco's voice trail off, "Don't forget, there's four of them."

David found no tunnel beyond the exit he took and, bursting onto a straight cobblestone road, a line from one of his favorite hymns popped into his head: . . . *through many dangers, toils and snares* . . . . But he also had bad vibes—vibes that required explanation, like the ones Kathy would get.

A block away, he stopped to ask a woman if she'd seen men running past her.

She nodded and pointed toward the cathedral which

was visible another two blocks ahead. She raised four fingers and said, "This many chase one big man."

He resumed his pursuit and for the first time since he'd gazed out the window, realized his actions were reflexive, not well thought out, perhaps the culmination of all the pent-up energies associated with the trip, with leaving the investigation at home, with reliance on the advice of others to visit Radonia. But he shook away those misgivings for, despite the head start of the four men, and a knee that was about to cave in, it became evident he'd caught up. In the distance, he saw a collection of horse drawn carriages assembled near the main entrance to the cathedral. Colorfully clad drivers bartered with prospective riders. Domes, spires and a bell tower rose up in stark relief to the commercial trade below. Four men darted from behind a carriage and entered a small side gate to a section that wrapped around the cathedral. David wiped his runny eyes on his sleeve and didn't know how, but he quickened his pace.

He opened the same gate and slid through, coming upon the cool foliage of a courtyard of orange trees. Courtyard City, he thought. He looked around, saw no one and entered the nearest of several king-size gates to the cathedral, imagining his breaths ricocheting off the stone walls of an antechamber.

Inside, he felt at once swallowed up by the sprawl of the gothic structure and disposed to genuflect or otherwise acknowledge its quiet solemnity. Although his eyes roamed over vaulted apses, scores of chapels, sepulchers and sacristies, and a gilded altar modeled after the Seville original, there was no time to dwell on them. Even so, how out of place for the task at hand, how out of character to be doing what he was doing in a godforsaken country he hardly knew existed, chasing through a rough imitation of a world-class cathedral, not at all certain of the identity of the man he was after. Maybe the man wasn't Hendley, after all. Was he a twin?

He did not walk, nor did he run. He hurried and could hear his footsteps in the main nave and in every alcove he entered at its periphery. The odor of must and incense was heavy but not offensive. His leg needed flexing and, for an instant, he leaned against a massive marble column and, running his hands over its surface, was struck by the seamless texture. Among the slow movers he passed, veiled parishioners and hooded holy figures, there was no one who resembled Hendley.

It was difficult trying not to be conspicuous, although he didn't care. And, what if he *did* reach them? Would they understand? He missed his Minx and Magnum and snubby.

David was tempted to retrace his steps and climb the tower but opted to scout around a second time. To the side of the main altar, he noticed a poorly lit alcove he didn't recall searching before. He entered cautiously and saw five confessional boxes strung along the far wall. Their wood was shiny and, even from a distance, he could smell lacquer. The curtains were red velvet and only the middle set was drawn closed. Up closer, the gloss of that box's trim appeared smudged. There was no priest around. David's eyes were drawn to a spot below the curtain. In the dim light, he couldn't be sure of what he thought was there. He inched closer and muffled a gasp. Dangling from the bottom of the curtain was a limp hand with only four fingers!

David wasted no time. He pounced on the edge of the curtain and flung it open. "What the . . .," he said, stiffening.

A big blond man—clearly dead—was wedged into a sitting position. His eyes were partially open and opaque. His face was blue, lips severely down-turned. There was no blood. A length of thin wire was wrapped tightly around his neck. At each end of the wire was a brass handle.

David felt his shirt turn sticky and his mind momentarily blank. Frantic, he focused hard. He was leery of becoming involved, of reporting the death to any authority figure he could locate nearby or, later, even to Saltanban. At home, he'd been sucked into criminal cases of international significance and now, a continent away, this was neither the time nor place to add to the load. Let Radonia handle its own justice.

He stole out from the alcove and limped as nonchalantly as possible through the cathedral, avoiding eye contact. He passed a nun seated alone in the back row of chairs facing a side altar and heard the hum of the rosary.

David left the building the way he came and walked back toward El Cielo, hunched over, weary, confused. The wrong man chased and a dead body found. The Camorra again? His shaky decision to remain silent. Kathy's quip about a wild goose chase. He thought it was a day without reason, an hour of surprise, but a moment for definition.

He walked by a phone booth, then back, and after checking his watch and several crisscrossing calls to South and North American telephone operators, was connected to Henderson Hendley's office in Westport.

Hendley answered!

By design, their conversation was brief, David's reporting he was in Radonia, the columnist reminding him to spend time with Molina's successor there. Before he hung up, David stated he was completing written profiles on everyone he'd interviewed to date.

"Do you have any brothers or sisters?" he asked.

"No, I was an only child," Henderson replied.

Back at El Cielo, David found Musco pacing along the road outside. It was 5:05.

"He had to leave," Musco said, "but we're supposed to meet him at this here club at six. It's five blocks from here." He handed David a card. He studied it while deciding whether or not to tell his partner about the body.

"How did you make out?" Musco asked.

"A wild goose chase."

"You really think it was that Hendley guy?"

"Not now." David didn't mention the phone call. "Was Saltanban angry?"

"No, but he seemed in a rush, too. All antsy, kinda. Did you know he wears pistols at his sides?"

"No."

"Yeah, and blue army fatigues."

David penned a line in his notepad.

*　*　*

After they had checked into the Husa and David had changed into jacket, shirt and tie—brown blazer, white button-down and green striped bow—they walked to the Club Rojo, arriving near the main entrance at 5:55. Musco's clothing was similar, save for the blazer, which was blue, and the tie, a bright red. They smiled at each other when they recognized American flag pins on their lapels.

It was a low flat building of red clapboard and red awnings. A crimson canopy jutted out from the entrance door to a point short of an elevated circle stuffed with red flowers—camellias, tulips, cannas, roses. David couldn't identify the prevailing fragrance.

Without warning, several men in military uniforms materialized from separate locations. One of them gave David and Musco a nod, and they were escorted through a corner door, into a corridor leading to the rear. To his left, David caught a glimpse of a spacious dining room with muted red walls and carpeting, chandeliers and red-clothed side tables of fruit, cheeses, fish and giant shrimp atop mounds of ice. He had to increase his stride to keep up, and Musco skipped once or twice. Spanish chatter rippled through archways into the corridor.

At the far end, two of the military men opened a double door with a flair and, after David and Musco stepped through, closed it behind them.

Juan Carlos Saltanban sat at a table in the center of a small, sparsely appointed room. The table, set for four, was the only one in the room, and the president faced the door. A woman sat opposite him, her back to David as he approached. Saltanban's expression was animated as he finished a rum and coke and set it down against a second emptied glass. He leaped to his feet.

"Well, my friends," he said, "welcome to Radonia. Welcome!" He patted the woman's shoulder, and she rose. "I would like you to meet my Chief of Staff," he announced. She was Gloria from El Cielo. David could sense Musco's eyes roll in his direction. After two handshakes, Saltanban shook Gloria's, too. "Why not?," he said, laughing. David chose not to shake Musco's.

The president was dressed in a dark suit with solid yellow tie. When he spoke, eyeglasses swung from a yellow cord around his neck. Gloria also wore a dark suit with red accessories that included a shoulder bag sparked with white metallic studs.

Saltanban took the lead, first with some amenities like inquiring about the flight, the hotel accommodations and the accuracy of directions, and then said, "David, I hated that you felt obliged to run so hard in my country, and I am sorry I could not wait for you to return."

So, that *was* a one-way mirror at El Cielo.

"I can understand your feeling," David said, "but it was my decision and it didn't get me very far." It was the finest answer he could muster on the spot, and he could have been done with it, but he elaborated. "I thought I recognized someone I know. It's a wonder I didn't create a stir with the guards in the alcove."

"Oh, them!" Saltanban threw his arms in the air.

David was surprised at the reaction and at the president's not pursuing the issue of the chase. Nor did he expect Saltanban to raise the question of the body in the confessional. David had already vowed silence on the matter.

The president pressed a button under the edge of the table and a waiter and wine steward came in. Drinks were ordered. And reordered. They talked about communications, military history, the tragedy of September 11, Gloria's role in the government, the Red Checker Cab Company, David's medical practice.

Saltanban was up to four drinks when he said in a commanding tone, "You did not make the trip to have dinner here, so I will say this. Gloria knows all my secrets and I assume your deputy knows much about you.

Nevertheless, after dinner, while they conclude with dessert or a cognac or whatever, let us retreat to the next room and have a private conversation. Just like at Manny's wake."

David nodded. He had piled up questions for Saltanban and wanted to be alone with him. It was the overarching reason for the trip.

* * *

The back room was not an ordinary room in a restaurant. It was a 30-foot square office with floor-to-ceiling books on the lateral walls and, ahead of them, a bank of windows with light green roll-up blinds made of see-through banana fiber. The carpeting was darker green. All available wall spaces were covered with brown silk fabric and the widest, between the windows, contained six vertically hung clocks that registered different time zones:

Radonia: 6:45	Paris: 11:45
New York: 5:45	Tokyo: 8:45
Sydney: 9:15	Tel-Aviv: 12:45

Short-wave radio hardware and a telephone switchboard were crammed into a small cubicle dug into the right sidewall among the books.

Circumscribing the room were eight cantilevered tables with mahogany tops and a line of ebony inboard of the surface edges. On the tables were telephones, replicas of satellite dishes, computers, monitors, printers, television sets, small plastic mock-ups of: a transistor, a phonograph, a telegraph; early and late model radios and copying machines; and a series of artificial satellites with gold nameplates at each base: Weather Satellite, Communications Satellite, Navigation Satellite, Earth

Observation Satellite, Military Satellite.

They stood at the door. "Quite impressive, Mr. President."

"Do you like it? This is my non-government office. I have everything I need here, but it is more my reading room." He pointed to an oversized club chair dressed in yellow and white striped ticking. "I am fortunate to have the owners of the Club Rojo as loyal friends."

They sat in the center of the room, on soft red leather chairs separated by a coffee table that held two glasses and a pitcher of ice water. David poured a glass and took a sip while Saltanban stuck to the last of the string of rum and cokes he'd consumed throughout the dinner. Once again, the president spoke first.

"I am most happy to have shared some of this special day with you, David, for I learned this morning that my book will be published."

"On cybernetics?"

"Yes, yes. Aside from Radonia, it is my love."

"Congratulations. Who's the publisher?"

"It is one of yours." Saltanban took a folded letter from his pocket and turned back the top just enough to read the letterhead. "Brower and Roberts from New York City."

"Very nice. Very good reputation."

Weighted down with questions he'd have to defer, David attempted to look pleased, his smile stiff. "Tell me more about it." It was a statement he regretted before long.

"I will never forget the other night when I overdid my explanation of communications, and I will not make the same mistake. Well now, I first met Norbert Wiener when he was winding up his teaching career at the

Massachusetts Institute of Technology, and I was just getting started. I was at a scientific symposium and he was on the program. He stimulated my interest in cybernetics. He had published the first book on it ten or fifteen years before."

"He's considered the father of that science, right?"

"That is correct. The science deals with how humans and machines can be similar and how controls can work in both. That is basically what my book is about."

"Would you mind explaining that again?"

"Controls or feedback. I believe that, eventually, we can build a machine to imitate human behavior but, until that time, we should concentrate on controlling that behavior."

"What's the title of the book?"

"If the publisher agrees, it will be, 'Mechanization: The Alternative to Cloning.'"

"It sounds very ambitious." David was stunned by the implications of the title but wasn't convinced Saltanban understood them.

"Not really. My premise is that machines should be able to accomplish more than the simple mechanization of work. After all, it is humans who are designing the machines."

"And?"

"And through feedback or control, the machines can become more human. I have chapters in there on institutional conditioning, on biofeedback in medicine and even on transcendental meditation."

How does one reconcile this dude's scientific preoccupation with the running of a third world country? "There," David said, "now we're talking."

"Now we are talking?"

"Yes, that's what I'm interested in. Transcendental meditation. T.M. In my medical field, there're so many patients,
say, with chronic infection, who also have high blood pressure or asthma or migraines. If we could only teach them
how to deal with their autonomic functions better. I know
there are centers for this sort of thing—stress reduction
techniques and the like—and they usually do a good job.
But not always. Do you think it can be improved on?"

"Yes, of course."

"Could you come speak to our state medical society
one of these days?"

"It would be my pleasure. If I could help someone, I
would be honored." Saltanban quaffed the rest of the rum
and coke.

David couldn't believe he had engaged in such conversation. Two murders at home, a third with the same M.O. as
the last and in a cathedral's confessional box, the specter of
organized crime, the puzzle of genetics, a quasi-emergency
4,000 mile flight—and he was talking about the virtues of
transcendental meditation with a prime suspect who also
happened to be president of one of the countries of the
world! Somehow, he had been diverted by a subtle switch
to medical talk. He shook his head imperceptibly, hoping to
regain focus and, uncertain of Saltanban's tolerance for
liquor, decided to pose questions rapid-fire after first offering a different reason for doing so.

"Mr. President," he began, "you were quite correct
when you said I didn't fly eight hours only to have dinner. So I'd like to get right to the point. If I may, I'd like
to clarify some of the things we talked about in the States
and also raise a few new questions." He took out his

notepad as if there would be no objection and there was-
n't. He entered the publishing company's name: "Brower
and Roberts."

Saltanban said, "I understand perfectly, and please feel
comfortable in doing so, for when one is comfortable, the
best results are obtained."

David hoped such maudlin concern for comfort
wouldn't invalidate the interrogation. The president's
eyes looked clear enough to him.

"Fine. Shall we start? First, where are all your government offices?"

"In the next city, Firma. It is but three miles from
here."

David harked back to Henderson Hendley's insinua-
tion. The seat of a shadow government?

Saltanban added, "And, in the next city, Trobajar—that
is where my telecommunications complex is located.
Where I hope to retire soon, God willing."

"What's your relationship with the company now?"

"I was the founder, and I still own it, of course."

"Forgive me for asking, but isn't there a conflict with
the fact you're the president of this country?"

"No, not at all. My profits have been put in trust.
Would you care for another drink?"

"No thanks."

"Do you mind if I have a cognac?"

"No."

Saltanban snapped his fingers sharply and a waiter
rushed in from a side door with a goblet of cognac on a
tray. David felt his eyebrow elevate.

"On another topic," he said as he wrote. "Will Barlow.
Would you mind if I paid him a visit tomorrow? As

Manny's successor, it seems the logical thing to do, as long as I'm here."

"Of course I wouldn't mind. Remember, David, be comfortable."

"And his office is where?"

"In Firma, at the Science Ministry building. I will have Gloria call him in the morning. Can you be there at eleven?"

"Yes."

"Good. If he is tied up, she will notify you at the Husa." David didn't recall ever mentioning where he and Musco were staying.

"Thank you. Now, back to the subject of your administration, Mr. President. How did you get from the private sector directly to the presidency?"

"Twelve years back—how time flies—I was hired by the military and then, soon, I instituted free elections." Saltanban studied the inside of his goblet for a moment, swished around the cognac, inhaled its fragrance and took a generous sip. He leaned back, expression pleased, apparently satisfied with the taste. Or with his answer.

David had arrived at the point he was aiming for: a head-on confrontation about discrepancies in remarks made over the weekend. He flipped to a fresh page.

"Regarding our mutual candyman friend, Adrian Clemente. He said you called him about Manny's murder, and you told me back in the States that he called you and then, after that, you saw the coverage on CNN." David, unblinking, stared at the president.

"Your point?"

"Who called whom?"

"What does it matter? The call was made."

If their roles had been reversed, David would have answered indignantly. Saltanban was matter-of-fact.

"Your flights to and from Connecticut last week. You said the terminal was in Hartford, yet it turned out to be in Boston."

"There were last minute changes."

"And your arrival and departure times. We checked with your embassy and the airlines—matter of routine—and the times didn't match."

Saltanban said calmly, "For security purposes, whenever I travel, we announce inaccurate times and, sometimes, inaccurate destinations."

"Your aide, Evilina. You said she came from Radonia but my understanding is she lives in the States."

"I forgot she moved near Boston. She came originally from Radonia." David was beginning to get the picture.

"And you said you fly to the U.S. once or twice a year?"

"I said 'year'? No, I should have said 'month'."

David waited for further comment but, since none was forthcoming, moved to an issue he thought might crack Saltanban's armour of self-assurance.

"As part of the investigative team in Connecticut, Mr. President, I was made privy to an e-mail exchange between you and Manny Molina in which you wrote that your government doesn't like your idea, but that you would prevail. Can you tell me what that idea is, or am I going too far?"

"No, you are not." Saltanban went through another cognac ritual. "My idea? My idea is to introduce cybernetics in all our elementary school classrooms because it is an important wave of the future. Our future depends on the minds of our children."

"And your book will no doubt be required reading?" David asked with a wink.

"No doubt." Saltanban's laugh crackled. "But, a simplified version."

David didn't believe the "idea" explanation for a moment. What intrigued him, though, was Saltanban's repetitive knack of sliding from answer to answer, undaunted, without effort, without worry of believability. David invoked a variation of a psychiatric term. *Perseveration?* But he was quick to admonish himself that it was a mechanism used by normal and disturbed people alike.

Thus far, a reading of Saltanban's personality was the key outcome of the South American visit. That and learning of Evilina's Boston residency, a surprise bonus. David surmised the president, given a minute or two—with or without an alcohol overload—could suction anyone to his way of thinking. He dubbed it a "Bermuda Triangle" personality.

Yet, the discrepancies remained and David's call on the current Minister of Health still lay ahead.

* * *

Musco agreed with his assessment when, later at the Husa, David detailed the entire conversation with Saltanban. He also shared everything pertinent to the investigation, from the first threatening phone call, to the conversation with Stonzo, to the discovery of the body in the confessional box. Everything except his hunches.

"For someone who don't want to know nothin'," the deputy said, "I sure know more than somethin'."

"Well, you've been promoted. I'll have to give you a badge one of these days."

Before falling into a deep sleep, David's last thoughts centered on the trip. Was the time consumed worth it? In the overall scheme of the investigation, did Saltanban merit such attention? If his command of Radonia were deteriorating, was that relevant? The answers came down to a single individual and his relationship to the country and its inscrutable president: the first victim, Manny Molina.

CHAPTER 11

✦ ✦ ✦

Wednesday, February 13

The person behind the desk in the half-empty office gave a wan smile. Through Hendley, the columnist, David knew that Will Barlow's days were numbered as Radonia's Health Minister, but he didn't yet know why.

It was 11 the following morning, Wednesday.

"It's always good to see a fellow American," Barlow said. Glancing at Musco, he corrected himself: "Two fellow Americans."

"Well, I'm glad you could fit us in on short notice." David and Musco sat opposite the desk, in the only other two chairs available. David was tired of office settings and was oddly happy to see filled boxes and crates as the principal décor.

"These days, there's no such thing as that. My official duties are just about over down here—I don't even dress the part, anymore. As you can see, I'm leaving the post." Barlow ran his arm across the room, over scores of containers brimming with books, wall pictures and office supplies. "And your visit wasn't a total surprise, anyway. Henderson Hendley phoned me last night. He said you'd be arriving to interview me, and he also filled me in on your background and your current investigation."

"Hendley *called*? He sure does have his nose everywhere."

"That's why he's so good at what he does, I guess."

Barlow was a stooped, twitchy man with a sallow complexion. His rimmed glasses matched the color of the circles closing in on his eyes. He wore a light blue sport jacket and shirt overlying a darker blue ascot.

David withdrew his notepad, explained Musco's role and trustworthiness and stressed that the questioning would primarily involve Saltanban.

Barlow twisted and untwisted a paper clip and said, "It's no secret that in recent months we haven't seen eye-to-eye very often, but I'll be as frank as I can." The clip snapped. "And, just for the record, I'm leaving as much on my own account as on his. You don't know the half of it—I'll be so glad to be back on my own turf."

"He certainly puts it away, doesn't he?"

"The liquor? Only recently. It's gotten way out of control, just like some other things." Barlow went to work on another paper clip and then added, "Which I'm itching to go into." He got up, looked toward the drawn blinds on a bank of windows, seemed to change his mind and sat, leaning forward, hands folded on the desk. "Let me level with you, David. When I heard you were coming, I began thinking of all the things I wanted to say. So if you don't bring them up, I will. But, please, one proviso: can we keep your source confidential? Once I get reestablished back in the states, I won't give a friggin' damn, but until then . . . well, you can understand, can't you?"

"Certainly."

"And your deputy there?"

"Certainly," Musco responded.

David thought the arrangement too good to be true and promptly asked a question for fear Barlow might change his mind. It was based on a headline he'd read in the morning's edition of *Radonia Hoy*. Husa's receptionist had helped him with the translation:

Camorra at Copa Cathedral?

"Did you read about the murder at the cathedral?"

"Yes," Barlow replied without emotion.

"The handiwork of the Camorra?"

"No doubt. Their violence isn't too uncommon in these parts, but it's the first time I ever read of a confessional being used."

"Do they rule the underworld in Radonia?"

"Not yet, I would say. The American Mafia does, but the Spanish version is gaining a foothold."

"Are they rivals?"

"That's putting it mildly."

"For what?"

"You name it: gambling, loan sharking, drugs, prostitution, extortion."

"How about corruption of public officials—and I don't mean you."

"I'm sure they've fought to gain favor, but I don't know how successful they've been. All I can say is the average person on the street believes organized crime is running the country."

David frowned as he made his first notepad entry, a brief one-liner.

"Do you think Juan Carlos is friendly with them?" he asked.

"I think he has ties. And knowing him, it wouldn't surprise me if he's playing one against the other."

"How'd he ever gain power in the first place?"

Barlow ran his thumb back and forth over his other fingers, signifying "money."

"I see."

Barlow obviously wanted to elaborate. "We're talking big bucks here. His company is big-time solid, and he was the pioneer in his field, so he got an early start."

"Does every important official come from wealth? Again, eliminate yourself."

"I'd say yes."

"Then where's the democracy?"

"They rationalize the country away as a democracy because, although all party candidates are rich, elections are held every two years."

"Seems to me that you have to pay to run."

"You got it."

"Pay whom?"

"The government."

"How many ran last time?"

"Six."

"What percent went for Juan Carlos?"

"About 25." Barlow flashed a contemptuous smile. "But there's another element to it," he said.

"Oh?"

"He may have paid some of the others to run—you know, to spread out the vote."

"I take it there are no campaign laws down here."

"What the hell are those?" They nodded in unison, including Musco, without looking up from his writing pad.

"And the seat of government—I take it that it's right here in Firma, not over in Copa where your president stays, right? And if so, why?"

"Uh-huh. Why? Because he's being kept under wraps. Some of the other Ministers are making all the key decisions, especially a guy named Diago Nogales—one hell of an economist. Despises Saltanban and any of his cronies. He knows I'm not one of them, so we've always gotten along very well."

"Radonia's run by a shadow government, then?"

"Exactly. David, Saltanban's behavior is weird. He has enough supporters who ignore it so he stays in power publicly, but privately others run the show. He's a scientist, not a politician, with everything black and white, no grays. Same as a fanatic." Barlow unfolded a sheet of paper.

"Here's what I wanted to bring up—I made a list. Drinks heavily now. I already mentioned that. He's become—well—a petty tyrant with a chip on his shoulder. At meetings, he rants and raves about cybernetics and rambles on about world affairs—when everyone else wants to talk about Radonia's problems, not others'. He takes secret trips, has secret visitors. Some people swear he conducts seances. His latest kick is to push for lowering the age for the presidency from 21 to 18, and if anyone opposes him on it, he goes into a rage. Last month, he had 500 tulips planted in the garden at Cielo, and the next day he had them removed." Barlow smacked the paper with the back of his hand. "There's more, but you get the point. As I said, though, he does have a substantial number of supporters, and they're extremely loyal."

"You mean here?"

"Here and, by all indications, all over the world."

David had made random notations in his pad, unlike Musco who had filled several pages. Aware of the time and of a scheduled 2:45 departure back to the States, David ended the interview with an emphatic snapping shut of the pad. The three agreed to meet again, once Barlow returned to the Washington area.

David thanked him for the information, and Barlow was profuse in his appreciation for their indulgence. "No one around here would ever dare listen to me about this," he said. "I think they're all a bit frightened." His upper lid fluttered.

"Of Saltanban?"

"Probably. If not, the mobs. It's the prevailing mind set: act frightened and keep quiet. That's why I'm out of here in a few days."

*   *   *

At the start of their drive back to the Husa, Musco said, "He played tough but that there's one scared fella. Could be why he let it all hang out. Maybe ain't seen nobody he could trust in years."

"Agreed. How would you like to run a cab service down here?"

"I guess I could play scared and keep my trap shut but, man, they'd have me handing over all my money. No sir, I like it where I am."

The rest of the ride was heavy with silence as David rehashed the events of the past day: the "stupid" chase after a fancied Hendley, the discovery of a dead nine-fingered body guard, dinner and conversations with Saltanban and another of his concubines, the revelations of a terrified, almost pleading functionary. He would reserve any interpretations, however, until later that night when he sat before the computer at Oak Lane.

David phoned Kathy from his hotel room and gave her an outline of the trip with assurances he was whole and a promise to contact her again when he arrived back in Hollings. But he rethought the promise, stated she sounded tired and convinced her not to wait up for a call. Besides, he expected to be tired, too; he would phone in the morning.

*   *   *

Ten minutes before their plane touched down in Hartford at 10:45 p.m., David and Musco rehearsed the plan to be used during their lunch with Anthony Stonzo the next day. Musco insisted it be called their "Operation" rather than "Plan". They settled on "Operative Plan."

David dropped his deputy off at the hospital's auxiliary parking lot and, during a mile stretch on the back roads, glanced repeatedly at familiar lights in the rear-view mirror, lights that veered in another direction before he realized his Beratta Minx and Blackhawk Magnum and ankle snubby were at home. He fast grew edgy, for Kermit had returned and, no doubt, the Asian Yakuza were still around.

CHAPTER 12

✛ ✛ ✛

Thursday, February 14

Davon awoke from a sound sleep at 7:30 a.m.—late for him. Soon after arriving home the night before, he had decompressed with a scotch and a hot shower and checked TV for a weather forecast. The consensus on three channels was, "Thursday—sunny, calm and dry." Groggy-tired, he had restocked Friday and laid out his side-arms on the dresser before dropping into bed at about midnight.

During coffee and toast, his thoughts about the upcoming computer entry jogged his memory of the discipline he'd acquired over the years—sometimes he felt it an obsession: documenting impressions and self-admonitions, originally in his own shorthand on three-by-five cards and, when computers arrived, in more detail on his home pc. The habit stemmed from his early days as an assistant pathologist at Hollings General when he would tackle problem cases of doctors who enlisted his help.

Occasionally, a diagnosis was so difficult to establish that only after painstaking reviews of his personal notes and periodic insertions of new laboratory data, could the problem be solved and proper therapy instituted.

In a roundabout way, the train of thought reminded him of how much he missed his medical practice after only a week's absence—but a week filled with three murders, repeated deception and intercontinental travel. It was detection of a different sort, one that siphoned his time away from the house calls and from the interplay with associates at Hollings General. He longed especially for contact with patients, people he could trust, those with no reason to be devious. There was no chance he'd abandon his new job, but the intensity of the week was something he hadn't bargained on.

David sat before the computer enveloped in a powerful urge to wrap up this latest criminal investigation and get back to medicine. His mind wandered to Kathy and to how much he would level with her about the discoveries in Radonia. And—he had no idea why—to Dr. Sam Corliss, Chairman of the Holling's Center for Behavioral Health, who had offered him valuable criminal profiling assistance before. Perhaps he should be consulted again? He decided to call Kathy after the entry and began typing:

Thursday, February 14

Molina and Crocker Murders, continued:

(A) Ongoing Summary

Echo-man phoned Hole: "Stay away from Brent."

Visit to Brent—Musco with me:

Ogleton furious with Weld. Latter ambivalent

about research initiatives. Strange he's
at Brent. Stated Ogleton opposed to
research, that Brent only a conduit for
grant money. Indicated Molina and Ogleton
argued a lot.
Molina's office: stack of "Radonia Hoy"
newspapers. Appt. book has meeting with
Ogleton day before murder. Molina and
Saltanban e-mails. What's so secret that
Molina wanted coded messages? Vague e-
mail from Agnes Crocker.

Hendley in Westport:

Knew Agnes Crocker. Believes Saltanban
knows something re murders, is losing grip
in Radonia. Advised I visit there, talk to
Molina's successor. Is up on organized
crime & nature of its interest in Brent-
type research.

Kathy:

Saltanban's flight discrepancies. Evilina's
residency.

Call from Anthony Stonzo—Echo-man? Likely
Mafia. Meeting set for this noon in NYC.
Operative Plan also set.

Radonia:

El Cielo. Military highly visible. Found
body of Saltanban's guard in cathedral—
likely Camorra job. Why? Dinner at club
with Saltanban. Published book re cybernetics. Bought the presidency? Answers
glib. Will Barlow: returning to U.S. Says
Saltanban lost marbles. Says shadow govt.

Barlow's safety?

Back home: Saw Kermit again.

(B) Action Review

Meet with Stonzo & implement plan.

Draw out Clemente more.

Locate Evilina & quiz her.

Big question: Organized criminals hired or acted on own?

The good news: Musco now my deputy.

(C) Considerations

Weld safety?

Barlow safety?

Except for one piece of information he'd forgotten about, the call to Kathy was perfunctory—a simple repetition of their last conversation but with his added lament about medical practice, hospital activities, even karate at Bruno's. She cautioned him to keep his cool with Stonzo in the Big Apple and stated she'd arrive at Oak Lane around six after stopping to pick up some fast food. The forgotten piece was that Evilina did indeed have a residence in Massachusetts. On Cape Cod.

In David's next and last call before departing for New York City, he learned that Belle at the Hole had matters under control.

"Dr. Castleman," she said "left the E.R. entirely and can devote all his time to house calls now."

"It's okay with the boss?" Alton Foster, the hospital's administrator, had initially agreed to relinquish the E.R. Director on an intermittent basis, to assist David during any long criminal investigations.

"In spades. He's even suggested you name your partnership, "Hollings General House Call Associates."

"Right about now, that sounds good. Good? It sounds great."

"Where have you been, by the way?" she asked.

"Out of the country."

"Really? For what?"

He checked his watch, indicated he was running late and would explain at a better time.

To him, Belle sounded like Kathy when she said, "David, do please be careful."

"That's part of my nature."

"Yeah, right."

David hung up after receiving answers to questions he thought he should ask. No, no new threatening phone calls and, yes, her daughter, Georgia, was fine.

He raised the shade in the den and stared incredulously at a swirling, steady snowfall which nullified all forecasters' predictions. Through the bedroom window, he checked the railing atop the park tower and, from the height of accumulated snow there, estimated it had begun to fall even as the prognosticators were speaking nine hours before. He wouldn't risk a traffic snarl on the Merritt; instead he would drive to the New Haven Railroad Station where he and Musco would board the Metro-North to Grand Central Station, then take a cab to the restaurant.

It was late morning in a near-empty passenger car. David assumed most of the commuters had taken an earlier run. Against personal sartorial dogma, he wore a tan trench coat. Musco was dressed in a high garnet turtleneck and gray heavy sweater. David guessed turtlenecks were making a comeback. The air smelled stale or, at best, electrical, and the ticktack of wheel on crosstie would have lulled him to sleep were it not for the abrupt changes of light streaming through windows or the anticipated swoosh of oncoming trains. He paid only cursory attention to his "inside man" who was expounding on the merits of never giving a straight answer during any form of bargaining.

Finally, David said, "It doesn't make any difference, Musc. We know what we have to do."

"Yeah, but it's still good to know how to handle your tongue, specially when the guys you're talking to are lookin' to cut it off." Musco did a double take at David's stoic stare.

*   *   *

They arrived by cab at the Sorrento Restaurant ten minutes early and, the snow dwindling, decided to walk twice around the block. Each man was silent as if the Operative Plan had already gone into effect. Snow-packed sidewalks were slippery and horns polluted the air. At twelve-thirty, they walked beneath a green canopy and entered the front door. David hung up his coat. Musco dusted some snow off his sweater. For the occasion, David had dug out his finest dark suit, together with hexagonally shaped cuff links and a matching tiepin. He held Friday in his left hand.

An attendant led them into a small side room, its walls plastered with murals of the Amalfi Coast, Sorrento and Mount Vesuvius. A balcony hovered above two sides; on one side, clouds of cigar smoke billowed from a partially opened door.

The room's only occupants were two men in pinstripes who sat opposite each other at a square table, two empty chairs between them. The one without dark glasses munched on a crust of bread. A saucer of green oil was at his elbow. He wiped his hands on a checkered napkin and stood.

"You must be Dr. Brooks," he said, his voice firm and resonant. "I can tell from your height. You're right on time. You and your friend came alone I see. You must not be too experienced in negotiations like this, but that's all right, we won't be too hard on you." He spread his hand over his chest and announced, "I'm Tony Stonzo and this is my associate, Rick Massialano. We call him Shades."

"How do you do, Mr. Stonzo. Yes, I'm David Brooks and this is Mr. Diller. We call him Musco."

"Musco?"

"That's right, Musco," Musco said.

"Don't look like a musco to me, whatever that is." Stonzo flashed a collection of crowned pearly teeth and adjusted a red handkerchief in his breast pocket. It coordinated with the tie he wore over a black shirt.

David, armed with Beretta Minx at his shoulder, snubby in his ankle rig and Blackhawk Magnum tucked away in Friday, had been troubled over the possibility of being frisked by a band of hoods and was relieved when it hadn't occurred, thus far. He'd been thinking about it, even during the train ride into the city, and concluded he would have resisted if such an attempt had been made, demanding to do the same in return. He still speculated over the consequences.

As Musco and Stonzo glared at one another, he checked out Shades who had never stood up. Chewing gum as if he would never have another chance, his massive frame overhung the chair and seemed bolted down to it. His face looked like the surface of the moon. David noted a bulge under the left lapel of his jacket.

"Please, sit," Stonzo directed. "It's cramped in here but cozy."

He was not a short man but a double-breasted suit gave that impression. Bushy black hair, sideburns and a small goatee outlined features too pronounced for his face. David guessed he was on either side of fifty.

"Now, for purposes of this discussion," Stonzo said, "first, let's all shake hands."

In the process, David noticed Stonzo's shiny fingernails. Musco tried to out-squeeze Shades but was unsuccessful.

"Second, here's my number if you need to reach me." Stonzo straightened his second and third fingers toward David. Wedged between them was a card which David took. It was the size of a business card but was blank except for a phone number written in pencil. He put it in his pocket.

"So far, so good. Now, third, please call me Tony and may I call you David and . . . uh . . . Musco?"

"Yes," David said. Musco didn't answer, too busy pulling out a notepad from beneath his sweater. Shades followed the move closely.

"Tony—it's 'Tony,' right?" Musco asked. He assumed a demeanor he might have used in a courtroom scene.

"Right."

"Okay for me—as the inner man, you know—okay for me to make some notes?"

"Be my guest," Stonzo replied, his eyes narrowing.

"Thanks a lot." Musco wet the end of a pencil with his tongue and said, "Now, how do you spell your last name?"

"That's S-t-o-n-z-o."

Musco wrote it down, his tongue following along.

"And 'Tony' is 'Anthony,' right?"

"Right."

"And, Anthony, could I have your address?"

"My address? Just put down Chicago."

"And what's the name of your service company?"

"It has no name."

Musco looked up. "No name?"

"Oh, call it 'Stonzo enterprises.' Can we get on with the meeting?"

Musco erased and wrote and erased and wrote. He looked up again, first at Stonzo, then at the other two, and said, "Sorry. I was right in the first place. I think 'Enterprise' is with an 's', not a 'z'."

"David, all right with you if we start?" Stonzo asked. His shoulder twitched.

"Yeah, sure. You got the notes straight now, Musc?" The cabbie nodded.

"Now then, David," Stonzo said, "I'm going to be as frank with you as I can." He leaned forward across the table. David smelled toothpaste. "You are publicly using harsh language about a segment of society which I happen to admire."

David folded his hands and placed them on the table. Musco followed suit.

"And you are making comments that are stirring up things we do not like stirred up."

"Like?"

"Oh, c'mon, David, let's not act stupid. Look, our schedule does not permit me to be less than open, as open as I can be. So let me say the following to you, plain and simple." He leaned closer and his voice became a whisper. "We could easily have you neutralized if I gave the word. I'm sure you understand that."

"Killed?" Musco exclaimed.

"My dear Mr. Musco . . ."

"Diller," Musco said.

"Diller . . . Musco. For your edification, one 'kills' when one has no good reason to, but one 'neutralizes' when one has every good reason to kill. Is that too confusing?" He kept his head dead-stiff but shifted his eyes from one to the other. "To either of you?"

"No," David answered. "What you're saying is that you could have, or you might still have me neutralized."

"That is correct."

"Just like you had Manny Molina and Agnes Crocker neutralized?" David held his breath.

"If it emphasizes to you that I mean business, yes. But only the scientist, not the broad. We heard about her. The Spaniards did that, not us. We're not in the business of neutralizing the female gender."

"Is what you did, though, because of your own motive or someone else's?"

Stonzo's reply was swift. "Now, now. Would I go around asking doctors about the personal affairs of their patients?"

David's interpretation was even swifter: Stonzo just screwed up. He as much as admitted it was a contract killing.

"I see your point," David said, masking a sense of relief. "On the phone, you said we'd talk about your friend, Juan Carlos Saltanban."

Stonzo glowered. "We're not friends anymore."

"Oh? Care to elaborate?"

"He's a lightweight, a bum, *un malandrino*." Stonzo tugged at his collar as if it were choking him. "You went to see him?"

"Yes. He seems to have a handle on things there."

"Really? Are you sure you went to the right country?"

David decided to go with a hunch. He fixed on a spot between Stonzo's eyes and said, "I hear all gangs like yours are fighting over turfs in other countries."

Stonzo's smile didn't finish forming until he'd completed the next phrase. "For your information, Dr. Brooks, we're not a gang. We have legitimate business interests, and they're strictly domestic."

"No interests in Radonia?"

"That little desert in South America? We wouldn't be caught dead there. It has no class."

"Okay, it has no class. But getting back to your interests, how can you say you neutralized someone and then claim your business is legitimate?"

"Simple. If someone is crazy enough to interfere with our legitimate interests, then bam! Get it?"

"I see that point, too. I don't agree with it, but I see it. So what are you asking?"

"I'm telling and I'm asking. Two things. I'm telling you to stop bellyaching—keep your trap shut about our enterprises. And I'm asking—maybe that should be telling, too—I'm telling you to withdraw from the case. Go back where you belong. I hear you have a nice practice, that you're a good doctor."

Stonzo didn't wait for a response but slid his hand under his jacket. David reached down as if to scratch his ankle. Stonzo withdrew a leather cigar case, paused, then inserted it back.

"I forgot about lunch," he said. "Well, do we wrap up a deal before we eat and maybe have a toast?" He picked up a menu.

"I don't know, Tony," David said, running his hand over the back of his head. "What's your connection with the Camorra?"

"Connection? Ha! I'll tell you what our connection is. We control them. We control them because they're small potatoes, and they're scared of us. They're all *citrullos*. Jerks. You want more particulars?"

David bluffed surprise in his face. "No, that'll do." He reconsidered. "How about the Yakuza?"

"You mean the Asians? They're not much smarter. We control them, too."

"Do you mean they'd agree to do whatever you requested?"

"Not 'requested', 'ordered.'"

"Like stalking to intimidate?"

"If that became necessary." The capo and Shades rolled their eyes and exchanged glances.

David chose not to pursue that line of questioning but believed he may have learned who was behind the Kermit headlights.

Stonzo continued as if the Camorra and Yakuza issues hadn't been raised. "Now, some of the underbosses and lieutenants thought of doing away with you entirely, but I talked them out of it. I'll be out front with you, my friend—and don't let this go to your head, either—you're too well liked and well-known now—and violence like that might have backfired and decreased the demand for our services. But if you become a smart aleck; if you decide to lean against the wind instead of with it . . ." He shook his head slowly from side to side. " . . . then that's a different ballgame. Know what I mean?"

David straightened his spine. "Thanks for your intervention," he said. "Tell you what, Mr. Stonzo—Tony—I'll think on it. Give me a week."

Stonzo's expression turned flint hard. "What?" he shouted, flinging the menu across the room. He pulled back as if to get a better bead, looked *through* David's eyes and, without benefit of a breath, said, "*Va fa'n culo!* You have 48 hours, Brooks. Saturday at noon. Chicago. Palmer House. No phone calls. Be there. Good day." He waved off a waiter who had arrived to take their orders and said sternly, "No lunch today, Carm."

Six men in black mohair emerged from the door on the landing and descended an open staircase at one end. They walked in single file and flicked cigar ashes, three preceding Stonzo and Shades out the door, three following close behind.

At the start of the train ride back to Connecticut, Musco tore up his notes into little pieces and threw them on the floor. David skimmed through a magazine he'd taken out of Friday. Grins stretched across their faces. Soon after, they reviewed what had transpired. The bulk of the return trip was taken up with a rehearsal of the next steps of the Operative Plan, every detail, every nuance, every contingency. David stressed the many gaps, the timespans for possible errors, the unexpected hurdles, lumping them all as emergencies that would have to be dealt with as they popped up. Creatively. On the spot.

He drove Musco to the usual location near the hospital. "I'll call you when I check things out," David said, leaning through the open window.

Musco approached his cab, turned, waved his hand and, smiling, changed it to a tight fist.

* * *

David ripped off his trench coat, threw it on the bed and carefully removed his jacket. He unclipped a tape recording device from the side of his waistband and peeled off strips of electrical tape from a wire leading to his hexagonal tiepin. He rewound the recorder, played it back and phoned Musco.

"Home run, Musc, home run!"

"I knew it was. You go wired . . . you don't get caught . . . it works. That's what they tell me. How did I sound?"

"Great. Good voice. You should be in radio or television. But I have to ask: how in hell did you keep your composure asking El Honcho those questions? It was eight to two in there, you know, and they didn't exactly have nail clippers in their pockets."

"Simple. There's an old saying: 'Do what you have to do when it's do or die.'"

"Like on the spot?"

"On the spot."

"Where'd you get it?"

"Made it up."

"See, you should be in radio and television."

They settled on a time to meet in the morning. David hung up and remained seated, fondling the tape and reflecting on whether it decreased or increased the risk of his survival.

CHAPTER 13

✛ ✛ ✛

David sat before his computer, reviewing the encounter at Sorrento's and waiting for Kathy to arrive.

Since Stonzo referred to underbosses and lieutenants, he must be the top boss himself. If so, how could he have made such a blunder by admitting complicity? And then demanding he pull out of the investigation? David reassessed: Stonzo could still be an underboss, a capo, for there must be other underbosses around.

He could have had a response of sorts for Stonzo right after reviewing the tape. He thought facetiously of having said to him at the restaurant, "Wait, give me some time alone in the next room. I'm wired and I want to see if our conversation recorded clearly. I'll be back in half an hour to suggest where we go from here."

He knew euphoria whenever he saw it, and he now felt it, for his "catch" in the city put him one up in a clash with the Mafia. More than that—maybe ten up. Based on Stonzo's recorded admission of guilt, he could arrange for an immediate arrest warrant. But, confident the killings were contracted hits, he concluded that such a step might be premature. A given was that the warrant could be issued any time. Another given was that a Stonzo arrest might send his client into hiding. Moreover, David didn't know whether or not a captured Stonzo would cooperate. What were the limits of Omerta? Did the code of silence pertain only to mafiosa members or did it also extend to clients?

An additional question was why mafiosi would be so open with law enforcement in the first place. His best answer was that they wouldn't show their face to "real" cops, but they would to an amateur detective, especially if they thought they had instilled fear in him.

David wasn't yet sure how he could use the new evidence, but he reasoned it might at least prevent further killings; thus he would keep the Chicago date. But what would be Stonzo's reaction when he learns of the tape? Who will be with him at the time? Some lieutenants and foot soldiers who might react impulsively to the news?

Despite the remaining hazards, he felt confident. Perhaps overconfident. The pieces were falling into place, but he was tackling an entity he viewed as diffuse. Stonzo was only one capo in a syndicate, and any offense committed against one would be an offense committed against the organization, against the "Black Hand." David once read there was a time when they wrapped the remains of those who opposed them in tarpaper. How many in Chicago will have stained black hands?

He got up and paced. He had thought himself into a muddle. Visions of gangsters, grotesque facial scars, rolling cigar smoke, gangland slayings. Thoughts of

Belle's admonition, "Do please be careful" and of his own declaration that emergencies would have to be dealt with on the spot. Then the image of Musco beside his cab, fist clenched, smiling. It was all there, locked in his consciousness, like a clump of tangled string. He had a firm grip on the string's beginning, but its end was nowhere in sight. David's leg tightened.

He hated such times: rhapsodizing one moment, blunted the next; over-analyzing; overloading. He had to experience a sense of order, of control. Or distraction. He booted up the computer and clicked to his last entry. Opposite "Meet with Stonzo and implement plan" he typed, "Done." Kathy would arrive soon. That would help even more.

The front door opened and slammed shut. Kathy rushed in and blurted, "Thank God you're here. I should have had you call me. What happened?" She removed her coat and tossed it on a chair together with a bag of McDonald's food.

David left nothing out, from the walk on the streets of New York, to Musco's bravura performance, to Stanzo's outburst, to the review of the recording. Even his collection of thoughts.

She pulled him to his feet and, in an embrace, whispered, "Thank God you're here."

"You already said that."

"I know. I hope I can say it again after Chicago. You're going, I take it."

"It's essential."

She withdrew a small heart-shaped box of chocolates from her purse and handed it to him.

"Happy Valentine's Day," she said.

"That's right, I forgot," he said apologetically. "Happy Valentine's Day. I do have a present I've been saving for you. It's at home, though. Let's celebrate another time."

He went into the kitchen to get Kathy's bottle of Chardonnay from the refrigerator and a bottle of red wine from the cabinet. Balancing them in one hand and two glasses in the other, he returned to the living room and sat on the sofa next to Kathy. He poured the drinks and offered a toast: "May it all work out." After their first sip, he again touched Kathy's glass with his. "I love you, Kath," he said.

She molded herself into his arms and said, "I love you, too, darling. I only wish I could help you more."

"You're busy enough so you do what you have to do . . ." He felt her nodding against his chest. ". . . when it's do or die."

She broke away and said, "Come again?"

"Oh, nothing. I was just reminded of another Muscoism." He took a second sip, peering at her over the glass. "You look bushed," he said.

"I am. I'm now doing Narcotics, too, and they say Nick wants me to oversee precinct squads, eventually." Her lip curled in disgust. "We're so short-handed, it's criminal."

Kathy, in a turquoise suit, got up and removed its wrinkled jacket. "I'm a mess, too—I came straight from work." She exchanged the jacket for the bag of food, and they ate cheeseburgers and fries and sipped wine while she chronicled the goings-on at the Police Department and he elaborated on Radonia and New York. During a lull, he pointed to the chair.

"The French fries odor might have transferred to your coat," he said.

Kathy rose, hung up the coat in the hall closet and returned next to David.

"Well, did it?" he asked.

"You don't miss a trick, do you?" she replied. She kissed the tip of his nose lightly and added, "Yes, it did."

"Talking about tricks, do you want to hear the tape?"

"Of course."

They listened to it in the den, Kathy wide-eyed, David, head bowed, deep in thought.

"That's incriminating stuff," she said. "I can make a phone call and we can arrest him now, because . . ."

"Not yet, Kath. Trust me. There's more than Stonzo involved, so timing is critical."

"Like Saltanban?"

"Maybe."

"Do you know what I can't figure out about him?"

"What?"

"If things are so out of sync down there, why did he invite you?"

"The guy's out of it. He's losing his power, and he's still strutting around. Doesn't have a clue. But he's got money and apparently plenty of it."

"You mentioned him in the same breath with organized crime more than once."

"Yeah, there's something there, but I'm not sure what, yet."

"And his girl friend, Evilina. Should we bring her in?"

"No. Timing, again. But see if you can talk to her on the phone. Ask if I can meet with her sometime in the next few days. We'll let her know when. I have a sneaking suspicion she'll welcome the opportunity."

David assumed a tutorial pose. "Here's the problem as

I see it." He spread out five fingers and counting on them, said, "If we have, say, x number of suspects—Saltanban, Clemente, Ogleton, Hendley, even Weld or Evilina or Barlow—then you have to be careful in *how* and *when* you question them, because some might be in cahoots and warn others. Then throw in the Mafia and the Camorra and the Kermit crowd and we have one helluva dilemma." He switched his hands to a clasped position behind his head, as if he were satisfied with his assessment. "It boils down to two parallel tracks, Kath. The enforcer or enforcers on one, the client or clients on the other. The only problem is, where do they connect?"

The phone rang. It was Belle.

"David!" she sobbed. "They've taken Georgia away! They left a note. I didn't see it at first, and I could hardly hold it and it said . . ."

"Wait, wait, Belle. Let's back up. Take it easy. Georgia's not there?"

"No. She normally comes home from school around 3:30. I don't know if she did or not, but she's not here and they left a note on the porch. It was in the corner." Belle sounded as if she blew her nose.

"Have you got the note now?"

"Yes."

"What does it say?"

"Tell—your—boss—to—play—ball—or –else," she said, enunciating each word in a tremulous voice. "David, I wanted to call sooner but I didn't see the note and I thought she was just being late or something. Should I . . ."

David put his mouth closer to the phone and said, "Belle, listen to me. Lock your doors, pull your shades and keep your phone line open. We'll be right over. Kathy's with me."

As they stormed out of the house, he spoke in ragged bursts. "As soon as she said it . . . I knew who was behind it . . . it's *got* to be Stonzo . . . it's got to be . . . that son-of-a-bitch!"

*   *   *

Belle's home, a mile from David's, was a red saltbox, its roof short-pitched in the front and sharply pitched in the back. It was set back from the street, at the end of a long torturous driveway lined with shrubs. A light rain began to fall, its fine drops and lingering snowflakes cast about in a howling wind that had kept its intensity since the morning.

At the door, Belle tearfully accepted David's and Kathy's embraces. She ushered them into her living room, which was furnished with two soft sofas and companion chairs, their slipcovers a tea-dyed print; a weathered pine cupboard with white lace pieces that draped over its shelves; square side tables with books stacked and blankets folded and layered; and an abundance of apparent heirloom treasures—china pitchers and teapots, stained boxes, oil paintings. Everything neat, clean and tasteful. David had never been there before but, knowing Belle's strong imprint on the E.R. and the Hole, it was about what he'd expected.

They sat on the soft pieces, facing each other. A cat brushed back and forth against David's ankle, uttering high-pitched plaintive sounds. Belle's upper cheeks were red, and she twisted a handkerchief as she spoke.

"What next?," she said. "I mean, what do we do?"

David replied, "There's a protocol we follow, and Kathy's already initiated it."

"The Crime Unit should be here any minute," Kathy said.

"Let's see if we can keep this under wraps, Kath, or the press will have a field day tomorrow," David added.

Eying a straight back chair next to the cupboard, he got up and dragged it in front of Belle and sat on its forward edge. He took her hands in his and said softly, "First, let me say, Belle, how sorry we are that your daughter had to be drawn into this. And, second, I'm quite sure I know who's behind it, and I have a meeting with him tomorrow. In Chicago. This is difficult for you to listen to, but you've faced crises before in the E.R.—not your own but ones you've had to make decisions about and live through. Think about them for a minute. We talk to people about preventing hearts from stopping and brains from swelling and lungs from collapsing and so on. All things frightening for parents and relatives to hear, right?"

Belle nodded.

"So, you have to keep your wits about you and have a game plan whether it's simple or complicated, right?"

Belle nodded again and rubbed the corner of her eye with a knuckle.

"Well, the 'or else' in that note refers to possible bad things, but I don't think any of them will ever happen."

David gave her the gist of the New York meeting—including Stonzo's statement that they don't harm females, mentioned the tape in his possession, stressed its value as leverage and, finally, explained that Georgia was the Mafia's leverage.

"When he learns about the tape tomorrow, besides blowing a gasket, he'll release Georgia. I promise."

"Should I stay here tomorrow or go to work?"

"Go to work. It'll be hard, but try to keep your mind busy. They know how to reach you if they have something to say, but I don't think they do. We have to sweat it out until Saturday."

On the way home, he said to Kathy, "I gave her the best case scenario." He turned up the speed of the windshield wipers.

* * *

Aside from the secret recording in New York City, David's Operative Plan was no more than a list of what he had scheduled in the investigation. He considered it a flexible document, easily adaptable to changing circumstances. There was one in place during the last string of murders, one he believed helped solve the case, although he was the first to admit it was a "plan plan" not a "schedule plan." This time around, the difference notwithstanding, and with a bow to superstition, he deduced that if it worked once, it would work again.

In their haste to be with Belle, he and Kathy had driven in his car when they should have taken two, for she didn't expect to spend the night at David's. They motored back to Oak Lane together and, from there, she left for her condo complex.

Shortly afterward, he downloaded the plan on the computer. He wanted his total schedule before him in order to assess the effect of a single event or a single interview on all its components. In addition, he had to incorporate the recent developments pertaining to Stonzo. It read:

OPERATIVE PLAN

Tuesday and Wednesday—Radonia.
   Saltanban. DONE
   Barlow. DONE

Thursday—To NYC with Stonzo. Wired. DONE
Friday—See Ogleton.

Molina house to check e-mail.

See Dr. Corliss.

Sunday—See Evilina. Cape Cod.
Monday—Reenter Clemente house.

Locked door (with Musco) .

Interview Clemente again.

Check on Saltanban's book.

Possible reinterviews—Weld, Hendley.
Reminder—Peak at right time. Congregate the suspects?

He added:

Find Georgia—Time is now more of an enemy!

Make duplicates of tape.

Chicago with Stonzo Saturday noon. Lv here Fri.
night.

David headed toward the kitchen for a nightcap. When he heard the phone ring, he had a strange feeling.

"Sorry to bother you so late. How are you feeling?" Echo-man oozed sarcasm.

"Stonzo, you bastard! What have you done with her?"

"The bubble gummer is safe, the last I heard, but my associates don't have the patience I have."

"If they as much as mess her hair, I'll come after you, pal," David said, his eyes raking the room.

"Now, now, let's not get carried away. Listen carefully. Your attitude today did not please me. I want you off the case and I want to read about it in the newspapers. You're famous now—they'll splash it on their front pages. Be smart, give them a story. Dr. Brooks Returns to Practice Full-time. Get the idea? You do that and I'd be much obliged. And your assistant will get her daughter back. Think about it between now and Saturday."

David was tempted to tell him about the tape but, in the way Stonzo put it, he appeared to indicate no harm would come to Georgia prior to the Chicago meeting. David also understood that with Georgia held captive, hauling Stonzo in was no longer an option. Even so, he wanted to keep the conversation going and said, "We could come get you, you know."

"You couldn't find me in a million years. The number I gave you? A cell phone. I move around a lot, and I change the number every month, anyway. Plus you try to make a move like that and the girl is history—gone."

David realized it implied a position of weakness but he asked anyway, "How do I know you haven't already . . . already . . ."

"Had her neutralized? You don't. You've heard of insurance, Dr. Brooks. She's my policy. Or maybe you understand 'ransom' better. No money here. Just honor my terms and you get her back. Simple, see?" David didn't comment.

"And if you don't, that's simple, too. But that would pain me. I'll let you in on a little secret—maybe I mentioned it before. I have no trouble neutralizing or even killing men—big tough ones, like you—but when it comes to women, you know, like my mother or sister, well, that hurts me. Hurts me badly. And with little girls, it would be worse. Fortunately, though, my associates don't feel the way I do."

"Why you . . ."

"And one last thing: if we cap the deal, and then we send her back, but then you flip—you know, fink on us or something—we have ways to deal with that, too. The syndicates wouldn't be happy. That's what the other side—your side—calls them. I like to call them interested parties. Either way, they're very loyal. *Very*. You have less than 48 hours, Dr. Brooks. Think hard. They say she's a nice little girl."

David heard a dial tone.

CHAPTER 14

✛ ✛ ✛

Friday, February 15

After another fitful sleep, David phoned the Hole shortly after eight a.m. Belle answered, her voice hurried.

"I've been here since seven," she said. "Any word?"

"No, I doubt anyone will call."

"I tossed and turned all night."

"I know what that's like. You'll catch up later."

"The police came after you left. Cordoned off the property. They must have been there for two hours. Took samples, took pictures, took the note. Sparky did most of the work. Nothing yet, I suppose."

"No. The department issued the usual bulletins. I'll check with the lab later, but I'd be surprised if they have anything positive. And Belle . . ."

"Yes?"

"Please understand, I have to proceed as though this didn't happen, so I won't be coming in. I'll be all over the place today but call me on the cell phone if you need to."

There was a silence at the other end. And then Belle said feebly, "I'll be okay. We'll just wait it out. Good luck today."

The words sounded vacant, but David forced himself to end the conversation.

"I'll check with you later on," he said.

He picked up Musco at the hospital and, on the way to the Hollings Police Department, filled him in on the call from Stonzo and on Georgia's kidnapping.

"Phew, we're lucky we have the tape," Musco said.

"But they don't know that yet."

"Why not call Stonzo and tell him?"

"Because it'll work better in person. He implied we have till tomorrow. The real question is, do his geek friends feel the same way?"

Minutes later, Musco's umbrella drawn, they stumbled against drizzle and wind along the cement walkway to the Department building, its bold new entrance harsh against walls of blanched brick and pitted mortar. The night's stiff steady rain had washed away most of the snow as if it had been an embarrassment while, off to the sides, dirty white map-like designs remained spread out on the ground.

Inside, three uniformed police officers maintained telephone switchboards behind the heavy glass partitioning of a dispatch window. Each of them waved, and David and Musco were buzzed through a heavy metal door. Raincoats in hand, they proceeded into a maze of newly decorated rooms with shiny modular furniture and partitions in textured teak and white, past benches of microscopes, chemical bottles, latent fingerprint equipment and the brothy smell of petri dishes. David gave Sparky's office door a tap, and they walked in.

The criminalist sat at a table inspecting a piece of paper which David recognized as the note left on Belle's porch. Sparky wore plastic gloves. Various wire baskets, magnifying glasses and stacks of documents appeared arranged for a neatness contest. A lamp dangled on a cord from the ceiling above the table. The lamp's green shade matched Sparky's visor.

"Morning, my friend," David said. "Anything startling?"

"Oh, hi, David . . . Musco. Wet out there, eh? Here, let's have those coats." He began to slide his chair back.

"No, we just thought we'd drop by. We're headed over to Kathy's."

Sparky rotated the paper, checked it front and back and tossed it aside. "No, nothing startling. The usual kind of staged writing," he said. "And no prints. None anywhere except Belle's and maybe the young girl's. Nothing to go on, I'm afraid."

"I didn't expect much, if anything," David said. "Two questions though. There was still snow on the ground last night. Could you make out any footprints?"

"Nothing distinct. They were all mushed together."

"Tire tracks?"

"No patterns at all."

On leaving, David wondered why he was being meticulous about possible clues at Belle's, for he was certain that Stonzo and his cronies were responsible.

Toward the other end of the building, Kathy's office was a ground-level rectangle with banging steam radiators and creaky floors, part of the original wing not included in the Department's renovation program. The walls were colorless and empty save for a calendar and a paper cup dispenser for the water cooler. It had a row of basement-style hinged windows beneath which a ledge was stacked with manuals, books, papers and cardboard boxes of all sizes. Fluorescent lighting fixtures were suspended from a high ceiling. One flickered. There was no door, only an opening the size of two doors.

Designated Kathy's chamber, it was far removed from rooms packed with sophisticated detection, communication and data base equipment, from the Firearm Storage Room and the Evidence Storage Room, from the Interrogation Room and the holding cells. Kathy's large barren space held but a file cabinet, swivel chair, makeshift serving table on casters, coffee maker, a couple of wooden chairs and a heavy metal desk that looked like an Army-Navy Store retread. Its surface contained little more than a stack of papers and a king-size telephone assembly.

Two rooms away, she shared a computer, printer, copier and fax machine with personnel in adjoining offices.

But while her chamber was reputed to be dull and antiquated, its corridor was the busiest in the building; most officers, detectives and technicians chose it over the two others that linked the new wing to the old.

Kathy stood at the serving table fixing coffee when David and Musco entered. She turned and David kissed her on the forehead. She shook Musco's hand.

"Do me a favor, Kath. Can you call Jack Ogleton? He usually gets in early. Ask if I can come over."

"When?"

"Now."

"Now make the call, or now come over?"

"Both."

Kathy handed them filled cups as if they had ordered them. "You used to make your own calls," she said. "You've graduated?"

"I didn't have the heart to ask Belle."

David's answer wasn't germane to the question, but Kathy looked wounded, anyway. "I'm sorry, David, I couldn't resist. Did you call her this morning?"

"Yes."

"And?"

"She's banking on tomorrow."

"You're all set? Musco, you'll be there?"

They both nodded.

Kathy carried her cup to the desk. She flipped through a telephone log and called Howerton University, working her way up through layers of answering menus until she reached the president's office and received an affirmative answer to David's request.

"Perfect," David said. "Now while I'm doing that, one more favor?"

Kathy pressed her lips together in a smile.

David removed the tape from Friday. "Could you have some copies made of this? How many, do you think?"

"Well, you'll have this original, so one for Musco, one for me and . . . maybe Belle?"

"One for Stonzo, of course, and how about my safe deposit box?"

"Absolutely—and give the key to your lawyer. What's his name?" she asked, snapping her fingers.

"Harold Flommer."

"Yes, Harold. We don't have to tell him the contents, just to have the box opened in the event of your . . . my God, I hate talking this way!" Kathy glanced at Musco, then at David, and her eyes revealed she would have sprung directly into his arms if they were alone. Musco faked a cough.

David responded, "Think of it as part of the Plan. So what do we have, five copies? Yeah, have five copies made ASAP. *Please*?"

"David, cut the . . . I mean the dig. I was just having fun with you before. I'll help out wherever you believe . . ."

"Great. Then get in touch with Evilina and set up a meeting for Sunday around noon. Cape Cod, right? I'll go there. I have a sneaking suspicion she'd be too scared to show her face around here."

"What makes you say that?"

"Intuition, that's all."

David saw Nick Medicore streaking by and almost called out to him, but the Detective Chief, once clear of the doorway, angled his body back on one foot.

"It is you," he said. "Any progress?"

"We're getting there," David answered.

"Is Sparky giving you your forensics?"

"Yes."

"Good." Nick didn't shift his weight, supporting it with his hands against the doorjamb. "Sorry, I'd stay to chew the fat, but I've got things to do," he added, and hurried off.

David looked at Kathy and shook his head. "He thinks we're chewing the fat?"

"David, that's just his way of expression. Don't be so sensitive. And stop reading into things."

"I don't mind expressions. It's the implications and innuendos that bug the hell out of me. And he's got a million of them."

"What would you rather have: a chief who sugarcoats

everything he says to you but holds a tight rein, or one who irritates you but let's you do your thing—completely? Don't forget, he's kept you in charge. And, believe me, darling, he knows he's lucky you're around."

"You want an answer?"

"I forgot the question but—yes."

"A chief who let's me do my thing and who doesn't bug me." David improvised a grin.

Kathy stared at him briefly and said, "Let's change the subject, because no matter where this is heading, I guarantee that you'll end up . . ."

"Where?"

"Where what?"

"Let's change the subject."

"I already said that!"

David lifted her up and smothered her lips with his, even as she'd begun a new sentence.

✳   ✳   ✳

The next town over, Howerton, boasted little except a university of the same name. The school was considered academically and socially progressive, but its reputation had been built on the size of its endowment with a growth history that placed it among the top five nationally. Expansion and diversification were thus affordable, the three-year-old Brent Institute of Biotechnology among its most recent additions. Jack Oggleton, MBA, Ph.D., the university's president for ten years, was given most of the credit.

By nine a.m., David and Musco were in his office. More accurately, it was a collection of offices that radiated off a central rotunda. Corinthian marble columns provided support for a domed ceiling. The green marble carried over to the floors and was again featured as keystones and springers in each of the arches to the surrounding five offices. Five women sat stiffly at five desk and computer stations at the periphery of the open rotunda. David was struck by their similarities: gray bobbed hair, dark-rimmed glasses and plain clothes. He speculated that Ogleton's wife interviewed and hired them.

All rooms were visible from the rotunda. In each, a lighted cigarette was perched on a freestanding ashtray. Four rooms were unoccupied. Ogleton called out from the fifth.

"C'mon in, David," he said. He sat at a desk, sleeves rolled up, cigarette in hand.

The room was a disappointment and reeked of smoke. The contemporary lines of its furniture and built-ins clashed with the classic design just 20 feet away. Scattered around were maple-slatted benches, contoured foam chairs with spindly steel legs, floor lamps with paraboloid-shaped aluminum diffusers.

"Jack, I don't believe you've met my associate, yet. This is Musco Diller."

Ogleton cleared his throat and said, "How do you do?" He pointed a finger at Musco. "Red Checker Cab, right?"

"Right on," Musco said, stretching his smile.

"I've heard of you. You own it, correct?"

With a critical squint, Musco replied, "Any chance you fixin' to hit me up for a donation?"

All three chuckled and Musco slapped his thigh. They shook hands.

Ogleton took a long drag on the cigarette and blew the smoke out the corner of his mouth, the same direction as the origin of his words. "Now why in hell would I do

that?" He pulled over an ashtray and snuffed out the cigarette in quick little twists, inspected it up close and
repeated the procedure. He cleared his throat again and
said, "Sit down, fellas. What's on your mind, David?"

Musco, instead, answered with a question: "Are all
those five out there your *own* secretaries?"

"Who, them?" Ogleton cupped his hand around his
mouth and said softly, "Christ Almighty, together they
equal, say, one, one-and-a-half. Yes, they're mine."

Notepads drawn, David and Musco sat before the desk
in armchairs tailored in khaki heathered upholstery and
supported on curved legs of aluminum.

David began: "Jack, I have no more than two minutes
worth of questions. I know you're busy." He waited for a
response and was taken aback when none was forthcoming. Why not a courteous dismissal of such a small time
constraint? David followed with, "I've been making the
rounds."

"I know. I hear you're working hard at it. If one of my
faculty members gets his fuckin' brains shot out, I would
expect to be questioned. It stands to reason."

"What did you think of him?"

"He was a damned good scientist but a misdirected
one. And he stunk with budgets. I can't say he was trust-
worthy, either."

"Oh?"

"The son-of-bitch had a habit of coming on to my
wife." Ogleton breathed out audibly. "But that's neither
here nor there now. On the professional level, we had our
little spats but always resolved them friendly-like."

"I see. Many of his personal effects have been seized by
the police and I've had a chance to look at them. His

appointment book states you had a meeting with him the day before he was murdered. Is that right?"

"We never had that meeting. I canceled it."

"Can you say why?"

"Sorry, I cannot."

David glanced at his pad as if he were consulting a series of prepared questions when, in fact, he was comparing the sharpness of Ogleton's answer with the sharpness of his question. He continued: "It's well known you oppose stem-cell research. Then why have a Brent?"

"Because it's the wave of the future. I hate medieval literature but we still have to offer it here."

David took down his first note. Musco had been writing at double his usual pace.

"And Agnes Crocker?"

"What about her?"

"Was she a friend of yours?"

"I can't say one way or the other. She opposed the research too and wanted Brent shut down. I didn't . . . don't . . . obviously."

Musco's eyes checked with David. Then, in a manner that spoke for them both, David said, "obviously?"

"Or else why would I have pushed to have it designed and built in the first place?"

David recalled Professor Kater Weld's opinion that Ogleton was funneling some of Brent's science grant monies into other university projects.

"That makes sense," David said. "Do you know Juan Carlos Saltanban?"

"For sure. He's a great man. And one of our greatest benefactors."

"You mean for Brent or the university as a whole?"

"He designates every nickel to Brent."

"A lot of nickels, I'd guess."

"A real lot."

"Are there any strings attached to the money he gives, or would that be confidential information?"

"It would be if there were strings, but there haven't been any. Thus far anyway." Ogleton cleared his throat. "And I think 'strings' might be the wrong word here. Very few people say to us, 'Look, either do this or that, or you don't get the money.' I think what you meant to ask is, 'Do they want their donation used for a specified purpose that the university's already established, such as curriculum or capital improvements?' The answer is that most people don't restrict the use—they don't tie our hands."

David decided to play dumb. "Isn't that unusual?"

"Why?"

"Wouldn't a good many donors specify how they want their money spent? You know, like for stem cell research or certain genetic studies?"

"On the contrary, as I said, most give to the unrestricted fund. Some people call it the general fund."

"Do you mean for Howerton or Brent?"

"I mean for both. If someone gives to Howerton, most of it's unrestricted for Howerton; if someone gives specifically to Brent, most of it's unrestricted for Brent."

David looked at his watch, mentioned again how busy Ogleton must be and joined Musco in thanking him for his time.

At the archway, David, in a Columbo-style turnaround, said, "By the way, Jack, did you ever have reason to believe that Molina was linked to the Mafia in any way?"

"Only in that they did him in. That's what the papers implied, anyway. From their description of the killing, it seems obvious it was a mob hit. I wouldn't expect that he was friends with them, though. If he was, look at what it got him."

*   *   *

David gunned the Mercedes over Hollings' back roads toward the deceased Manny Molina's house. He thought some of the answers given by the university president were too quick. And too long. He remembered him as one who spoke in sentence fragments, but that seemed to have changed within the past week.

"So, what did you think of him?"

"I like the guy," Musco answered.

"That's because he knew about your company," David deadpanned. "Do you think he's hiding something?"

"Doesn't everybody? But you're right, probably him more than everybody."

David peered at him through the corner of his eye.

He punched in Kathy's number on his cell phone. "Well we met with Ogleton and . . ."

"How did it go?"

David was startled at having his own words stepped on. Where did she pick up that habit?

"He was pretty tight-lipped, but it went about as expected. Molina was apparently interested in his wife."

"Did she reciprocate?"

"He didn't say, and I couldn't tell. He said he canceled a meeting with Manny the day before the murder but wouldn't say why. Maybe he intended to confront him with it and changed his mind. Anyway, we're on our way to Molina's, and I have a whole bunch of details to clear up between now and Chicago."

"When you say it that way, it means only one thing. What do you want me to do?"

David segued into the list on his mind. "First and fore-most—I can't believe we goofed on this—we never arranged for the flight to Chicago. See if you can book one for us for today. Second, make sure the tapes are ready before we fly out. Call Flommer and level with him about the safe deposit box and key. Then get in touch with Dr. Corliss at the hospital. Psychiatry, remember? He helped out with profiling last time around. Don't you agree he might help again?"

"He can't hurt."

"So, find out if I can meet with him sometime this morning. Call me either way." He paused before adding, "And Kath?"

"Yes?"

"All of that with a great big *please*."

"There you go again. Consider them done. And I think you need a good night's sleep."

* * *

David could have obtained a key to Manny Molina's house at the Police Department but, with Musco along, there was no problem gaining entrance. They walked into the study, directly to the computer which David booted up. As was the case in Molina's office at Brent, no password was needed to gain access to the files and to old e-mail messages. Only one from the in-coming mailbox stood out. It was from Professor Kater Weld and was received the night before Molina's murder. It read:

If Washington demands accounting, I believe we have to go with it, yes. On the superbug issue, I think the genetic maps are nearly complete for the ones we discussed. But Lord help us if the info gets into the wrong hands. Imagine the possibilities. Imagine the enormity of the bioterrorism!

Molina's reply, sent the same night, was:

Thanks for your note. Right now, I'm caught in the middle—boxed in. Not sure what to do. Will elaborate in person.

Musco, who had read the messages over David's shoulder, said, "Superbugs? What the hell are they?"

"Germs made stronger," David answered

He knew he had to speak with the professor, preferably in person, not so much about Molina's stated dilemma, for Weld had already informed him about that, but about the superbug and bioterrorism references.

Instead of waiting for Kathy to call, he phoned her and learned that an 11:30 appointment had been made with Dr. Corliss, and that she booked a flight out of Hartford to Chicago for 4:30 with a return departure the next day, Saturday, at 4:05 p.m. David checked his watch. Plenty of time. He called Brent. Weld told him to come ahead.

They were about to leave the study when David noticed something peculiar about the wall behind Molina's desk, something he didn't recall seeing when he was there shortly after discovering the body. In a grouping of four pictures, the upper right one was missing. A well-demarcated space remained, lighter in color than the wall around it and with an empty hook at its center. He examined the other three closely: a shot of Juan Carlos Saltanban at his desk in Radonia, one of the exterior of El Cielo and one of the president with a woman about the same age, presumably his wife. What David *did* recall was taking many photos of the murder site. Had he failed to pay attention? Later, he would check the series to be sure.

* * *

They sat on the same cherry benches as before. David's knee throbbed, and he tried to straighten the leg but, feeling a twinge in his lower back, returned it against the other leg.

"Kater, thanks for seeing us again. Here's why we're here: can you give us a rundown on superbugs?"

Like a lightbulb switched off, Weld's smile vanished. He rose and buttoned his long white laboratory coat from top to bottom as he once again paced in a narrow path before them. Musco inspected the path, presumably checking for worn spots.

"Let me begin by saying that genetic engineers, who have spent many years fighting diseases, now face—since September 11—a terrible paradox . . ." It was as if Weld had bottled up a lecture and the cork had just been removed. ". . . because some of their impressive break-throughs can also be used for sinister purposes. Genetic maps of many pathogens are publicly available—on the Internet, for example—and certain techniques, notably the splicing of drug-resistant genes into microbes normally defeated by vaccines or antibiotics, may help terrorists develop biological weapons laced with genetically altered superbugs.

"But there's nothing new about biological warfare. Back in B.C. times, Greek armies contaminated their enemy's wells with the bodies of dead animals. A few centuries later, other armies did the same thing with the rotting corpses of dead soldiers. Things got more sophisticated during the Renaissance when attacking armies used catapults to launch diseased bodies into walled fortifications."

Weld sat and crossed his legs hard, the equivalent of David's slamming his notepad shut. "That's it in a nutshell," he said, his expression a strange cross between satisfaction in the delivery and depression in the message. "But, shall I go on?"

"Yes, please do," David said. Neither he nor Musco was taking notes. Each had folded his arms over his chest.

"Take mousepox, for instance," Weld continued.

"Mousepox?" Musco queried.

"Yes, a cousin of smallpox. Last year some researchers with the most altruistic of intentions accidentally engineered a super potent strain of it. Take the Malta fever pathogen. Just three months ago, scientists in Pennsylvania published its genetic blueprint. Or E. coli. One of its strains was made 32,000 times more resistant than the conventional variety. Thirty-two-thousand times! I'll tell you, fellas, it's scary. And I haven't even gotten into the possible creation of brand new diseases."

"So what do we do?" David asked.

"Fortunately the feds have reallocated some funding to several biotechnology companies. This, by the way, ties in with using grant monies more prudently—you know, the theory I put you through the last time you were here? Anyway, they're studying such things as designing multi-disease vaccines on the premise that a common ground among pathogens can be found in RNA, the middle substance between DNA and proteins. It's interesting. One group is working on a nasal spray that might boost the immune system to fend off numerous agents right after an attack."

David had the impression that Weld could continue for hours. "I'm sure you're aware, Kater, that all of Manny's possessions have been confiscated, including his computer."

Weld nodded. "Routine, right?"

"Right. Well, in that same e-mail you mentioned Monday, you referred to Washington's demanding accounting. What did that mean?"

"We at Brent Institute were about to plunge more aggressively into embryonic stem-cell work and even into cloning, but then came the President's decision: federal funding would be limited to already existing stem-cell lines. We don't have those here. They do give us funds for other kinds of basic research. The accounting thing means we wouldn't even get *that* money if we continued to dabble in the other business I just mentioned."

"Your words, 'more aggressively.' I think I know the answer but I want to be sure. Does that imply you *had* been doing embryonic stem-cell research?"

"Yes."

"And cloning?"

"Yes."

"And all of it came to a crashing halt?"

"If we continued, that would be breaking the law, plus, as I've stated, all other funding could be cut off."

"What if you received private funding?"

"We'd still be breaking the law."

"Could anyone here conduct any of this . . . let's call it forbidden work . . . on the q.t.?"

Weld straightened his bow tie. "I suppose it's possible but, sooner or later, it would come out. No, I believe that would be highly unlikely, and I can't imagine anyone here trying such a stunt."

"How about someone who *was* here?"

"Who, Manny?"

Weld's face grew pensive. "I can't see it," he said.

David got up stiffly and flexed his leg a time or two while the others rose. He felt for his notepad, realized it was in Friday and removed it. He scribbled in a couple lines, at the same time addressing Weld: "You've been most helpful, Kater, and I thank you."

"Any time, David. It's always good to see you. And you, also, Musco."

In the car, Musco asked, "Do you think the guy's leveling with us?"

"Probably, but I'm not 100 percent sure. It could be he's leveling all right, but only with what he selects."

"That mean he's holding back?"

"You got it."

In the course of David's interrogations, he never minded receiving lectures; he preferred them to snappy predictable replies. And more elaborate body language was a bonus. He was certain he'd receive another lecture from Dr. Corliss.

On the way to the hospital parking lot, David said, "I can handle this alone."

"Beautiful. Shrinks and I don't mix," Musco quipped.

Had he let on that there was some experience there? In his wino days?

"The flight is at 4:30," David said. "Security's tight so I'd better pick you up at 12:30. And, don't forget, no sidearms on the plane."

"Oh Christ, that's right. Stonzo and his boppers will have their heaters; we'll have nothin'."

∗   ∗   ∗

Dr Samuel Corliss' office was in Rosen Hall, the smallest building in Hollings General's psychiatric unit—The Center for Behavioral Health—located in an annex to the main hospital complex. Most visitors, including medical staff, entered through its central door. David chose again his shortcut through the basement, past the pharmacy with its amalgam of chemical odors and through the laundry room, not too far from the Hole and the elevator shaft where Dr. Tanarkle, the pathologist, was found dead but weeks before. He didn't have time to visit again with Belle.

He knifed his way around corners, leading with Friday, ducking at imaginary ceilings and crossing the lowest ramp to Rosen Hall before taking the elevator to the third floor. The paging system didn't include the basement or the psychiatric unit itself so he avoided the operators'curt pages which he always considered a distraction whenever his mind was on other things. And the usual inhabitants in the corridors upstairs who would only detain him with questions about the crimes: doctors writing while they flitted by, nurses in pairs, technicians with their lab trays of vacutubes and tourniquets.

It wasn't that David was anti-social, only that his mind was on other things: the upcoming visit with Corliss, the caper with Stonzo in Chicago, and also the irony of sticking to scheduled meetings lately. It was all a matter of better time management. Since the hospital murders, he had subjugated a long-held belief that calling ahead ruined the setting. He connected it to Nature. Unannounced keeps everything as it should be. No pretense. No makeup. Nothing staged. All raw and true and natural.

As he neared the door to the psychiatrist's office, another thought was that the Chairman of the department should have been accorded larger rooms, all two of them. Inside, an empty waiting room contained three soft channel-back chairs placed equidistant around a triangular table with neatly piled magazines. Posters of Paris highlights dominated the walls, and a vase of freshly cut purple flowers rested on a corner table. It was common hospital knowledge that Dr. Corliss had brought flowers to his office every morning since his arrival at Hollings General decades before. And that he stuck a sample in his lapel as that day's boutonniere.

David knocked on the inner door.

"Come in, David," Corliss said.

David looked around. No mirrors. He opened the door and walked in.

"Hi, Sam. How did you know it was me?"

"Why, didn't you know you have a distinctive knock?"

David inspected his knuckles.

"Sit, David, sit. I haven't run into you since you hauled in the killer last month. How can I help you?"

The room was a shade larger than the outer one and just as basic: brown leather couch, two matching recliners, a maple desk and a high-back chair. Ivory sidewalls were sprinkled with diplomas, certificates and family photographs. Paintings of Sigmund Freud and Karl Menninger hung on the wall behind the desk, framing Dr. Corliss where he sat.

The psychiatrist looked the part, with a white beard that seemed trimmer since their last meeting; pince-nez; frumpy gray suit and purple flower; clump of white hair at the temples. A star key medallion, another Corliss trademark, dangled from his neck. David conjectured it was used as a metronome in therapeutic hypnosis, and he was determined to cry foul if he ever saw it begin swinging in his presence.

David settled into the recliner before the desk but kept it upright, feet on the floor, knees higher than his hips. For some reason, he would have felt uncomfortable taking notes in a personal meeting with a psychiatrist. He gave a thumbnail sketch of his trip to Radonia and a brief description of Saltanban, Barlow, Ogleton, Molina, Crocker, Hendley, Clemente and Weld. Dr. Corliss stated he knew or heard of all of them except Saltanban.

"From the last time," Corliss said, "you know my feelings about this, but, since you're a colleague and confidant, I can share with you that none of them has ever been a patient of mine." His stare pinned David to the near wall. "Let us proceed, shall we?"

David remembered the last time well—the "ethical canon" speech— when Corliss spoke of a breach of medical virtue and his own conscience if he were to reveal whether or not a person was a patient of his. He had explained with passion how the mere identification of such a patient branded him with a psychiatric label. And how a natural extension of that would be even to reveal that someone had *never* consulted him professionally. His harangues could take up the greater part of a morning, and his more formal lectures to house officers and to audiences at Howerton were delivered extemporaneously and without effort, as if he'd memorized every word, practiced every inflection. The hospital staff dubbed him "Demosthenes with a Flower."

David leaned forward. "Sam, what I'm after is a quick

summary on personality types."

"What types? Paranoid? Passive-aggressive? Cyclothymic? Narcissistic? Obsessive-compulsive? Antisocial?"

"Forget cyclothymic and obsessive-compulsive."

Dr. Corliss wrote down the remainder on a sheet of paper. "Okay, then, let me put it this way. I'll tell you what: stop me when you've heard enough about each type. Just say 'enough.' It won't upset me."

Here it comes, David thought.

"Those with paranoid personalities tend to react with suspicion to changes in situations and to find hostile motives behind other people's trivial and innocent acts. When they believe they've confirmed their suspicions, they might act in ways that surprise or scare people. They then use the resulting anger or rejection by others—we call that 'projective identification'—to justify their original feelings."

"What about how they might act in the workplace?"

"These persons may be highly efficient and conscientious although they usually need to work in relative isolation."

"What if they have some kind of cause, some kind of crusade?"

"They often do, and sometimes we can't tell what came first—the cause or the paranoia."

"Enough. And passive-aggressive?"

"I go along with the term but only for classification purposes. I prefer 'passive-assertive,' and only because many of them are so passive at times that they can't quite complete the slide into aggression. But they do reach the assertive stage. These folks use their passivity to control or punish others, and some of their idiosyncrasies serve to deny or conceal hostility."

"Enough."

The psychiatrist consulted his paper. "Next, narcissistic. Persons with this disorder are grandiose—that is, they have an exaggerated sense of superiority. They have a need to be admired and are extremely sensitive to criticism or defeat. In point of fact, when confronted with a failure to fulfill their high opinion of themselves, they can become enraged and . . ."

"Enraged to the point of killing?"

"Oh, yes. That turns on many things: on the kind of failure, on the level of their grandiosity and, of course, on their degree of rage."

"Enough."

"This is all helpful?"

"It's just what the doctor ordered."

David grinned. Corliss didn't as he looked again at his paper.

"Last—Antisocial. We used to call this 'psychopathic' or 'sociopathic.' These people callously disregard the rights and feeling of others, and they exploit them for personal gratification or materialistic gain. They're often chronically dishonest and deceitful and tolerate frustration poorly. Sometimes they act out conflicts in impulsive and irresponsible ways, often with hostility and serious violence."

"Like murder?"

"Right again. And again, it depends on the degrees of their personality traits."

David wished he had taken out his notepad. "What's the difference between a psychopath—what you're now calling 'antisocial'—and a narcissist?"

"Pychopaths, as I said, exploit for personal gratification and narcissists exploit because they think their superiority justifies it."

"Can someone have . . . well, to put it simply . . . a little of each?"

"Yes, indeed. Various combinations are probably more common than, say, a pure paranoid or a pure narcissist. But David, there are other considerations that are relevant here. For example, when we come to examine various adaptive techniques that help individuals protect their personality structure, such as from tension or from unacceptable impulses that must be restrained, we find them of such standardized types that we call them defense mechanisms. These anxiety-reducing devices are normal in normal people and enable them to meet the needs of their personality without resorting to the extreme measures that psychotics use. If the defenses aren't successful, though, they may appear as psychiatric symptoms or as attempts at adjustment that disturb personal relations. As anxiety increases, the defenses against it tend to become less efficient and less rational. Sometimes anxiety may participate in what we call a vicious reaction-circle. Aggressiveness, for example, may generate anxiety, while anxiety, in turn, generates aggressiveness."

David shifted his weight on the recliner and Dr. Corliss noticed.

The psychiatrist said, "Well I've given you some generic psychological autopsies. You're applying them to your suspects, no doubt?"

"No doubt."

"Then, let me conclude by saying that destructive personality disorders—like the narcissistic or the psychopath—are the primary foundation of criminal behavior. These types have an uncanny skill for hiding their disorder. They often sense it, and they work on it. If they do, indeed, become criminals, then, in their minds, all the world's a stage—one on which criminal activity allows them to play the role of master and satisfies their consuming need for power. 'Power' is one of the key words, and I should have mentioned it more often.

"Specific to your cases—and understand, David, I only know what I read in the papers or see on television—don't forget the role of jealousy or revenge in tipping the balance in any of these types. I hope I've been helpful."

They got up at the same time. David shook the psychiatrist's hand, careful to relax his elbow which relaxed his grip some. "You certainly have, Sam, as always. Now I'll see what I can do with it all. How can I thank you?"

"You can thank me by making an occasional house call for me."

"No, don't do that to me! I don't make psychiatric visits" David responded, winking.

"Why not?"

David hadn't anticipated the question and came up with, "Because I think I'm sometimes nuttier than they are."

Dr. Corliss retorted, "But surely you must have visited a patient with a stomach ache when, in fact, you had one, too."

David reveled in such innocent sparring. "So, with all due respect, you're saying that if you treat a psychotic, then you yourself might . . ."

"Hold it there! I surrender."

David left the office believing that any of the categories could apply to all the half dozen people on his suspect list, and perhaps to some who, as yet, were not. He shook his head, as frustrated as a three-ball juggler with six balls in the air.

*   *   *

David and Musco landed at O'Hare Airport in the early evening and took a cab to the Sheraton Hotel. Before their departure from Bradley, David had stopped by the Police Department and secured a copy of the tape, leaving the original and four other copies with Kathy.

Chicago was clear and blustery, its carbon sky gloomy, portentous. It was their first time there. The streets were like those of any huge American city except, to David, the honking was less than in New York, for example, and there appeared to be a disproportionate number of restaurants: all heights and sizes, independents and chains, fronted and recessed, gaudy with lights or elegant with courtyards. He'd heard that the food in Chi-town wasn't all meat and potatoes, either, its culinary diversity among the lofty handful. He thought he caught the smell of fried fish wafting through his cracked down window.

And the music! Faint strains filled the frenzied scene of Rush and Division Streets, into the posh French-Moroccan setting with its mellow world beat and on past a martini bar and a string of nightspots pumping out live blues, all working their way up to a louder, even more frenzied weekend.

The cab crossed Milwaukee Avenue. Musco read the street sign and whispered, "Now I don't know. We're in Illinois, right?"

"Right," David said, girding for a laugh.

"Milwaukee's in Wisconsin, right?"

"Right."

"And we're on Lake Michigan, right?"

"Right."

"Well, why ain't there at least a Lake Illinois? If I lived here, I'd raise holy hell."

David laughed and gave a thumb's up sign. The cabby looked at Musco in the rearview mirror and said, "Not bad, pal."

Over dinner, Musco dwelled on how O'Hare got to be the busiest airport in the world ("their lockers rent cheaper"), why the Sears Tower was the tallest building ("they miscalculated") and why a host of governmental and social agencies there were unnecessary. He named them individually, but David knew Musco had taken liberties with the ones he'd heard of in Connecticut ("Now let's take the Department of Revenue Services of Chicago . . .") David also knew that Musco was trying his best to keep things loose.

CHAPTER 15

✝ ✝ ✝

Saturday, February 16

David was awakened by Musco's phone call. It was an hour after daybreak. He heard the weather channel in the background. He checked the clock on the bedside table and was barely able to manage a response. "It's too early. We've got a big day ahead of us. Go back to sleep."

"No, it's time to get up anyway. Goddamn storm headin' this way, you know. Late this afternoon. That's when we fly again."

David yawned. "I hope we make the flight."

"What!" Musco exclaimed. "We're as ready as we'll ever be, long as they don't pull out a chatterbox or a pineapple or somethin'. So, knock it off."

David, now fully awake, said, "What I meant was, I hope the flight doesn't get canceled."

It was the first time he could remember such an edge to Musco's voice but chalked it up to an adrenalin rush, one shared the moment David opened his eyes.

"David, my boy, I thought you were gettin' soft there, for a minute."

"Not me. And for your information, Musc, Chicago machine guns went out in the thirties, and if we stay close enough to our hosts, they won't detonate a bomb." He'd found Musco's street talk amusing.

"Where did you learn that kind of language anyway?"

"I picked it up. Why?"

"Curious, that's all."

With time to kill after breakfast, they took a bus tour of the city. David looked out at the lakefront, Grant Park, the Loop, the Art Institute, Soldiers' Field, the Field Museum and the Sue Dinosaur Exhibit. He looked, but he saw none of it. If ever there was a time for the three-by-five card, it was upon him. He took it out of his wallet.

Do not force issues.

Know when to roll versus when to take stock

Do not outpace circumstances. Let things settle out.

The time to roll was an hour away.

At noon they arrived by taxi at the Palmer House and strode into the lobby. David wore his scarf, no gloves. Musco, in his raincoat, carried a satchel containing a copy of the tape for Stonzo, a notepad, several pencils and a pencil sharpener. They were greeted by a man who came out of nowhere and looked like one of the cigar smokers in New York. "Follow me," he said in a loud raspy voice. He held a toothpick in his mouth.

They wound through corridor after corridor, deep into the bowels of the venerable hotel, past the usual house-maids and snack areas and ice machines and water cool-ers, until they reached a set of double doors. The man knocked four times, and the doors opened. Before them, an enormous room looked like the painting of an early morning fog around a duck pond. David counted nine people in his quick glimpse around. All smoked cigars, including Anthony Stonzo. None of them had removed his overcoat.

The greeter took a seat in the first of two rows of five others behind Stonzo. He sat at a glass-top table. Two empty chairs were on the opposing side. The men in back resembled those in black mohair at the Sorrento Restaurant. Shades Massiliano sat to the right of Stonzo. To the left was a new man in a chesterfield, his head turned as he conversed with the row behind. Musco sat down first and placed his satchel on the table. David paused a moment to allow for handshakes or greetings or nods, at least. None of it happened. As he began to sit, he braced for a throb or a twitch or for his knee to ache. None of it happened. And he was surprised. But once in his chair, after tucking in his left arm to check for the Beretta Minx—and meeting no resistance—he felt his knee act up.

The new man faced front.

"Oh, my God!" David shouted. It was Henderson Hendley, the Westport columnist. "You? You're *with* them?" Hendley lowered his head without responding. Stonzo ran his tongue over his teeth.

David flashed back to his two encounters with Hendley, then flash-forwarded through the substance of their talks. He rubbed his decision scar more rapidly than usual. *Do not force issues. Know when to take stock. Let things settle out.*

"I'll do the talking, Brooks," Stonzo said, sternly. "There are more people than him who are with us. You probably know a few."

"What's in the bag, Fusco?" Shades asked.

"That's 'Musco'."

"I open it, not you."

"What if it blows up in your face?" Musco asked, his head moving with emphasis.

Shades stroked his pockmarks. "You open it, I watch. But move those hands slow. V-e-e-r-y slow."

Musco didn't move.

David glanced at Hendley who appeared to be taking notes. David was certain it was an act.

Stonzo slammed his fist on the table. "This here meeting is now in session," he said. The resonance of his voice was diminishing. "Now let's start from the beginning, Brooks. My name is Anthony Stonzo and I'm telling you to bug off, *sta zitto*, stop badmouthing my people, mind your own fuckin' business. Dig? What's your fuckin' answer?" The veins in his neck popped like varicosities.

"Would you open the satchel—excuse me, the bag— Mr. Diller?" David said, calmly.

Musco went for the satchel in slow motion, his eyes rotating toward Shades whose eyes, in turn, were riveted on Musco's hands. Shades' own hand and those of all the men behind slid in unison into their overcoats.

David announced that he had been wired during their last meeting whereupon a hum rose from the men in back. David nodded to Musco who handed him the tape. He pretended to study it, and Shades made a stab for it as if he were clawing through the bars of a cage.

"Uh-uh," David said, whisking back the tape. "This is for your capo, Buster, not you." He handed the tape to Stonzo, snapping his wrist with a flourish.

Stonzo turned it over and back, then over and back

again. He inspected both ends. "What's this supposed to be?" he asked. David knew the capo was stalling for time while he figured out what to say. Or do.

"It's a tape of our delightful conversation in New York. You may keep it. My fiancée detective, my secretary, my lawyer and a few others also have copies." David felt his face tingle as he glared at Hendley. "I was even thinking of sending one to that little twerp next to you. And don't get reckless, Stonzo. You want to go on a rampage? You'd have to neutralize them all at once—you know, swoop down?"

Stonzo swept his eyes over everybody in the room.

"What do I want?" David continued. "I want that little girl back. And I want to know who hired you to kill Manny Molina."

"Or else you go to the cops?"

"Maybe. Maybe not. You'll have to take that risk."

"Your girlfriend *is* a cop."

"We think alike."

Stonzo screwed up his mouth. "Are you a gambler, Brooks? You've got the tape; we've got the girl. Should we see who blinks first?"

"Forget the blinking. I'm telling you, pal, if any harm comes to the girl or to Mr. Diller here or to me, you and your tidy little empire will be kaput—sayonara—finito."

Stonzo's breath welled up as he stiffened in his chair and, with a once hollow voice turned to gravel, he said, "Why you . . . you . . . punk! You think you can get away with this? You're an amateur! A fuckin' hick amateur! *Ti rompo le ginocchia, le gambe.* You hear? I'll break your knees, your legs."

Trembling, he leaped up and buttoned his coat. He

swung around to David's side of the table, planted both hands on it and, his face inches away from David's, whispered loudly, "You'll be hearing from us, amateur, one way or another." He stormed out of the room through a side door, the others in pursuit. David wiped a fine spray of spit from his forehead.

He and Musco exchanged wry smiles and David, content to sit for a moment, watched as Musco opened the double doors.

"Where are you going?" David asked.

"I need some water. I think I saw some right down the hall."

David remained seated and flopped his arms onto his thighs, caught up in the relief of the moment and the verge of a beginning-to-end review of what had transpired. Instead, his mind wandered to the codes of the mafiosa, like "Omerta" and its mandate that, "If you talk, you die" and the sworn and deadly promise that any offense committed against a single member is considered one against the organization. To the evolution of organized criminals and why some remained low-ranking picciottos and others rose to become sgarristas or capodecinas or even a capo crimini. David had learned the chain of command well, and he'd often questioned how a gang of mobsters, one as narcissistic, amoral and impulsive as the next, could adhere to what they had sworn to in blood, to keep silent and to protect their own, even if it meant death.

And then, strangely, he shifted to the instinctive codes of the animal kingdom, ones shared by most classes, most species. Providing shelter for their young. Protecting them and sometimes their mates from danger. He envisioned them in self-protective modes: color changes, mimicry, flight, freezing, playing possum. He thought of more than lions and tigers and bears, conjuring up wolves, bison, fox, apes. And rats. He wondered whether rats protected their own.

David straightened up from his chair just as he saw Musco returning through the double doors. And at the same time he saw the barrel of a Colt .357 Magnum poke out from the side door. The door swung open and Shades appeared, his Brobdingnagian body awkward in a spread eagle stance as he leveled the gun toward David's head.

"David! No!" Musco yelled, hurling himself between David and the gun.

A percussive shot echoed through the room.

Musco somersaulted onto his haunches and tipped over.

David, who had ducked, heard the bullet snap into the wall behind him and smelled gun powder.

Shades turned and fled.

Unsure whether Shades had backup, David dropped to the floor and scrambled on hands and knees over to Musco. He rolled him over, looking for blood and detected none. David's breathing felt unimpeded but was fast and deep, and he blurted, "You okay?"

"Yeah, twisted my ankle but that's no big deal, considerin'. You?"

"I'm fine—now stay down for a second."

David stared at the open door feeling vulnerable for the two of them. But no one came into sight, not even hotel personnel who he'd expected to burst in. A frequent Chicago occurrence?

Grimacing, he raised himself, holding his knee out straight, then lifted Musco, propping him on his feet and scrutinizing him with the rapid finesse of a physician. Musco flashed a toothy, triumphant smile.

"If we had our hardware, we coulda gone after the bastards," he said. "You sure you're all right."

"Yes."

"No broken bones?"

"No."

"No holes?"

"No."

David had an urge to hug his sidekick, and he did, silently, without verbal thanks. He backed away and said, "You know you could have gotten yourself killed?"

"Yeah, I guess. But like I said, what's a deputy for? No, wait. You can always buy me a medal."

"Musc . . ."

"What?"

" . . . Never mind."

They both brushed off their clothes.

"What should we do now?" Musco asked.

David flicked lint from his jacket. "Go on with the investigation."

"But what about all this that just happened?"

"About the hotel or the shooting?"

"Screw the hotel—where the hell were their people?"

"We don't forget about it. Attempted murder. One more thing."

They hobbled out of the hotel, their faces reflecting no pain, no cares, no desire for retribution but, although David couldn't vouch for Musco, his churning stomach registered a different picture.

While hailing a taxi at curbside, he said, "Do me a favor, Musc?"

"I just did."

"Let's not give Kathy the details for awhile."

"Cool."

*   *   *

Chicago escaped the storm by the time they flew out, but back in Connecticut, another snowfall legitimized the claim that, through Friday anyway, its mild winter weather had been a fluke.

Their plane landed without incident. They retrieved the Mercedes from a park-and-fly facility and David sloshed along Interstates 91 and 84, Musco asleep, snowbanks hood-high on either side. He puzzled over whether or not the tape and his demands would drive Stonzo underground, particularly in view of the fired shot. Did he even know about the shot? And what of Georgia? And Hendley, the Slippery Spy? Why would he even show his face there? Will Stonzo call or should he be called? By when?

There had been other times like these, when one question led to two more, when their total seemed greater than the sum of their parts, and David would postpone any resolution for there could be none. As in days past, it was all cryptic and shadowy and nebulous, requiring fresh dissection, a sorting out. But that would come.

He called Kathy on the cell phone and was greeted with as many questions as he had put aside. He recounted the essentials of the confrontation minus the shooting incident.

"What about Evilina—are we on for tomorrow?" he asked.

"Yes. Harwichport at noon. Mulligan's Restaurant. She said it's midway between the trampolines and go-carts."

David felt a burst of nostalgia but was too tired to bring

up his early days there. Instead, he inquired, "How did she sound?"

"Relieved."

"How could you tell?"

"Is 'Thank you, Lord' enough? She's one frightened young lady, David."

"I thought so."

Kathy returned to the Chicago scene. "After you gave them the tape, did they still hang tough?"

"In general, yes. Especially that creep, Shades."

David turned and looked at Musco. One of his eyes was open, looking back at him.

CHAPTER 16
✦ ✦ ✦
Sunday, February 17

Davidhad slept dead to the world and at nine a.m., he left for Cape Cod, Massachusetts—three hours away—*his* drive-time. He hadn't been there in nearly 30 years. Alone, he drove east from the snow drifts of Connecticut to the sand dunes of the Cape, not as plentiful along the stretch he knew as a youngster, more so at the claw of the peninsula, in Provincetown especially, where the family would spend a day during each summer's vacation. There in P-town, David would be bored accompanying his mother to antique shops in search of her favorite satins and embroidered pongees, or inlaid tables and boxes or any article of exquisite carvings in rose-wood, ivory and sandal-wood. But invigorated once they rejoined his father for a stroll along endless docks, to observe dark men diving for coins or to pile into boats for an afternoon of whale watching.

He looked forward to this kind of venue for a change,

not a sprawling metropolis—a New York City, a Chicago, or a Boston which he would demand as a place to confront Stonzo again—but a more serene escape-land on the other side of the Bourne and Sagamore Bridges. Upon leaving Hollings, he recalled the old *Lone Ranger* radio show and the announcer who would implore its listeners, "Return with us now to those days of yesteryear . . ." And then, despite the gravity of the mission, he let his mind regress for the first hour, to the late sixties, early seventies, during his pre-adolescence when the family would rent a cottage for two weeks. He remembered the excursions to Nantucket and Martha's Vineyard, flying kites on the beaches, surfing the frigid waves in Eastham—all of which he liked—and the band concerts at the gazebo, craft shows at the Triangle, the last day with its clean-up chores—all of which he didn't. But his favorite was to ride the go-carts and jump atop the trampolines; they were the reason the family eventually moved from a rental on the northern bay side, south across the belly, to one along a broad blue sweep of ocean. Once in awhile, he would return, though, to be with his father at the edges of the fish ponds in Brewster and Orleans, where pickerels and black bass flourished. He remembered their early morning travels past a red defunct windmill and seeing cart loads of sun-bonneted women and wide-brim hatted men en route to the cranberry bogs. And feeling wind-burned on their return trips back to the cottage when, even as a boy, he marveled at the panorama of the heavens, radiant in violet, amber and rose.

But for most of the ride, David dwelled on sorting out the particulars of the Chicago episode, just as he had promised himself, and going over the queries he would put to Evilina.

He arrived at noon on the button and, with Friday in hand, walked toward Mulligan's entrance from the parking lot in the rear. The air was crisp, the sky sapphire clear. He was in one of his turtlenecks and a blue blazer. His lips tasted salty and that, together with the distinctive and not-totally-unpleasant odor from the swamplands and the cooing of mourning doves, again reminded him of innocent days, certainly not ones filled with murder, mobs, terrorism and once unfathomable genetic manipulations.

Its interior was plain, with several tables in the middle, a bar at one side and booths along the other three. Four women sat at one table, a man at the bar and several couples in the nearest booths. A corner one was occupied by a woman whose back was toward David as he approached. She was sipping coffee.

"Evilina?" She jumped and began to rise.

"Please stay," David said. "How are you doing?"

They shook hands; hers were cold and moist.

"Fine, Dr. Brooks. I'm glad you're here. I want to start by . . ."

"No, no. Not till after lunch. I'm in no hurry, and we can cover whatever you want. I have some questions, too. Would you like a drink?"

"No, thank you."

She seemed shorter than he remembered, but more comely. Her hair was frosted, a departure from what he recalled as auburn or purer brown. And the smile seemed less ready than before. David thought her eye shadow looked ridiculous as did the rings on most of her fingers. She, too, wore a blazer—green—and black slacks.

They each ordered New England clam chowder and a

club sandwich. While they ate, David explained how he happened upon sleuthing and, in answer to gentle queries, she summarized her background. It turned out she was born and raised not in Radonia, but in nearby Boston and graduated from one of the colleges in the Fenway. She worked as a sociologist for only a year, quit, took up hairdressing and was hired by a popular salon in Hyannis where she'd been employed for the past four years.

Evilina volunteered that she met Juan Carlos Saltanban three years before while on a vacation in Cancun, Mexico—"The saddest day of my life." David decided not to press the point since it would be part of his line of questioning later on.

After lunch, David apologized for withdrawing his notepad from Friday. "With so much going on lately, I forget half of it," he said.

In view of Evilina's obvious fear-generated anxiety, he wanted to avoid having her hold back or even fabricate information. He thus labeled their meeting a preliminary one.

"I hope to have a larger meeting in Connecticut in a couple days where we might air things out better. Trust me when I say all the parts have to come together at about the same time. Would you be willing to come?"

"Do I have to?"

"No, but it would sure help."

"I'll think about it."

She had seemed to become calmer, but that changed.

"I'm scared, Dr. Brooks."

David reached over the table and took her hands. "Let's do it this way," he said. "You know there have been some killings in my state, and because of your ties with Juan Carlos, I've come here as part of the overall investigation. I'll ask you some questions now, and if you feel uncomfortable answering any of them, say so—and perhaps if you decide to join us in Connecticut, you might have a different outlook. Okay?"

Her eyes were trained on her rings, which she twisted. She looked up. "Okay. I'm so sorry. I think I'll be okay."

"Good. First, have you ever been to Radonia?"

"Never."

"I'm going to skip around, Evilina, so don't let the order bother you. Do you think Juan Carlos still has power there?"

"He thinks so. I don't."

"How do you know that?"

"Clemente."

"Do you talk with him much."

"Yes."

"You consider him a friend?"

"Yes."

"And if I say he'll be at the meeting in Hollings, you'd be more likely to come?"

"Yes, it would make it easier."

David jotted down something in his pad. "The wake last Sunday. Juan Carlos arrived the day before and left for Radonia later than he'd said. Do you have any idea why?"

"All he told me was that he had important meetings with some people."

"Do you know who those people were?"

"No, I don't."

"And all those security men at the wake. Where did they come from?"

"Boston."

"Do you know them personally?"

"Only to say 'Hi' to when they're with him."

"Are they with him frequently, do you know?"

"Around here, they're *always* with him."

"How do you know they're from Boston?"

"Juan Carlos told me."

"He seems to have friends all over the place. Do you know how come?"

"I can't answer that now." Evilina breathed faster. David made another notation.

"Still on the wake. Why did you attend?"

"He wanted me to. It's that simple."

"Did you want to?"

"No, why should I? I didn't even know the guy."

"Did Saltanban give a reason why you should attend?"

"No."

"He apparently sends chocolates to friends all over the world. Do you know why?"

"Only that he always wants to look like the good guy."

"Do you know Henderson Hendley?"

"I've heard of him."

"Can you elaborate?"

"I can't say much more about him right now." A notation.

"About his visits to the States—Saltanban, that is—he says he comes here infrequently. Is that your understanding?"

Evilina put on an incredulous look. "He comes at least once a month."

"How long has that been going on?"

"Ever since I met him."

"So he comes to see *you*?"

"Primarily."

David twirled the pencil in his fingers. "Now understand, you don't have to answer this, and I don't know how to put it more delicately, but does he fly here to see you for sex?"

"Yes." She looked down at the table.

"I see. And again, don't answer if you don't want to, but you said awhile ago that meeting him was the saddest day in your life—so why the sex?"

"Because he terrifies me, and so do all the people around him."

"Like the criminal elements?"

"Yes." She appeared to be on the verge of tears.

"Have any of them ever bothered you?"

"No."

"I hear he's had a falling out with them. Does that ring a bell?"

"I wouldn't be surprised." Another notation.

"Do you think he was involved in the two murders in Hollings?"

"I wouldn't be surprised about that, either. I mean it, Dr. Brooks." Notation.

David sensed she'd had enough. As he had. He had asked what he wanted and even the unanswered questions had some meaning, he believed.

"Not much more, Evilina. What can you tell me about Saltanban's son?"

"I can't talk about that right now." While she blew her nose, David recorded his final note and put away the pad.

"Okay then, does he have any other children?"

"Yes, two daughters."

They got up, hugged and David thanked her for her cooperation. At his request, she gave him her phone number.

"I sincerely hope you'll visit with us later," he said. "The Candyman will be there, maybe one other. Maybe just the two of you."

"Will Juan Carlos?"

"Definitely not."

As he walked to his car, he flipped back to his notes. He had printed: "SALTANBAN'S FRIENDS. HENDLEY. MAFIA. MURDERS. SON."

He then realized he'd forgotten to ask Evilina if she knew whether or not Saltanban had a wife.

✳   ✳   ✳

By late afternoon David was at home, pleased with the preliminary meeting at the Cape and hopeful Evilina would attend the upcoming meeting. But at the same time, he felt disgusted with himself over two issues. One was his compulsive nature: constant concern over the thought of making mistakes or of leaving things undone; entanglement with tiny details; trying hard to remove the unpredictability from all he encountered; recording everything, from mantras on three-by-five cards or in his notepad, to computer entries and operational plans. Visual records for a goddamn visual person. He wished he could wallow in disorder, laugh at perfection and thumb his nose at perseverance. But wishes aside, compulsions aside, he queried himself: if certain habits—computer entries, typed out plans and mantras—if they worked in the midst of the last murder spree, why not again? Why stop now? A variant of, "If it ain't broken, don't fix it." His idea was to crack the case as soon as possible, therefore returning to his practice as soon as possible—and, of course, preventing further killings. And if these required humoring compulsive urges . . . well . . . humor them, damn it.

The other issue, perhaps an offshoot of the first, was the resurrection of an old problem: the perceived need to contact Kathy with the results of each meeting, each incident, each phone call. Some of it, he believed, revolved around the necessity of keeping Detective Chief Nick Medicore current, and Kathy would do so. But many times in the past, David had given himself a scolding about informing her of every fresh development, and once again, he decided to heed it. The Cape details could wait till later.

The decision suddenly became academic: the phone rang, and it was Kathy.

"Welcome back," she said. "How did it go?"

Because of his frame of mind, he gave her a whittled down version of what had occurred and said he would elaborate in due course. He stated he was about to enter some data in the computer and afterward he'd be more certain about his schedule for the next couple days.

"Hopefully, we won't have to go beyond that," David said.

"So you're still making those . . . what are you calling them? . . . computer entries?"

"Yes."

"When do I get to see them?"

"Any time. For me, they help clarify what happened and what might happen. I get more out of typing the stuff than in reading it later. Kind of crystallizes it, you know?"

After expressions of their love and assurances they

would spend the next night together, he was about to hang up the phone and said, "Barring anything catastrophic."

Kathy replied, "Wait a minute. Regardless, you have to sleep sometime."

∗   ∗   ∗

David spent 20 minutes reviewing his next computer entry, getting the chronology straight, referring to his notepad, writing down some facts. He then typed:

Sunday, February 17

Molina and Crocker Murders, continued:

(A) Ongoing Summary

Meeting held with Stonzo at Sorrento Restaurant, NYC. I was wired. He wants criticism of Mafia to stop, my withdrawal from case. Admitted he had Molina murdered. Won't say who hired him. States Camorra killed Crocker. At odds with Saltanban. Blew up when I acted lukewarm re his requests. Demands meeting in Chicago.

Recording "took" perfectly.

Kathy wants Stonzo arrested. Not yet.

Georgia kidnapped.

Stonzo called. Admitted they have Georgia. Meet same demands or else, he said.

Ogleton interview. Said Molina had "thing" about his wife. Won't say why his meeting with Molina was canceled—by Ogleton. Justified Brent's existence even though he's opposed to their mission. Neutral in opinion of Crocker. Admires Saltanban who gives

Brent big bucks.

Visited Molina's house again. E-mail received from Prof. Weld wrote of super-bugs and bioterrorism. Picture missing on wall of back room. Forgot to compare with my photos and enhance if nec.

Weld interview. Superbugs rundown. Didn't fully dismiss embryonic stem-cell and cloning research capability with private funds. Federal funds non-existent for them.

Dr. Corliss interview. Personality types run-down. Paranoid, passive-aggressive, narcis-sistic, antisocial, combinations of each. Psychological defense mechanisms. States all capable of murder.

Held meeting with Stonzo at Palmer House, Chicago. S... hit fan when told I was wired. Gave him copy of tape. Hendley there! Stonzo stormed out. Stated would contact me. Shades took potshot. Missed. Musco risked life.

Evilina interview, Cape Cod. Born in States. Answered some questions but held back re Saltanban's friends, Hendley, Mafia, the murders, Saltanban's son.

(B) Action Review

Await Stonzo contact.

Georgia's safety.

Arrest Hendley as possible accessory?

Arrange APB for Shades?

Schedule The Meeting with at least Clemente and Evilina (if willing).

> Update Operative Plan.
> Check Clemente's locked closet.
> Check on Saltanban's book on cybernetics.
> Check photos taken at Molina's.

"The Meeting" under "(B) Action Review" was David's way of highlighting its pivotal role, a throwback to his college undergraduate days. Generations ago, the football classic between his alma mater, Yale and its arch rival, Harvard, had been designated The Game. Yale's success was gauged not by its earlier performances each year but by the outcome against the team from Cambridge. Similarly, the success of David's criminal investigation hinged on the outcome of The Meeting on Wednesday.

And while he was at it, he decided to revise the Operative Plan for the following day forward. Why he called it that, he still wasn't sure, for it amounted to nothing more than a brief schedule with a fancy title. And most of it was already in his previous entry. Compulsion is thy name! He snickered at himself as he typed:

OPERATIVE PLAN

Monday—Reenter Clemente house.

Locked closet door.

Check on Saltanban's book.

Tuesday or Wednesday—Hold The Meeting. Who? Where?

Remember still—Peak at right time.

Georgia a concern.

Stonzo's contact critical.

Pray he makes one.

If not, what?

By when?

David went to his file cabinet and found a large envelope containing the photos he'd taken in Molina's study. He sifted through them until he discovered a close-up of Molina's dead body and, over his left shoulder, a clear view of the wall behind him. On it was a grouping of *four* pictures! There were only three when he and Musco checked on Friday. David examined the photo under his desk lamp and decided he needed neither magnification nor enhancement techniques to confirm what seemed obvious: the upper right one was a family photo depicting Saltanban and three women in a formal sitting. They appeared to be his wife and two young daughters.

He was still scrutinizing the photo when the phone rang.

"Dr. Brooks?" It was Anthony Stonzo's unmistakable telephone voice.

"Yes. Tony? How are you?"

"Super. I just want you to know I'm not ready to talk yet. I have a few important details to settle first, but please expect my call tomorrow morning at about eleven. You'll be home?"

"Yes."

"Until tomorrow, Dr. Brooks. Goodbye."

David had wanted to bring up the Shades incident but there was no chance. Funny, he didn't let a day go by.

He pulled out a TV dinner from the freezer and, dismissing the Nutrition Facts on the box, placed it into the microwave.

He downed a scotch while waiting, then ate without tasting, and the last thing he remembered before falling asleep in his recliner was running his fingers through his hair several times over. The phone ring startled him awake.

"David, this is Henderson Hendley. I want you to know
. . ."

"Hendley! Why you little creep! I should have had you
brought in hours ago."

"David, listen to me. I know. I know what you're thinking. But I want to talk to you. Can we meet someplace
tonight? I have some information on Georgia."

The bastard knows her name. "Sure you do," David
said. "You've sweet-talked me before, Hendley." The
thought of a missed opportunity flashed through his
mind. "And how do I know it wouldn't be a setup for
your scumbag buddies? Did Stonzo hear the tape?"

"I don't know and I don't care. Setup? You'll just have
to take my word for it. How do I know you wouldn't plan
an ambush with the police?"

"What place are you talking about?" David considered
bringing Musco.

"Have you ever been to Seaside Park in Bridgeport?"

"I forgot about that place. Yeah, maybe 30 years ago."

"What was the old pavilion in those days is now an ice
skating rink. We have to meet after dark. I want most
people in bed. Make it midnight. There's a parking lot
behind the rink. And please come alone."

No Musco. David hesitated. His instincts about the
columnist had failed him before but Georgia was not
gone then. "I'll be there at midnight, and there had better
be no tricks."

"No tricks. And remember, come alone."

"For that little girl, I come alone."

Hendley hung up first.

David didn't phone Kathy, although it crossed his
mind. If he did, he expected he might have had a battle

on his hands over her insistence on bringing reinforce-
ments, or over even going at all.

*   *   *

It was 11:15 p.m. when David, fully armed, stole out into
the frosty night air. He drove the 40 miles to Seaside Park
with an eye in the rearview mirror, not in the mood for
reminiscences—as in the case of Cape Cod. A dirt road
led to its entrance, a tall black gate of wrought iron, as
tall as the level of elm trees that funneled into it from
right and left. The dirt became blacktop as he inched
through the open gate and off to the side where he
parked but kept the motor running. He opened Friday
and eased out his Blackhawk Magnum, then laid it on the
seat between his thighs. He shrugged his left shoulder to
feel the Minx and patted the snubby at his ankle, conscious of moisture on his palm.

The park rested in a deep depression, its far rim rising,
then, like a camel's back, sloping to the sea. David shifted into a lower gear for a more controlled descent. He
had always associated evenings at Seaside with fog, thick
fog that he was convinced stuck to his skin. But there was
none to be seen or felt, nor any stars, only the hint of a
moon veiled by clouds. He pounced on his Blackhawk
when he heard the guttural meows of cats in an apparent
standoff. Easy now.

He continued down the roadway some 200 yards.
Where the land leveled off, the light smell of fish and a
surge of waves below triggered brief memories of swim-
ming and frolicking in that area during his teens. He
spotted the pavilion whose facade and veranda had been
retained and drove around the back, surprised the stan-
chion lights surrounding the parking lot were still on.

Perhaps skating ended late. David parked alongside one of the stanchions, turned off the ignition and waited, all the while weighing his options should a convoy of cars converge upon him. His leg twitched and he slapped it.

Ten minutes later, he saw the headlights of a car moving rapidly in his direction. Once it veered sideways toward him, he could make out the outline of a driver. It was short. Hendley is short. But as the car came closer, he saw another shadow on the passenger side.

"Son-of-a-bitch, I knew it!" David screamed. How many are in the back seat?

As he reached for his guns, the car came to an abrupt stop diagonally in front of him, and he realized the passenger was a young girl. "What on earth . . ?" he muttered.

Georgia burst out the door.

"Dr. Brooks! Dr. Brooks!" she shouted, running to David's car. Tears streamed down her cheeks.

David flung open his door and scrambled out. The girl leaped into his arms. "Geor—gia," he said, spirits buoyed. He held her gently at first, then pulled her in closer, in anticipation of a half-dozen men piling out of Hendley's car. It didn't happen.

"Surprised?" Hendley asked. He was at their side, alone.

"Are you kidding?" David gave Georgia a quick once-over. "Are you okay?" he asked. She nodded yes and sniffled. "They didn't hurt you?" She nodded no.

He glanced toward the rear seat of Hendley's car. "You're alone, I take it?"

"Yes, I'm alone. And unglued, I'm sorry to say." Hendley glanced around.

"Look," David said, "Thank God she's safe and sound, but what in hell's going on?"

"May we sit in your car while I try to explain some things?"

Georgia climbed in the back, the other two in front. Hendley wasted no time.

"First, let me say I was at the kidnapping itself. There were three other men. Georgia cooperated, and there was no struggle. They forced me to put her up in my apartment building in Westport. Stonzo's orders, of course."

"Wait up. What about your wife?"

"I have none. I live alone. Georgia was kept in the basement, in a room the maintenance man used to live out of—when we had a maintenance man. Yes, it was kept locked, but it has a TV, and there's a john there."

"How about food? You starved, honey?"

"No, but I'm sick of sandwiches and potatoes. Mr. Hendley was really very nice to me. He apologized to me a million times." Georgia sounded younger than her years. And weary.

"I hope you'll believe me, David, but I wanted no part of this. Nor of anything else with those guys. Listening to them . . ." He grunted. ". . . they're all animals. You see, for reasons I'm too embarrassed to talk about, they got me over a barrel about ten years ago and pretty much had their way with me. I'm changing all that." He looked wistfully through the windshield. "They wanted to put me on their payroll, and I refused. But I had to play along because I had no choice. And as far as my being in Chicago, I absolutely hated facing you, believe me, but they wanted me there after giving me some gobbledygook about solidifying their hold on me. How stupid! But I wasn't about to argue.

"I was told, in no uncertain terms, to paint Saltanban

in a bad light whenever I could, even if it meant denigrating organized crime in the process. The mob knows it has a bad name to begin with. Saltanban had a serious rift with them, and that's why he turned to the Camorra. Actually the Camorra was the reason for the rift. It was a turf war."

"Did he hire them to kill Agnes Crocker?"

"I can't be sure, David. I really can't, but it would make sense."

"And Molina?"

"The same thing. I'm not sure."

"You're telling me you're not one of them?"

"That's what I'm telling you. Now and again, they had me writing columns that would indirectly serve their purposes. I guess I was considered a consultant who would never flip. But I always threw in a dig or two."

"And you've soured on them because . . ."

"It wasn't a question of souring. I was never in their corner to begin with. I abhor what they stand for and what they do. It's just that they had me in a blackmail stranglehold."

"So you want to get even because of that and because of another thing, I'd guess—the murder of your good friend, Agnes Crocker?"

"Yes."

"But the Camorra probably committed that crime."

"I know. But I happen to be pissed off at *all* mobs."

David thought the columnist didn't have that word in him.

"Why are you telling me this and, incidentally, does Stonzo know you've returned Georgia?"

"No, not yet. But he calls me everyday."

"What are you going to tell him?"

"Beginning sometime tomorrow, I won't be there. I won't be anywhere as far as anyone's concerned. I'll be in hiding. Moving in the shadows, to be melodramatic about it." Hendley released a sick smile. "But getting back to your original question, I'm leveling with you because of the reasons I gave, because I want to apologize for my role in the kidnapping—though God knows I had no choice in the matter—and because of one other thing. I don't know, maybe we're birds of a feather, but back there when I first met you at the wake? I wasn't kidding—I've followed your exploits carefully. Between the wire services and what the mob dug up about you, I got a fairly complete picture. And that scare tactic garbage—the cut wires, the canary—they told me about that. I think you've been terribly wronged, and you're just trying to do your job. Two jobs, in fact. So before I fly the coop, I want to help you."

"Are you awake back there?" David asked.

"Yes."

"Go on, Hender, please."

"At first, you were so . . . so tentative in the papers, that is, in your rare interviews. Then you changed . . . really changed. As you were becoming a big league crime buster—I don't know any other way to put it—you gained resolve. You were assertive. Even in Chicago, you showed it, eyeball to eyeball with Stonzo. I loved it. Outside, I suppose I looked stoic, but inside I was gloating. That's what Hamlet was all about, you know. Self doubt versus revenge. But forgive me, I'm rambling."

"That's pretty complex stuff. You sure I'm that complex?"

"You're not, but your life has been, and you've handled

it beautifully. You've changed in the process. Anyway, that's my view."

David thought the columnist acted whipped. Hendley turned his head forward and in the illumination, his eyes glistened.

"Thanks," David said, reaching over to shake hands. "I believe you. I mean about the mob and how you were involved. Sounds like you got sucked in deeper and deeper. Those other abstract things though—the self doubt, the resolve—I don't know. The revenge? Oh, yeah, I'll buy that."

"So to finish up," Hendley resumed, taking out a handkerchief and dabbing at his nose, "what I propose to do—and I've thought about this over and over—is to assist in gathering firepower against them. Understand, I know these fellows and they're no fools about certain things. If they see enough firepower, they'll back off. And probably for good. They'll simply move elsewhere, out of the territory, way out. That's how they operate."

Hendley's voice took on the quality of a personal manager. "Here's what I'll do. I have connections with the electronic media. Tomorrow morning, I'll arrange bookings on the major TV talk shows so you can tell what you know about the mob. I won't word it that way, of course, just that you have news of major proportions. I'll fax you the confirmation sheets by tomorrow night. Then you inform the mob and get their cooperation—about anything you want. You'll be talking with them soon?"

"Yes."

"Then if they comply, you cancel your appearances. Second, I'll include in the fax the column for my syndication network. It will be a blockbuster exposé. In my

other one—about your interview at my Westport office—
that should appear the day after tomorrow, Tuesday—I
wrote a last line that said something like, 'coming next, a
major exposé of a national tragedy and travesty.' Stonzo
will see it, or he'll be told about it, for sure—one more
worry for him. And all of this, together with your tape,
should be plenty." He took a deep breath. "Now, just in
case . . ." He looked across the lot and down the roadway.
" . . . I think we should leave. What do you think about
the ideas?"

"I think they're brilliant."

"And anywhere along the line, you can back out. In
fact, the column won't even mention you."

Hendley took down David's fax number on a piece of
paper. They shook hands again, and Hendley stretched
back to shake Georgia's.

"Thanks, my friend, and I wish you luck," David said.
"You know you can call me if you think I might help."

"Certainly."

Hendley opened the door as if he didn't want to leave.
Head bowed, he walked toward his car but stopped and
circled around to David's window. David opened it.

"A couple other thoughts," Hendley said. "You realize
that if you sink that branch of the Mafia, others may or
may not retaliate. My feeling is you're better off if you let
sleeping dogs lie, but that's your decision. Let the professional law enforcers peck away at them. By the way, I'll
also mail you the original copy of the column. That's better than a fax for your scrapbook. Good night and all the
best to you both."

"Good night, Mr. Hendley," Georgia said.

"Thanks again, Hender. I can't thank you enough,

especially for giving Georgia back in time."

For the moment and until he'd had a chance to digest what Hendley had revealed, David believed the strategy would be helpful, but it still had to coincide with trapping the person or persons who ordered the killings.

David floored the accelerator back to Hollings while Georgia filled in the details of her captivity.

"With a man like Mr. Hendley, you're really not scared," she said. "But those other men—they were spooky. They made me real scared."

"They didn't hurt you, did they?"

"No, but they talked funny. They said, 'You be nice, little girl, and we be nice.' Stuff like that."

"They didn't touch you, did they?"

"One of them grabbed my arm—at the beginning—it didn't hurt much."

David roared onto Belle's street at 1:15 a.m. He switched to high beams as he turned into the long driveway, hoping Belle might be awakened. When they got out of the car, he slammed his door for good measure. It worked. A light went on in one of the front rooms and Belle raced out of the house before they reached the front door.

"I looked out the window! I looked out the window!"she screamed.

"Mommy!"

Belle snatched Georgia off her feet and twirled her daughter in a circle.

"Tell me I'm not dreaming," Belle said, placing her down like a precious vase.

"She's fine," David said. "Let's go inside."

Belle turned on more lights, and they sat in the living room.

David explained what had transpired and apologized for not notifying her of the trip to Seaside Park ahead of time.

"I would have tried to persuade you to let me come along," she said.

"Oh sure," David said. "You say that now that you know things turned out okay. But what if you thought . . ." In an instant he changed what he was about to say. " . . . what if you thought carloads of mafiosi were there?"

Belle replied, "But I never said I would have succeeded in persuading you. Either that, or I would have depended on your not *letting* me persuade you."

He could tell she felt airborne. He ran his fingers through one side of his mustache and said, "Final answer?"

"Final answer."

They laughed lustily, David less from the repartee than from his own exhilaration.

He got up and stretched his arms. "I have to go," he said, "but, Georgia, do you have school tomorrow?"

"Yes."

"No," Belle said. "I'm bringing you to work with me. We'll find a cot for you to rest on."

"Look at the time," David said. "Why not stay home tomorrow? We can have one of the switchboard gals handle our calls."

"No, I'll be there. I won't sleep anyway."

"As you wish, but I'm going to need her when Stonzo calls. He's supposed to, at eleven in the morning."

"Why Georgia?"

"To talk to him on the phone."

Georgia's face blanched. "Mom told me about that man. I won't know what to say."

"Don't worry, it'll be written out for you. He'll be impressed." David winked at Belle who responded with an I'm-not-sure-about-this look.

"I don't want to impress that man," Georgia whimpered.

"The reason is, we have to prove you're here. Until then, he'll still think you're in Westport and, remember, Mr. Hendley said he might not be around anymore. So relax, Georgia, you'll do fine."

✳ ✳ ✳

It would have been an unusually late hour to phone Kathy but the news of Georgia's return was too vital to keep until later in the morning. David called and kept it short. Kathy reacted with more excitement than David could have mustered had their roles been reversed.

CHAPTER 17

+ + +

Monday, February 18

Over the span of a frenetic week, the Candyman had crossed David's mind more than once. This was one of the times, but he had planned the call while typing his last computer entry. He phoned Clemente's store at 9:05 a.m. He had a dual purpose.

One was to invite him to the upcoming meeting whose details David had settled on. He was confident by now that the murders were ordered by a single individual and that Evilina and Clemente held the keys to the identity of that person. Hence, he wanted them there—and only them—since they would be more inclined to "open up." It would be held on Wednesday, the day after next and would take place at his home, 10 Oak Lane, the least intimidating of all the locales he considered. Clemente agreed to attend.

"Believe me, Adrian, I can't go into it now but by the time we meet, Anthony Stonzo won't be a danger to you or

Evilina." David was on the verge of crossing his fingers.

He ended the conversation citing the formidable task of "having all the pieces come together at the right time." After hanging up, he thought about how difficult it must be to describe something technical—an EKG machine, say—without using your hands.

The second purpose of the call was to ensure that Clemente was at the candy store and not at his house.

David had contacted Musco at home at 7:30, chided him about taking Sunday off and arranged to journey with him to the Clemente homestead.

Before leaving, David made his third telephone call of the morning—to an old family friend, Harold Flommer, a curmudgeonly attorney who wore tweeds year-round and had not ordered the last five editions of his dusty law book collection.

"Hello, Harold?" David shouted into the phone. "David Brooks, here. I won't keep you long. You must be busy."

"Yes, I'm busy with transactions. Who did you say this is?"

Since when was a nap a transaction? "David. David Brooks."

"Oh, yes, David. For the love of Mike, what have you been getting into? At least you're alive. Up to now, anyhow. Why not cut your losses and live in peace and tranquility? Albeit the papers imply you never will. Got to hand it to you, though. You know, you're tougher then your father, and smarter—or dumber—depending on which side of the railing you're assessing the matter."

"Thanks for the advice, Harold, and my dad sends his regards. Look, if I may, I have a special favor to ask of you.

Tomorrow morning, right about this time, I'm driving up to a key meeting in Boston, and I was wondering whether you could come along. While we're there, I'd want you to draw up a short statement on your letterhead that attests to the fact a certain party was involved in a murder."

"Why? It might not stand up in court."

"Meaning it might—you know, the other side of the railing. Regardless, I really want it for another purpose."

There was silence at the other end; David thought Flommer was starting one of his transactions.

"Could you, Harold?"

"Now wait, let me get this straight. You mean what you're saying, correct?"

"Correct."

"And you want me to, as we say, officialize that a man there—man or woman?"

"Man."

"That a man there was allegedly involved in a capital felony? Like murder one?"

"You can write it that way, but leave out the 'allegedly'."

"David, my good friend, I will take this on if my schedule permits. But with one caveat."

"Shoot."

"What's that?"

"What's the caveat?"

"Simply for mutual understanding. Things are always in a state of flux whether it's in medicine or politics or the apple business. Even the law. New rulings, don't you know. I can't even keep up with last week's changes. So if anything I write for you is challenged under what we call the rule of duress—Clyde versus Trumpet, nineteen-aught-nine—in this instance as it would apply to a document signed under duress, if so found in court, it might be voided. We might have to seek out consultation with an expert in the aspect of the law. Understood and agreeable to you?"

"There won't be any duress but understood and agreeable. So, can you come?"

"Let me check my schedule. Julia, my secretary, is off for the rest of the year, but the fine woman down the hall in McFadden, McFadden and Brown has been very good about keeping my schedule. Let me check, and I'll see if I can fit it in. You say tomorrow around now?"

"Yes, I'll pick you up there at 9:30 if I don't hear from you before then."

"That would be a good way to handle it. I'll have to check it, of course, but I'm sure you won't hear from me. Nice talking with you, David, and take care of yourself."

✳ ✳ ✳

It was a day meant for golf and David arrived at the hospital lot in the convertible with its top down. Musco hopped from his cab, walked up to the car and shook his finger.

"Secret duty, remember?," he said.

David put the top up. On the way to Clemente's house he spoke about Cape Cod, the call from Stonzo and the rendezvous at Seaside Park. The cabby registered little more than a frown over the first two but upon hearing of Georgia's safe return, a toothy grin blossomed on his round face.

"Amen for the little girl. And amen for us too, because looks to me like there goes Stonzo's leverage."

"We'll see."

"So the newspaper guy cooked the old goose, eh?"

"That's 'cooked his own goose,' Musc, if I read you right.

And why do you say that? He's decided to go into hiding."

"That means nothin'. He's as good as cooked. Like they say, 'The hiders know where the hiders hide'."

David cocked his head. "Okay, I'll bite. Where did you get that? You made it up."

Musco nodded.

David parked beside the same row of hemlocks, his car hidden from the quiet streets of the neighborhood.

"It's only the locked closet we're here about," he said, "so it shouldn't take as long as last time."

Musco had no trouble with the back door of the house and, inside, trailed behind David who strode directly into the living room. He thought the chocolate and old wood aromas were pungent this time, the walnut clock louder, and he attributed these heightened sensations to a redirection away from the jitters he experienced during the last venture there. For he felt calmer. Some of the unknowns were gone and even Musco at his side was a factor, a reassuring one of shared vulnerability.

At the closet door to the left—still locked—David turned away and faked a whistled tune as Musco unlocked it.

"Simple," he whispered, stepping aside.

David opened the door to a foul-smelling, semi-dark room, no bigger than a pair of phone booths. He tried a light switch on the wall, and it didn't work. Sidewall shelves were crammed with books, pots, pans, crusted glasses and other assorted tableware. He blew dust off one of the shelves, coughed, spit and waved at the air. He couldn't recall ever tasting dust before. Or feeling so many cobwebs against his forehead as he took two steps into the closet. The boxy structure against the back wall reached to the level of his knees. It was a dark green metal safe. There was no dust on it.

He called Musco into the room. "Can you still crack these?" he asked.

"Are you kiddin'? Can you still ride a bike?"

"Do you want a flashlight? I have one with me." He pointed to Friday, which he had placed at the threshold of the door.

"Don't need no light, just my ears." Musco looked like a kid about to bite into a glob of cotton candy.

David walked out, leaned back against a wall and massaged his decision scar. He rationalized that it would be more criminal for them to find cash in the safe than just personal papers and documents. But what about drugs? And silver canisters as in the last investigation?

"Looks like a bunch of papers and things," Musco said as David was about to relive the intrigue surrounding the old drug lords.

He rushed in with Friday. The door of the safe lay open. Envelopes bundled with frayed elastic bands were stuffed sideways on both sides of a pile of larger envelopes and folders. David opened Friday, slipped on a pair of surgical gloves and went straight for the pile in the middle of the safe. He rummaged through an assortment of insurance papers and other legal documents. But it was the single yellow folder among the usual beige that attracted his attention: the one which had printed across its front:

1—PROPERTY DEED
2—WILL
3—SECURITIES
4—MANIFESTO FOR NEW WORLD ORDER

David opened the folder. He found the house deed, the will and various stock certificates. Number 4 was missing.

Manifesto for New World Order? If the Candyman didn't bring it up at the showdown, David pledged he himself, would have to, despite the illegality of entering the house. Much less one's personal safe! It sounded too critical to keep under wraps.

On the other side of the ledger, however, was David's vision of a courtroom and a prosecutor who queried, "Tell me, doctor, did you make an effort to notify the police so that a search warrant might be obtained?"

"No, sir."

"Did you think the finding of a so-called 'manifesto' was a matter of life and death?"

"It could be, sir."

"Are you a professional detective or an amateur detective, doctor?"

"An amateur, sir."

"No further questions, your honor."

David changed his mind about the pledge. Rather, he would wait and see. The scenarios were multiple, but the decisive ones hinged on whether or not Clemente would mention it. If he doesn't, he's probably involved in whatever the "New World Order" comprises. If he does, he's probably not, but knows who is. This was one of those issues that qualified for David's mantra: *Do not outpace circumstances. Let things settle out.*

* * *

The completion of the mission at Clemente's left plenty of time to be ready for the phone call at eleven. As they motored toward 10 Oak Lane, David's concentration alternated between what he might expect from Stonzo and what the manifesto was all about. He'd soon have the answer to one—if the capo, indeed, calls him. But he'd have to wait 48 hours for the answer to the other—if Clemente refers to the document. Or if there is one in the first place. It wouldn't make sense to call the Candyman right then and there for that would admit to trespassing. And a possibly disturbing call wouldn't be compatible with David's decision to limit the number at The Meeting; to hold it in a non-threatening environment like his own home; and to be as deferential as possible throughout the discussion.

He had that hemmed in feeling once again. He needed a quick change of pace, a laugh, an instant distraction, something. Three blocks from the homestead, he pulled the car over. He looked toward Musco for silent permission, then lowered the top and drove off with soft Broadway hits playing in the background.

The gentian sky was laced with four parallel contrails. David knew they were tiny ice crystals that formed when water vapor from the exhaust of airplanes condensed in cold air. But what fascinated him the most was that the crystals could seed surrounding clouds to form rain.

"See those thin lines up there, Musc?"

"Sure. Contrails."

"Just floating there. Good for nothing, right?"

"Oh no, my boy. They can make you put your top back up."

"My top? Really?"

"Sure. Crystals. You dig?"

"Dig what?"

"The suckers hype up them clouds and here come the rain, baby, here come the rain."

In view of his sidekick's savvy, David didn't know whether or not it was appropriate, but he got his laugh.

At the Hole, he greeted Belle and Georgia and, pointing to a cot in the corner, said, "You located one, I see, but it doesn't look slept in."

"I'm not tired," Georgia said, timidly. "Do I really have to talk on the phone, Dr. Brooks?"

"It's not much. See?" David spread out a sheet of paper on the desk. Words in uppercase lettering read:

HI, MR. STONZO. THIS IS GEORGIA. MR. HENDLEY WAS VERY NICE TO ME, BUT I'M GLAD TO BE HOME WITH MY MOTHER. I HOPE YOU HAD A VERY NICE VALENTINE'S DAY.

At first, only Georgia and Musco were to accompany David to his house to await Stonzo's call, but Georgia begged her mother to come, too. Belle contacted the hospital operator to provide telephone coverage for the Hole.

For all his earlier kibitzing, it was Musco who paced at Oak Lane while Georgia lay prone on the floor reading over her lines, and David sat before his computer, pondering. He was determined to force the issue of who retained Stonzo for Molina's murder and would do so either during the phone conversation or possibly at a future meeting. He preferred the latter for it would provide better circumstances for an arrest, if he were to go that route. As kernels of Hendley's advice danced in his mind—"if you sink that branch of the Mafia, others may retaliate . . .let sleeping dogs lie . . . let the professional law enforcers peck away"—David anticipated coming to a decision on the capo's fate later that night when Kathy arrived.

At 11:05, the phone rang.

"Hello, is this Dr. Brooks?"

"In person. Who's this?" Who's kidding whom?

"Dr. Brooks, this is Tony Stonzo. You know, I've been thinking it over. Maybe it's good for everybody if we have another discussion, you know, one more high-level job. And if I may be a little blunt—I've always been up front with you, you know—let me say that I've spoken with my associates, like in Hollywood and New York—Florida— and where else?—Canada—and they all agree with me. If you release those tapes in your possession, you're a dead man, and so is your girlfriend." He hadn't changed his cadence or his emotion and David visualized his expression hadn't, either. "And so, I'm out here in Hollywood, and I was wondering about you coming out here. Might be a nice trip for you. Ever been to Hollywood?"

"Thanks for the threat. Here, listen." David handed the phone to Georgia who read her lines firmly.

David took back the receiver and said, "Nice, huh?"

"You'll pay, Brooks!" Stonzo yelled. His voice sounded like one screened through a tight filter.

David said, "Now, to answer your question, no I've never been to Hollywood, my schedule's tight, that would be out of the question, you ever been to Boston?" He spoke rapidly before Stonzo had a chance to interrupt.

"Yes, I've been to Boston! Yes, I've been to Boston!" His voice jumped an octave: "*Mannaggia a te!* I don't like it there. Too many busters!"

"Busters?"

"Yeah, busters." The voice leveled off in disdain. "Young punks trying to make it in our business. They'd rat on me over a piece of cheese. And the cops there don't know their ass from a hole in the ground. They say

they're gunnin' for me for mingling with the busters.
Well, I'm not a player—I don't mingle. That's how much
they know. You better make it Hollywood."

"Forget it, Stonzo. Goodbye . . ."

"Wait! Frankie, bring me my calendar. When you talking about, Brooks?"

"I'm free tomorrow. Make it the usual time—noon. I
like the Sheraton Boston. It's in the Prudential Center on
Dalton Street. That's more of an address than your goon
gave me for Sorrento's. See you then, Stonzo. If you come
with more than two men, I walk out. I'm bringing Musco
Diller and my attorney. And remember this: an ambush
wouldn't have a chance, so don't even think about it."
David slammed down the receiver.

Belle asked, "Wasn't that kinda abrupt? He's a powerful
figure, isn't he?"

"Belle, I don't give a damn. It's *my* turn now."

✳   ✳   ✳

After lunch, David placed a call to Harwichport from his
home.

"Hello, Evilina, this is David Brooks."

"Where are you?"

"Home."

"David, I knew you'd contact me, but I thought it
would be tomorrow. Adrian already called about the
meeting Wednesday. We went over the whole thing—
God, many times—and we're ready to explain a lot of
things—so I'll be there. I'll go right to the Clemente
house—I know it well. He said you want us at your
house—at 1:30?" She spoke with clarity and purpose.

"Yes. That'll give you plenty of time if you leave from
the Cape that morning."

"No, we decided I'd better arrive the night before. I'll stay with Dolores and Adrian."

"That's even better. How much does she know?"

"Not much, I don't think. We'll tell her tomorrow night—and she'll probably have a stroke." There was a brief silence. "Just like I'll have if this phone is bugged. More than that, I'd be a dead duck. So would Adrian."

"I would have told you, Evilina, whether you said that or not, but I'm arranging to have Clemente's house staked out before you arrive, and you'll have a police escort from there to here on Wednesday."

CHAPTER 18
✢ ✢ ✢

Through Kathy and the Police Department, David secured the home phone number of a senior editor at Brower and Roberts Publishing. He had put off checking on Saltanban's book long enough—ever since the visit to Radonia when something about Saltanban's excitement over his book didn't ring true. David apologized but explained the urgency of his Sunday call.

"Yes, I've heard of you. You're the doctor who only makes house calls. Let me know if you write a book about your cases—uh—not the medical ones—the murders. You've certainly had your fill up there in Connecticut, from what I've been reading."

David asked him about a manuscript submitted by Juan Carlos Saltanban, the president of Radonia. "It was on cybernetics."

"Whoa, *that* one," the editor said. "Ordinarily we don't hand out information about individual manuscripts on the phone. In fact, we normally can't keep them straight—there are so many—but that one I do remember because of who the author is. One of our readers showed it to me and, Dr. Brooks, it was pure jibberish—written as a schoolboy would. And what he did to cybernetics—it was utterly awful."

"So you didn't accept it for publication?"

"No."

"He knows you didn't?"

"I assume so. I recall we sent him our standard rejection letter."

"How long ago?"

"Maybe ten days."

David wasn't stunned by the news, only more determined, alert—for with additional ammunition against the president, he was eager to hold The Meeting. He considered this latest fabrication another stitch in a pattern of lies that seems to have shaped the anima of the man. Or have they been denials, subconscious ones, mental shields of a sort, a variant of Freud's old formula that certain defense mechanisms are erected to protect the ego from being overwhelmed or disorganized from the effects of hate or guilt or rejection? Perhaps the mechanism hadn't worked for Saltanban through the years, and the disorganization component prevailed. Translation? The president's mind was a mess. He had mastered the field of communications, dabbled in cybernetics, bankrolled his way into a national presidency and, who knows, tried to understand all the potentials of genetics. Had he been trying to "find" himself, this while the Konzertmeisters of organized crime were orchestrating a role for him in their designs?

✳   ✳   ✳

David had to get away. He'd had his fill—almost. It was mid-afternoon, a time he knew some of his colleagues at the martial arts studio were just arriving there from work, ready to fend off serious injury in tae kwan do: cat-like maneuvers, snappy kicks and flying elbows, slashing of hands and feet. For David, however, it was more than that—a cocoon away from turmoil, where his senses could be piqued again by the smell of sweat, the taste of talcum and the give of the shiaijo mat beneath his bare feet.

He would go there every Tuesday night for combat, every Thursday night as an instructor. But now he would go there straightaway, a few hours before Kathy's arrival at Oak Lane, when they would work out plans for the following day in Boston. He felt as if he were in a bit of denial himself as he cast aside the powder keg with Stonzo, not altogether shaking his mind free of The Meeting the following day. He had a vague inkling of how it would turn out, with a single nagging exception: motive. M.O.M. The means and opportunity were obvious; the true motive remained an enigma. Yet, if the meeting hatched the motive and the murderer, he could return to his medical practice, a practice he considered a daily adventure—one that, yes, dealt with life and death, but not his own.

With Friday in one hand, a canvas satchel in the other, David left for the studio. Confident about the next 48 hours? About as confident as some male spiders after mating.

At 3:30, he cursed as he usually did when climbing three flights to Bruno's Martial Arts Studio. How about an elevator, for Christ sake? Black belts aren't supposed to have bad knees? The door at the top of the stairs read:

CHINESE—JAPANESE—KOREAN—AMERICAN
MARTIAL ARTS
Bruno Bateman, Grand Master

He walked down a long corridor directly toward the room Bruno routinely used for his classes. David stood at the doorway.

"David!" Bruno exclaimed. "More damn murders. How's it shaping up?"

The Grand Master was as tall as David but a string of a man with cheekbones that appeared inverted and graying hair gathered in a ponytail. When not in combat, his movements were economical, and he kept his hands at his sides like lethal weapons. His smile took a full sentence to form but a period to dissolve.

"Getting there, Bruno, getting there. Okay to join the others across the hall?"

"Absolutely. See you tomorrow night?"

David wasn't sure he'd even be whole tomorrow night. "No, probably not. I'm aiming for Thursday."

"I'll tell the guys. It'll be good to have you back," Bruno replied, one eye on David, the other on a student he had in a head lock.

At his locker, David changed into simple gray sweats, not the pajama-like costume of white cotton jacket and pants he wore for his instuctional sessions on Thursdays. He used to teach bujutsu, a form of Japanese martial arts that emphasizes swift and violent moves and a willingness to face death as a matter of honor, but now, in deference to his knee, he limited his workouts to non-percussive aikido—to neutralizing opponents without striking them.

The next hour was filled with teases and loud chatter

while dodging, feinting, spinning, grabbing and trying to out-fox friendly combatants. It went fast. He took a shower knowing the pain would come later.

Outside, as David eased into his Mercedes, he noticed a flat box on the front passenger seat. Its cellophane wrapping glistened in the glow from the dashboard. He switched on an overhead light and leaned over. It was a box of chocolates with the logo, *Candies by Clemente.*

* * *

Kathy's condo unit was never more inviting. Nor Kathy. David had phoned ahead and asked that she surprise him with "something nice." That always signaled a request for what she should wear, and she always understood the signal.

They held hands as they walked into the living area. He swung Friday in his free hand. A CD player emitted soft love instrumentals while two lighted vanilla-scented candles burned on the top of a bookcase, their glow shimmering off the ceiling.

David pretended he hadn't noticed her outfit, and she tried to appear casual. He put Friday on a console table, removed his jacket and folded it neatly on the attaché case. Once they became engulfed in her puff chair, he ran his hands over its faux leopard nylon and said, "I never realized before how good this feels. Silk or nylon, isn't it?" He transferred his hand to the border of her neckline and rubbed the material between his fingers.

Kathy watched him, mouth twisted, silent.

"I'll be darned," he said, "they feel the same."

She wore only a short black negligee and black quilted mules.

He held her shoulders at arm's length and said

thoughtfully, "Now let me see, you once told me that was a . . . a . . . a camisole, I believe."

They laughed with the relief of a bottle of fizz whose cork had just been popped. David led a tight embrace.

She got up, put on a matching robe that was draped over a chair and returned to his side.

"I was waiting to see how far you'd go with that," she said. "Your little funny for the day?"

"It wouldn't take much lately."

"I know," she said, caressing the back of his neck. "But can I ask you a serious question?"

"Sure," David said, gearing up for something about murders, suspects, motives. The Mafia?

"How come women have to wear sexy clothes while men wear . . . well . . .whatever men wear?"

David had relished his karate break and now at Kathy's had looked forward to additional time away from the surfeit of worry. He wasn't ready yet to resume his investigative mentality, to retighten. That would come later when he expected to review the plans—and get Kathy's input—for handling Stonzo in Boston.

And then there was the issue of the chocolates in his car. He had walled it off in his mind, an uneasy refusal to interpret it as more than intimidation. He wouldn't even attempt to trace the sender. Another difficult decision, but with burdens mounting and time trickling away, he had to be selective.

He was therefore relaxed by Kathy's question and gave what he thought was a dopey but easy response.

"Who knows, but I like it."

He spread out his arms and looked over his clothes—blue wool button-down, charcoal corduroys—and said,

"Do you want me to take these off?"

"David!" She smacked his shoulder.

"Well?.," he said, as if it were the logical question to ask.

"Well?" he repeated.

"Not now," she replied demurely.

Pulling hard on his mustache, she said, "I have another question for you. Why is it that so few blond males have one of these things? Dark hair, yes, but not blond."

"I never notice."

"I do."

"So answer the question: why do you have one?"

"That's why I'm different."

"You can say that again," she retorted.

The puff chair did little to support their backs, and Kathy rocked until she righted herself and planted her feet on the floor. David lounged behind.

She spied Friday nearby. "Why did you bring that in?," she said.

"Oh." He swung around and latched onto the handle of the attaché case with two fingers. "I nearly forgot." He opened it and pulled out a thin package wrapped in red-flowered paper.

"Voilà!," he said, "Belated Happy Valentine's Day."

"Well, thank you." She began unwrapping. "I don't think it's chocolates. And I don't think it's another gun. That took care of my birthday last month."

Kathy held up a white garment that resembled a sleeveless blouse. She stretched it out. "What on earth?," she said.

"It's a shirt holster. See the pocket? That's where you hide your pistol."

"Thank you, again . . . I think. Am I supposed to wear this . . . this thing . . . as a blouse?"

"No," he answered emphatically. "You wear it underneath something. Instead of keeping your pistol in your purse, it's on you at all times when you're out."

"Look, David darling, this was very sweet, but you gave me a new .45 last month, and I already had one, and now this. I don't think I'd be comfortable in it." She folded it up and returned it to the box.

"I gave you the Beretta Cougar because it's state of the art with the Cam–loc that gives you less recoil. That's very feminine, if you think about it. Good for fragile hands and wrists."

If Kathy's eyes were daggers, he would have felt the stab.

"Just like your purse," he continued. "You're alone in a restaurant and some thug comes up to you. You want to be prepared, so what do you do? You say, 'Excuse me, sir, would you hand me my purse?' No—you've got to have a holster of some kind."

"Oh for heaven's sake!"

She took out the shirt holster again and inserted her hand in the pocket. "What if I'm wearing a dress? It'll show."

"No it won't. The pocket's under your arm. And you wear jackets 90 per cent of the time, you know."

"Hmm."

"You've always complained you can't wear a shoulder rig or a clip. This is *perfect* for you. Do you think I'd go out and buy something that wasn't totally functional?"

Kathy peered down her nose at him. "But I hate guns in the first place."

"Kathleen, how the hell can you be a cop without a gun?"

"I have a gun."

"Where is it?"

"In my purse."

It was David's turn to peer down his nose, but he had never let exasperation interfere with desire. He pulled her to him, falling back with her into the middle of the puff chair. Their kisses were alive and found their favorite spots. He rocked forward and helped her to her feet, then clutched at his knee as he righted himself. He limped as they walked into the bedroom.

Fifteen minutes later, they came out. The limp was gone.

* * *

Kathy had prepared a tuna casserole together with David's preferred dessert: pumpkin pie. But it was far short of a leisurely dinner as David dictated the pace, anxious to go over the details of the Boston meeting scheduled for the following noon. Like stumbling upon a eulogy, his mood darkened. And it appeared to rub off on Kathy. They cleared the dishes and returned to the table.

"First off, Kath, could you have one of your people keep an eye on Georgia for awhile?"

"Done."

"And you put out an APB on that Shades character?"

"Yes."

"Now, before Evilina arrives tomorrow night, could you please have Clemente's house staked out, then make sure they have an escort to the meeting at my house the next day?"

Kathy nodded. "Are you ready for that meeting?"

"Yes."

"Just you, Clemente and Evilina?"

"Yeah, I think they'll be more forthcoming that way."

"What happens if a hitch develops in Boston tomorrow?"

"Real bad?"

"Real bad."

"We call off the meeting at my house."

"That sounds good. Now, Musco's going with you to Boston. Anyone else?"

"Harold Flommer."

"The lawyer? Why?"

"Because I want Stonzo's signature on Flommer's letterhead swearing Saltanban paid for Manny Molina's murder. And I want an attorney there witnessing the signature. Then I show the paper to Clemente and Evilina the next day, and they're convinced we have Saltanban dead to rights."

Kathy got up, walked around her chair and sat down. "Now let me get this straight," she said, "You're going to convince a big time capo to—in effect—sign an affidavit that the president of a country paid him to have someone killed? Is that right?"

"Bingo! We could also use it later on in court."

"What if Stonzo refuses? Refuses? He'll laugh in your face!"

David hesitated. "Don't forget, I'll be handing him the TV confirmation sheets and Hendley's exposé. Besides, it's a gamble we have to take. It's not even that. The worse that can happen is we have to endure Flommer in a two-hour ride and Stonzo ends up saying 'no.'"

"'Get lost' is more like it."

"We'll see. If the idea bombs, it's one less thing we'll have to reassure Clemente and Evilina. Anyway, give Harold a buzz and remind him. We'll pick him up around 9:30."

Kathy went to a drawer for a legal pad, sat back down

and made some notes. Meanwhile, David flipped open his own pad, crossed off three lines of writing and skimmed over several more.

David resumed. "Now, before we talk about the Boston police . . ."

"The Boston police?"

"Oh, yeah—I haven't mentioned them, yet. I will in a minute. Just bear with me. If they do arrest Stonzo, we can't let them publicize it until after the meeting at my house. They should be, like, undercover agents. And, likewise, they can't say they'll nab Saltanban and try to extradite him."

"Okay, they arrest Stonzo but keep it quiet. Why?"

"Because I'm not sure he'd be telling the truth. Those guys are so goddamn loose with their tongues when it comes to fingering people who happen to cross them. And he *hates* Saltanban because he cut the Mafia out of Radonia and probably all of Latin America. So he'd sign anyway—he couldn't care less who killed Molina. What I'm after is getting the goods on Saltanban from Clemente and Evilina the next day."

"He'd sign and then expect to leave?"

"Exactly. He snitches on Saltanban and then hopes to disappear, even though he really doesn't implicate himself in the statement."

"But since the murder looked like a certain mob hit, wouldn't the conclusion be that he did it?"

"Not really. It will be worded something like: 'I, Anthony Stonzo, have it on reliable authority that Juan Carlos Saltanban ordered the killing of one Manuel Molina.' Something to that effect. 'On reliable authority' is the important phrase. He'd claim that a rival gang did it—maybe even from Boston. Remember, he operates out of Chicago."

"I'm sorry, darling, but I have to understand this. If Clemente and Evilina know Stonzo's arrested, won't they be more apt to open up? Isn't the arrest better than a signature?"

"No. Stonzo might be arrested, but Saltanban might not be guilty."

"Now you've lost me. If Saltanban's not guilty, what good is what you learn at Wednesday's meeting? Comprend?"

"Comprend. The answer is that I'm not even sure yet whether Clemente or even Evilina is the killer."

Kathy's eyebrows shot up.

"If one of them is, in fact, the killer, then knowing Saltanban will be in custody will make that person more relaxed, with his or her guard down. He or she might make a mistake—a lot will depend on how I run the meeting. The key to all this is the signature, not the arrest. Clemente and Evilina know that, too."

"But, David, the tapes. Aren't they as good as a signature?"

"No. They would help in court, but remember the original came out scratchy. Stonzo could deny that was his voice; then experts would have to be brought in and all of that. The quality was fine enough to scare the bum, but he'd fight its authenticity if it were used against him. A scratchy tape without a witness isn't as good as a bona fide signature witnessed by a respected member of the bar."

"Let's hope so."

David glanced at his pad again. "The Boston police. Here's what I have in mind. You'd have to arrange it with their undercover people, as I said—give them all the details, tell them not to make the arrest unless they receive a call from you—and it would have to go like clockwork. If everything goes according to Hoyle—no surprises, we get the signature, Stonzo shows in the first place—then I'll phone you and simply say 'Red Alert.' You then contact the police who are waiting in the lobby for him to come out and they make the arrest. One problem I see . . . "

"Among many."

"Yeah, among many . . ." David's voice sounded wooden, struggling with a solution. ". . . is reasoning with the police to let a crime boss go loose. I mean if we don't give them the word."

"Not such a big problem. They'll simply put a tail on him if we ask them to. And I won't give them so much detail to begin with, like the tapes."

"Got it. I'll have to judge whether or not to give the code. And don't ask for any explanation because I may not have time. Remember, the code is, 'Red Alert.'"

"Red Alert."

"Okay, then. Here it is in a nutshell: what Stonzo wants is, one, to finger Saltanban whether he ordered the hit or not; two, to threaten me about the tapes; and, three, to leave the hotel unharmed. What we want is, one, the signature from Stonzo; two, to have him arrested; and, three, to have the police keep it under wraps. Otherwise a chain of events will be triggered that would go something like: big media splash, Clemente and Evilina find out, they assume Saltanban is apprehended, they fear for their lives because of reprisals, Wednesday's meeting at my house is canceled."

"Won't they fear for their lives later anyway, after Saltanban's arrested on their say-so?"

"Not as likely. Assuming Saltanban's guilty, they'll verify all the crazy things about him and hopefully reveal more. Then once that's made public, his sympathizers should melt away. We want information from Clemente and Evilina *before* the announcement of Stonzo's arrest in Boston and *before* Saltanban's arrest in Radonia."

"I think I have it, except what will you say to me if you don't want the police to move in?"

"I won't call."

"What would prevent you from calling and giving the code?"

"If he somehow slips through our fingers or . . ."

"Or what?"

"If I'm in no condition to call you."

* * *

When David got home, he found faxes of the text of Hendley's "blockbuster exposé" of the Mafia and confirmation copies for appearances on five of television's most popular talk shows including Larry King Live and Oprah. He scanned the blistering exposé; it was peppered with Stonzo's name.

CHAPTER 19

✛ ✛ ✛

Tuesday, February 19

At seven a.m., David fetched the morning edition of the *Hollings Herald* from the box out front. He turned directly to the editorial page. Henderson Hendley's column was not there.

At eight, he called Musco and briefed him on background and strategy for the meeting coming up. The presentation and queries mirrored those of the night before with Kathy. They went over the strategy a second time and included contingencies.

"On the spot," Musco said.

"On the spot," David agreed.

At nine, he decided to phone the *Herald*. The Managing Editor stated that no one there had heard from Hendley in some time. David called Hendley's home several times, leaving messages on his answering machine. He contacted his Westport office and recognized the voice of the secretary who wore the red suit.

"I'm concerned, Dr. Brooks. There must have been 100 newspapers calling about where his column was. He came in bright and early yesterday and stayed only a minute or two. On the way out—he was rushing—he said he'd be taking a year off from work, and that he'd be back at eight this morning to clean out his desk. It hasn't been touched."

At nine-thirty, David picked up Harold Flommer at his office and Musco at the parking lot. The attorney and the cabby stated they'd heard of one another and echoed each other's compliments about being the best in the business. They rolled onto Interstate 84 toward Boston. The weather was clear and sunny, 40 or 50 degrees.

Flommer, in blue tweeds, flowery tie and brown shoes, sat in the back and checked his pocket watch every ten minutes. Up front, Musco, like David, wore his usual blue blazer. David noticed the cabby running his right forearm across his beltline every so often. And that he fiddled with an attaché case!

"You have a new friend, I see," David said.

"Bought it yesterday."

"And I suppose you have a name for it?"

"I do."

"What?"

"Monday."

"Is what's in it what I think is in it?"

"Forty-five and forty-five equals ninety, man."

David cracked a smile, Musco didn't and Flommer shook his watch opposite his ear.

They drove through suburban Brookline. David lowered his window: the air smelled new, clean. He addressed Flommer. "Can you write down all the conversation that takes place there? I mean as it happens, on the spot? Like taking dictation?"

Flommer straightened his tie and said, "I was a reporter before I went to law school. I've done it a substantial number of times."

"With a guy lookin' at you who's packin' an automatic, and he's got an itchy finger?" Musco asked.

"Uh . . .not really, no."

David's voice deepened. "Harold, I'd like the statement written up nice and legally, on a single sheet of paper, and I want the pleasure of seeing the bastard sign it. You brought some of your letterhead?"

"Yes." Flommer held up his briefcase.

"So there's a laptop in there?"

"Correct. I have a world-class typist available to me at a moment's notice, but I prefer to transcribe the majority of my work myself, wherever that work takes me."

Musco looked at David and said, "How come you didn't have that stuff put down there on paper ahead of time?"

"Pleasure again, my friend. Call it warped . . . call it whatever you want . . . but I want Stonzo to know the wording came from me, not my attorney. Pardon, Harold. I'll dictate it to you right there. I want him seeing you typing it. It's my own little ritual, my own little formality."

David ticked off the brief statement, just as he had to Kathy before.

It was eleven-fifty-nine. They drove into the Back Bay section of Boston, past old townhouses and an assortment of colleges, their quadrangles teeming with students. A snowman was melting in one, and nearby, a handful of students pelted each other with snowballs. Chimes pealed in the distance. Modern high-rises stood out against the skyline, and the sprawling Prudential Center loomed ahead. David had attended several medical conferences at the Sheraton Boston so had no trouble finding it.

In a wing of the lobby, Anthony Stonzo paced behind the backs of Canfield chairs which circled a 12 x 12 expanse of Persian carpeting. David was almost fooled. The capo wore a gray fedora, wraparound sunglasses and a camelhair coat with pulled up collar. He was clean shaven this time. Light reflected off a line of sweat under his nose. A tall, broad-shouldered man in black mohair sat in one of the chairs studying his fingernails. His hair looked like gray paint. Across the carpeting, a seedy, middle-aged man sat tapping his foot, an abraded brief case on his lap. It vibrated in rhythm with the foot.

David led Musco and Flommer toward Stonzo who waved his men over.

Stonzo's hollow voice hadn't changed. "Ah, Dr. Brooks, there you are," he said, his smile plastic. "I believe you and Frankie here have met by telephone."

The tall man took a step back, then addressed David. "You're bigger than me. Your voice don't sound that way on the phone."

Stonzo shoved his arm across Frankie's midsection. "*Adesso basto*, Frankie. That's enough."

Frankie looked like a kicked dog.

"And this is Bernie Greene" Stonzo said. "I use him in our east coast operations. Good man."

David followed with his introductions and they all shook hands. No one came close to matching David's grip, even Frankie.

"I'm not sure why we have mouthpieces here" Stonzo said. "It's not like we need a contract among friends."

"But you sure use them among enemies," Musco said. Stonzo answered with a feeble smile that quickly turned to one of annoyance.

"Where's Shades?" David asked.

"He's been transferred. That was foolish conduct on his part."

David only wanted to touch on the subject. At this juncture, any efforts to make it a cause célèbre might hinder the purpose of the trip.

He switched. "I'm curious, Stonzo—why show up here? You, yourself, said it might prove dangerous. I take it you're not too well . . . uh . . . supported in these parts."

"Because I want to be sure that rotten bastard Saltanban gets what's coming to him. I must admit to you: back in New York, I lied—no not lied, it skipped my mind—we *did* have some important business going on and Saltanban took it away from us. He pushed and pushed for the Spaniards and he's still pushing. He ruined our interests in South America, in Central America, in . . ."

"Like what countries?"

"Columbia . . . Mexico . . . Panama . . ."

"The drug cartels?"

"I don't believe too much in that."

"You don't?"

"No. That's why my consigliere handles . . . why are we into this, anyway? Saltanban! That's what we should be talking about. He's the fink I'm after."

"Okay," David said, "you said back in New York that he hired you to have Manny Molina killed. Are you willing to put that in writing?"

"Yes."

No hesitation? No argument? Something's fishy.

"I'll go see if we can rent a conference room," David said, walking along the marble-columned length of the lobby toward the registration desk. The others followed in formation, Musco lagging behind as he checked around plants and behind opened newspapers, especially those obscured by swirls of smoke.

At the desk, Stonzo said, "No, I'll handle this." He snapped his fingers. "Frankie?" He extended an open hand which Frankie filled with a crisp hundred dollar bill.

They were directed to a small room on the second floor. It had a table, eight chairs and a service bar of coffee, soft drinks and a bucket of ice.

David sat at the head of the table, Stonzo and Musco to his left. On the right were Frankie, Flommer and Greene. Without a word, David handed Stonzo a folder containing copies of the television confirmation sheets and of Henderson Hendley's column. Typed under "Subject" on each sheet was "Dr. David Brooks: Commentary on Organized Crime." Along the top margin of the exposé article, David had scrawled, "To be submitted."

"In case you hadn't figured it," David said, "there's also a copy of the tape in my safe deposit box at the bank."

Stonzo gave each page a cursory examination and handed them back.

"I don't need any of this, Dr. Brooks. The tape you gave me was enough." He mopped his forehead with a paper napkin. "So let's not waste your time and mine. I realize it's tough doing business with you, so let's straighten some things out and move on."

Musco's eyes flitted toward Frankie with metronomic regularity. Greene, like a failing student during a final exam, tried to see what Flommer was writing. David fastened his gaze on Stonzo and motioned him to continue.

"I have a proposition," Stonzo said. "We call it a tie. You go your way, and I'll turn around and go mine. Now, you wanted our mouthpieces here so they can be our witnesses. No hard feelings"—he looked at the attorneys—"but as long as God is our witness, that's all that counts for me." He made the sign of the cross. "Therefore, you go ahead and lay it out, everybody will listen, we agree—or disagree until we agree—we shake on it, and we'll be on our way. Agreed?"

David glossed over the preamble. He said, "Agreed. First and foremost, I want you to sign a document that Mr. Flommer will type out for us. I've already briefed him on how it should read, but you'll hear me saying it in a second."

"A document?"

"Yes. A short one stating, in effect, that Juan Carlos Saltanban, President of Radonia, engaged a certain party to have one Manuel Molina murdered. In return for that signature, I cancel the TV shows and have the exposé pulled." David dictated the statement to Flommer, pausing as if he were putting the words together for the first time. Flommer wrote on a legal pad.

"Clear?" David asked.

"Clear," Stonzo replied.

"Second, I'm telling you that if, by virtue of that document or of some afterthought of yours or your friends, any kind of retaliation is made against me or my friends, I've arranged to have the tape and the exposé made known to the public. Also an outline of my remarks for the TV shows. Clear?"

"Clear."

"And third, if you have Henderson Hendley, I want him released immediately."

Stonzo flared his hand between them. "Dr. Brooks, I must stop you there. The treatment of those associated with us who decide to take things into their own hands is a private matter of our organization. It should not interfere with what we decide here today because it has nothing to do with you."

"Oh, but it does."

"Well, I'm sorry to hear that because it's too late. The order was given."

David looked at Musco, then back at Stonzo. "You're a bloodthirsty animal, Stonzo!"

Frankie reached inside his coat.

"Better not!" Musco shouted.

"Leave it there," Stonzo instructed Frankie.

David had thought there was a slim chance Hendley might still be alive, but he wasn't surprised by the revelation. He rationalized that at least he had the opportunity to give Stonzo a proper label. Mute, David stared at him without expression.

Stonzo finally said, "Well, do we let that personal matter botch up our deliberations or not?"

David gave no reply but spoke to Flommer. "How long will it take you to make out the document, Harold?"

"Two, three minutes on my laptop. Then, I'll take it down to the business office and have it printed out."

The lawyer removed the laptop from his briefcase and while he typed, David and Musco looked out one window and Stonzo, Frankie and Greene looked out another.

When Flommer returned from the business office, he

handed the document to Greene who proceeded to read it over several times, mouthing the words. Stonzo raised up and snatched it away.

Without sitting, he read each line. David handed him a pen. Stonzo looked at the pen, then at each of the others. He leaned over and signed his name.

"Now!" he screamed. David and Musco jumped up as Frankie and Stonzo trained their guns on them.

"We got what we both wanted, Brooks," Stonzo said, his breathing quickened. Frankie shoved both attorneys to his right, around the table. Stonzo backed up.

"This is just in case you have something up your sleeve." He used the gun to wave directions. "You three get together. Easy does it, now. We walk out nice and slow." Stonzo nodded to Frankie who edged closer to him from his position at the other end of the table. They began to insert their hand-held guns in their coat pockets. What followed was like the herky-jerky action of an ancient movie clip:

David yelled, "Spot, Musc, spot!"

Stonzo and Frankie pulled out their guns and stiffened their arms toward David.

Musco tackled Stonzo and somersaulted to his feet. The gun popped up.

At the same time, David gave Frankie's wrist a karate chop. The gun squirted down.

Flommer grunted as he scrambled to the floor, picked up the guns and handed them to David.

* * *

When David phoned Kathy, he said, "Red Alert, modified."

"What's that supposed to mean? Are you okay?"

"We have them ourselves. Musco's got both his forty-fives on them out in the hall."

"What happened?" David could hear the sighs accelerating.

"A little scuffle."

"You sure you're all right, David. You sound funny."

"I'm fine."

"Musco, Flommer?"

"They're fine. You should have seen Flommer. He wasn't even in on what we had planned. Wish we'd had a video."

"How many men did Stonzo bring?"

"Two. I'll tell you about it later. It would have been better to have them think someone tipped off the cops downstairs, but this will have to do. They pulled guns on us. We're not about to let them walk out of here, so we'll turn them in."

"They pulled guns? Promise me you're all right."

"Promise."

∗ ∗ ∗

High-fives, accolades and a lengthy post-mortem monopolized lunch on the Massachusetts Turnpike and the drive back to Connecticut. Flommer was dropped off at his office, and David headed for the hospital parking lot.

"The big meeting tomorrow's at your place?" Musco asked.

"Yes."

"You want me there?"

David spelled out the many sides of a reluctance on the part of Clemente and Evilina to cooperate fully, to tell all they know. "So you're welcome to come, but I think the fewer the better."

"Gotcha," the cabby said.

"I'll see you sometime tomorrow then—after the meeting."

"Regular place?"

"No, at Red Checker. Unless you'll be out hacking."

"Uh-uh. Too much paper work."

* * *

David's drive to the Police Department was slower than usual, and Hollings at dusk was darker than usual. The sky was layered with middle and high clouds as a northwest wind became chillier.

Kathy was standing at her desk as if she had stationed herself there hours ago, waiting for David to arrive. Her hug was clutching, not tender.

They remained standing as David summed up the events at the hotel, twice describing the "spot" sequence. "It was beautiful, Kath, beautiful."

Kathy, impassive, said, "What if, after all this is over, there's retaliation against you—not by Saltanban but by Stonzo's people, like that Shades guy? You think that's possible?"

"Possible."

"David, don't say that!"

"You asked—I answered." They embraced for a few seconds, and he drew away. "You're a cop, Kath, you know how it works."

David gave his best in trying to appear unconcerned. The look on Kathy's face was hardly that of a cop.

He slouched into a chair and let his arms hang down. She went to him and brushed his hair back with her hand.

"Why not go home, David—rest, chill out. You've got another big day tomorrow."

She was good that way, he thought. Advice born of instincts he didn't possess. He blinked his eyes and nodded yes—both slow by a beat.

At the door, he said, "I've got to admit, I'm still uneasy."

"Why?"

"I don't know."

*   *   *

Two nights before, after Georgia was returned by Hendley, David dropped into bed at two a.m. and was up by seven. Last night, Monday, his sleep was, at best, time consuming.

He had a theory about mental fatigue and its effect on good sleep and on bad sleep. Even if one is mentally whipped, good sound sleep is curative, but the combination of mental fatigue and restless sleep is a disaster. David was in the throes of a disaster. And whenever he got that way, he'd think about the same questions: Why the need to sleep at all—why wouldn't rest alone suffice, as in the case of insects? Why not be able to sleep while standing, like cows? That way, one could catch a few winks in a check-out line.

He also believed sleep was additive. If he were behind by, say, four hours, he could make up for it within a day or two, and his body wouldn't notice the difference. David didn't know whether he'd theorized himself into it, but that night he slept for 11 hours.

CHAPTER 20

✛ ✛ ✛

Tuesday, February 20

The rains had come and stayed, even as towering, black cumulus clouds gave way to a thick low cover with ever-widening gaps. The gaps were like corkscrew chutes, and David viewed them as precursors to better weather, maybe even within the hour when The Meeting would start.

He greeted Evilina and Clemente warmly, ushered them into the living room and took their dry raincoats. He smelled cigar smoke. Earlier, David had brought two easy chairs nearer the sofa. Clemente jingled change in his pocket before picking one of the chairs to sit in. He placed a shiny black briefcase beside him. Evilina, dressed in a beige blouse and stirrup pants, kept her purse on her lap as she sat in the other chair. They sat forward as if eager to begin, yet kept their arms relaxed.

David, in light blue sweater and dark blue trousers, sank into the sofa, and after they refused tea or coffee, he said, "Evilina, Adrian—thank you both for coming. I'll get right to the point. Obviously we're here to talk about Juan Carlos Saltanban. My suggestion is we say or ask about whatever's on our minds. As you know, my main purpose is to get to the bottom of two murders, not to sit in judgment of either of you based on any information you might have shared earlier. The whole question of fear comes into the picture and Evilina, you already expressed that to me up at the Cape." David decided to dispense with his notepad in keeping with a less threatening, more casual approach to the proceedings.

Clemente said, "Dr. Brooks, let me assure you—and I believe I speak for my friend—we want very much to cooperate, and we know *plenty*. As they say, we've about had it up to here." He planted the edge of his palm on his forehead and added, "But we don't want any trouble."

"How shall I say this?" David continued. "I'm trying to put myself in your shoes, so let me make it easier for you." He stretched toward Friday, which lay at the opposite end of the sofa, took out Flommer's letterhead bearing Stonzo's signed statement and gave it, first, to Evilina.

She perused it and handed it to Clemente. He ran his finger along each line as he read it. They leaned back in their chairs and smiled at each other conspiratorially.

David felt he might be jumping the gun, but he judged the reaction as one sparked by relief, not by the complacency of participants in a cabal. He took out a copy of the tape and dangled it before them.

"This is the secret recording of an interview I had with a guy named Anthony Stonzo. You know him?"

"Oh, yes," Clemente answered with a sardonic grin. Evilina nodded.

"Well in the interview, he fingers Saltanban as ordering

Manny Molina's killing. Just like that written statement."

Clemente leaned forward again, arms resting on his knees. "Dr. Brooks, you have no idea what we've been through—for a long time now. His wild schemes, and I mean wild. His demands. Saying he'll have us killed." The Candyman sounded like a hundred-pound weakling having sand kicked in his face by a beach bully.

"Did you and Evilina speak to each other often?" David asked.

Evilina replied, "Regularly. Daily, I'd say. At least."

Clemente said, "Whenever Saltanban called either one of us, and that's probably every single day. I used to talk to my cousin, Manny, quite a bit, too."

"So Saltanban would call and you'd discuss the things you just mentioned?"

"Yes, one thing after another," Clemente replied. "And usually there would be a threat."

"To keep you quiet?"

"Yes."

"Why tell you in the first place?"

Evilina seemed more anxious to answer first. "Because we were both part of his plan. Me more than Adrian."

"His plan? We'll get to that in a minute. How long had all this been going on?"

David realized they all spoke in the past tense, as if the ordeal were over.

"Two years or more," Clemente said.

David almost went for his notepad but changed his mind. "Do you think he had Manny murdered?" he asked.

"Yes," Clemente said.

"I agree," Evilina said, separating the bangle bracelets on her wrist.

David looked directly at Clemente and asked, "Now what was the plan?"

"Cloning."

David turned to Evilina.

"Cloning," she said.

"What do you mean?" David asked.

Clemente spoke. "He wanted to be cloned."

"*What?*" The room was seized by silence. David stood, put his hands on his hips and repeated the words in disbelief. "He wanted to be *cloned*?"

"So he could lead Radonia forever."

David sat slowly, shaking his head from side to side. "What about his son?"

"He has no son."

"But he talked about him. Luis, I think is his name."

"He talked about many things," Clemente said, "and you couldn't believe most of it."

They traded brief stares.

"What about the telecommunications business?" David asked.

"*That*, you can believe. He was an expert and should have stuck to it."

David pushed himself up, walked around to the back of the sofa, faced them momentarily and began pacing. "We've got to get into the cloning thing," he said, "but before we do, where does cybernetics fit in? You know, don't you, that he's saying he has a book out on it? I checked and there's no such book."

Clemente answered. "He talked over and over about machines doing the work of humans, but I didn't know about the book."

"I didn't either," Evilina said.

"I think he has what they call a love-hate relationship with science . . ." Clemente said.

Evilina interrupted. "That's a good way of putting it."

". . . especially since Manny refused to go along with him on the cloning business. Manny refused other things, too. Saltanban felt most of science let him down and that machines could be built to imitate human behavior. He calls them friendly machines."

David was reminded of Aldous Huxley's novel, *Brave New World*, and its totalitarian society that disregarded human dignity and worshipped science and machines.

"So if he can't have cloning, he'll take cybernetics?"

"Right. And it's crazy, but he thought that could still give him some kind of control. Over what, I'm not sure."

David couldn't stand it any more: he had to take notes. Weren't they both more relaxed by now, anyway? He returned to the sofa, removed his pad from Friday and said, "You don't mind, do you?"

They shook their heads no.

"Okay," he said, "You mentioned you were part of his plan. How so?"

"I was supposed to keep tabs on Manny," Clemente said, "and to mail chocolates to all Saltanban's friends around the world."

"What kind of friends?"

"He has a network out there."

"All over?"

"All over but especially here in the States . . . in Canada . . .South America . . . Asia."

"Afghanistan?"

"Yes, Afghanistan."

Clemente turned sarcastic. "As if chocolates could

keep them on a leash. He had a funny thing about chocolates. First of all, he hated the taste himself, but he used them for everything. Sent them to friends. Sent them to people he was going to kill. And even though he was bossing me around, I think he wanted to help me out by ordering hundreds—thousands—of boxes."

"Did you send them out very often?"

"Yes, very often."

"On your own, or did he pay for them?"

"He paid—and on time, too. I must say, Dr. Brooks, that many of the people really believed in him, with or without chocolates."

"How do you know that?"

"Dr. Barlow told me."

"Barlow? You mean Manny's successor?"

"Yes, he called me last week to offer his sympathies. He said he'd just learned from Saltanban that I was Manny's cousin. We talked. He said that Saltanban was losing power down there."

David made a note or two before continuing. "You said that Manny refused other things. Like what?"

"Saltanban wanted him to create superbugs at Brent."

"Superbugs? Christ Almighty!"

"That was why, he said, he had Stonzo by the . . ." He checked with Evilina. "Well, you know what I mean. He told Stonzo he had a vial of superbugs, and if he tried anything smart, his supporters were instructed to retaliate against him with bugs Brent had changed so that no medicines would work. Told him they were like those killer bees in South America. He said those guys aren't afraid of guns, but they're scared to death of disease."

David shuddered. "It gets worse and worse," he said,

"but let's go on with the cloning. Tell me more about it."

"Two years ago, I guess my cousin promised Saltanban that cloning could take place even if it was illegal in the U.S.—because he could depend on his colleagues in Europe to do him the favor. Well, as I'm sure you know, Dr. Brooks—and I only know because Manny told me—the government cut off money for cloning research. And whether or not he went to his friends—who knows—he told Saltanban 'no dice.' So the bastard had him killed."

"He told you that?"

"Not in so many words. But he killed him, I'd swear to it."

Clemente lowered his head, then raised it higher than usual and swallowed hard. "And you know, here's the clincher: even if they cloned him, this nut was willing to wait 20 years for the clone to grow up and take over his country."

"Amazing. But about the superbugs—with all his network in place, I assume he kept touch through his telecommunications hardware?"

"Yes."

"On the superbugs specifically though—was he going to use them as part of a bioterrorism attack?"

"I'm not absolutely sure, but he referred to it in something I brought you. He made out a stupid list of instructions for this new son of his." Clemente was about to open his briefcase.

David figured it must contain the manifesto; he motioned with his hand as a sign to wait. He first wanted Evilina's input on the cloning issue. Her body language had showed that she'd been privy to all the infor-

mation Clemente was disclosing, and that she agreed
with his opinions.

"Evilina," David said, "what was your role in the
plan?" He drew a line across a page of the notepad. With
every new notation, he had been adding a word or two
about previous comments.

"Simple." Her eyes moistened and she took out a handkerchief.

"I was to be the mother of the clone." She began to
tremble. "Not the mother . . . the carrier . . . the bearer.
The oven." Tears spilled over her cheeks before she could
reach them with the handkerchief.

David didn't want the tempo to slacken. "In other
words, your egg, your womb?"

"Yes."

"Why not have a natural pregnancy with his wife?"

"Because," she said, gathering composure, "he wanted
an exact duplication of himself, not a child that dared to
have anyone else's characteristics."

"And his wife, I take it, didn't want to be part of the
cloning."

"No. They argued over her carrying the embryo that
way. I don't blame her. That's making her as crazy as he
is."

"Of course," David said. He wrote more in the pad and
closed it. "Let's see what you have there now, Adrian."

Clemente opened the briefcase and removed a framed
photograph and a Manila folder.

"This is a picture Saltanban asked me to remove from
Manny's wall. As you can see, it's a family portrait—wife,
daughters, but no young boy."

"You took it down after the murder?"

"Yes. He told me to, and I did."

"So you obviously had a key to Manny's house."

"Yes, he wanted me to keep an eye on it whenever he traveled out of the country."

"Did he ever go to Radonia?"

"Yes. He was there three weeks ago."

"Hmm, Saltanban said a year ago."

"See? A goddamn liar."

"And in the folder?"

"He asked me to keep this under lock and key and, in case anything happened to him, to give it to his . . . ah . . . son when he was old enough. Here's the original in Spanish and I typed out an English version for you. Some of his words had double meanings, so my translation is rough. I even had to use the dictionary."

He removed two sets of papers from the folder and handed them to David who counted four sheets, each single-spaced in English and four sheets, each single-spaced in Spanish. He laid the Spanish version aside on the sofa and skimmed through the others. At the top was what David had anticipated: **MANIFESTO FOR NEW WORLD ORDER**. What followed were lists of people to avoid and a lesser number to trust in Saltanban's administration; rules to abide by in running the government; individuals to maintain ties with in other countries; strategies for winning elections; secrets for maintaining a friendly military; and other principles, regulations, mandates, directives, guidelines, formulas and tips.

But what caught David's attention were the beginning, the end and a few paragraphs at the top of page three. He returned to the beginning and reread:

My beloved son, Luis. You have received a legacy that I began many years before you were born. Handle it wisely with the skills you inherited from me. If I am unable to be with you, your most valuable contact is Adrian Clemente in Hollings, Connecticut, U.S.A. They call him the Candyman. He can especially assist you with altered bacteria and viruses.

David crossed his legs hoping it would help the chill disappear. "Have you read this?" he asked Clemente.

"Yes, many times. So has Evilina—I sent her a copy."

"I'm just curious. Why didn't you come forward a long time ago?"

"Fear. And I knew Manny wouldn't budge on cloning. He never would have agreed to make superbugs and try to harm anyone, either. He loved this country. He loved people from all countries."

Starting on page three, David also reread several tirades against big business, the media, "oppressed minorities", "governments too capitalistic for their own good" and a section about politicians:

When they speak, do you not for a moment know they are politicians? Do they? Certain corporations try to buy election results and the beneficiaries are favored politicians. If a "good" politician need be good in the art of compromise, then truth, honesty and loyalty are compromised. Contrariwise, if a politician shuns lies, deception and betrayal, he can achieve only ordinary status—a stranger to the inner circle and unable to accomplish much. Thus, the stuff of politics is such that it either attracts scoundrels or eventually creates them.

But none of this pertains to you, Luis. You are different. You are my son. Be my son. Be strong.

David sensed his face had turned ashen while reading the ending:

The struggle will take years, if not generations. But you will have the temperament, individuality and determination of your father.

He skimmed through all four pages again and found no other reference to "the struggle"—with whom, about what, using what. He gave the pages back to Clemente and puffed out a breath before speaking.

"A maniac. A smart one, but a maniac. I feel exhausted and I'm sure you two are, also. But while we're together, I have to end with a couple of quick questions. David flipped to the back of his pad and pointed to the top of a page. Adrian, you said last week that you consulted with Dr. Skopey, the heart specialist."

"Yes."

"When was that?"

"Over a year ago."

"Good. And you said once before that Spanish newspapers are delivered to your house?"

"Yes. Saltanban has them sent to me."

"Good. Do you have any idea why Agnes Crocker was murdered?"

"Saltanban said she was working hard to have Brent shut down. And there was some connection with Howerton's president. Something about illegal use of funds and Crocker was going to blow the whistle. I never understood it."

"Good. When I was down in Radonia, a man was found murdered in a cathedral there. I think he was one of Saltanban's bodyguards. Any knowledge about why he was killed?"

"I was told he knew too much and was about to become a spy."

"Against Saltanban?"

"That's what he told me."

"Last question, folks. I mean it. Adrian, this is the umpteenth time I've asked you this, but did you call Saltanban about Molina's death or did he call you?"

"He called me."

"Are you sure?"

"I'm 500 percent sure. I remember seeing it on my phone bill as a collect call. That's how he'd call to order chocolates, and at first I thought that's what he was doing."

"Why didn't you notify the police after he called?"

"I was very upset and not thinking straight at the time. I suspected Saltanban was behind it but was afraid of him and what he might do to my family. And I was afraid the police might arrest me if I called them. All the things I knew about him bothered me and made me feel guilty— so I just kept quiet. I was confused, Dr. Brooks, that's all I can say."

"And that's all the questions I have. Shouldn't we give ourselves a standing ovation? Whoops, that's another question."

The comment ignited a smile on Clemente's and Evilina's faces. They rose and David put both his hands around theirs while thanking them.

"Will you have him arrested?" Clemente asked.

"It looks that way. Just a couple details to clear up first."

David bent over to put his notepad back into Friday. "How about staying for a sandwich?"

"No, no, thanks—I have to get to the candy store."

Evilina added, "And I'm driving right to the Cape from here." She checked her watch. "Maybe I can beat the rush hour traffic on the Mass Pike. Thanks, anyway."

"Well, thank you both, again. And please don't worry. I'm sure everything about this terrible nightmare will be ironed out soon."

As soon as they left, David phoned Kathy at the Police department.

"They opened up completely," he said. "Saltanban's a psycho. I don't know where to start, but how's this for openers? Are you standing or sitting?"

"I'm pacing with a cup of coffee in my hand."

"He has no son, so he wants to clone one."

"*Cloning?*" He could picture Kathy sliding onto a chair, maybe switching the phone to her other hand. "That's incredible!"

"The manifesto? It's a scorcher."

David described the session, speaking more rapidly the further he got into it.

"But in spite of all that," he said, "I'm still uneasy. He certainly had motive. And with the Mafia and Camorra involved, opportunity and means were there. But that doesn't prove he's guilty of the crimes."

"I think we have *more* than enough to nail him for engineering both murders," Kathy said. "Clemente, Evilina, Barlow—they'll all testify. We have the tape, Stonzo's statement, subpoena power, you name it. And extradition should be a snap. By the way, we'll have to let the State Attorney's Office decide whether Clemente and

Evilina have to answer to any charges."

He rubbed his decision scar. "I don't know, Kath, I have something on the tip of my brain. I'll call you back." He hung up without allowing Kathy to ask when.

David went to the computer and reviewed the Operative Plan and every entry about the case—five in all. Next, he pored over each page of his notepad and scrolled through a list of other suspects in his mind. Then, like a Gestalt, it exploded in his mind: the 500 percent sure—phone bill statement by Clemente. He called the Candyman at the store.

"Adrian. Your phone bill and the Saltanban call. Do you keep your bills there or at home?"

"I keep all my bills here, why?"

"Would you mind checking it for the time the collect call came in? I'll hold on."

In three minutes, Clemente was back on the phone. "It says 1:10 p.m."

"Thanks, I'll be in touch. Bye."

David called Kathy. "Go ahead and have him arrested and extradited. I'm glad you agreed with me. Bye, I'm calling Musco."

"Wait! David, hold on! What are you talking about?"

He explained that Clemente looked up the time of the call made to him by Saltanban on the day of Molina's murder.

"He gave Adrian his condolences more than two hours before I discovered the body. So he knew about the killing before anyone else except, of course, the mob he hired. They must have notified him with the news of a successful hit. Then he claimed he heard about it by watching CNN."

* * *

David invited Musco to his house and reiterated everything he had shared with Kathy—from the moment Clemente and Evilina arrived to the time listed on the phone bill. He peeled four fifties from a wad of bills he took from his pocket and handed them to Musco along with a check.

"What's this?" the cabby asked.

"I didn't have enough bills."

Musco read the check and reached up on his toes to force it into David's breast pocket.

"That's too much, old buddy. It was fun."

David kept Musco at bay while he inserted the check into the headband of the cabby's cap. "But you earned it many times over. Just the Boston trip alone. The spot maneuver. You were fantastic."

"Nah, like I say, 'You do what you have to do . . .'"

They stepped on each others words. ". . . when it's do or die."